THE KING'S MEN

The horseman was rubbing his hand over his thickening cock, its outline clear through his britches. 'I've seen you looking at me, young master,' he murmured in a throaty whisper. Ned's gaze jumped to the stranger's crotch. The rounded triangular outline of the head of his cock was clearly discernible. Ned's blood pumped through him like a river of fire. He licked his lips.

'I know what you want,' continued the stranger in his honeyed, sensuous voice.

Ned cleared his throat, hoping this might make him sound a little superior. 'And what's that?'

The horseman pulled at the laces which held together his leather britches, exposing the beginnings of a delta of dark, wiry hair.

'You want me.' He continued to unlace his trousers until they hung loose around his hips. 'You want me now, don't you?'

THE KING'S MEN

Christian Fall

For all in the Rump Parliament ...

First published in Great Britain in 1997 by
Idol
an imprint of Virgin Publishing Ltd
332 Ladbroke Grove
London W10 5AH

ISBN 0 352 33207 7

Cover photograph by John Dietrich

Typeset by SetSystems Ltd, Saffron Walden, Essex
Printed and bound in Great Britain by
Cox & Wyman Ltd, Reading, Berks

SAFER SEX GUIDELINES

These books are sexual fantasies – in real life, everyone needs to think about safe sex.

While there have been major advances in the drug treatments for people with HIV and AIDS, there is still no cure for AIDS or a vaccine against HIV. Safe sex is still the only way of being sure of avoiding HIV sexually.

HIV can only be transmitted through blood, come and vaginal fluids (but no other body fluids) – passing from one person (with HIV) into another person's bloodstream. It cannot get through healthy, undamaged skin. The only real risk of HIV is through anal sex without a condom – this accounts for almost all HIV transmissions between men.

Being Safe:
Even if you don't come inside someone, there is still a risk to both partners from blood (tiny cuts in the arse) and pre-come. Using strong condoms and water-based lubricant greatly reduces the risk of HIV. However, condoms can break or slip off, so:
* Make sure that condoms are stored away from hot or damp places.
* Check the expiry date – condoms have a limited life.
* Gently squeeze the air out of the tip.
* Check the condom is put on the right way up and unroll it down the erect cock.
* Use plenty of water-based lubricant (lube), up the arse and on the condom.
* While fucking, check occasionally to see the condom is still in one piece (you could also add more lube).
* When you withdraw, hold the condom tight to your cock as you pull out.

* Never re-use a condom or use the same condom with more than one person.
* If you're not used to condoms you might practise putting them on.
* Sex toys like dildos and plugs are safe. But if you're sharing them use a new condom each time or wash the toys well.

For the safest sex, make sure you use the strongest condoms, such as Durex Ultra Strong, Mates Super Strong, HT Specials and Rubberstuffers packs. Condoms are free in many STD (Sexually Transmitted Disease) clinics (sometimes called GUM clinics) and from many gay bars. It's also essential to use lots of water-based lube such as KY, Wet Stuff, Slik or Liquid Silk. Never use come as a lubricant.

Oral Sex:
Compared with fucking, sucking someone's cock is far safer. Swallowing come does not necessarily mean that HIV gets absorbed into the bloodstream. While a tiny fraction of cases of HIV infection have been linked to sucking, we know the risk is minimal. But certain factors increase the risk:
* Letting someone come in your mouth
* Throat infections such as gonorrhoea
* If you have cuts, sores or infections in your mouth and throat

So what is safe?
There are so many things you can do which are absolutely safe: wanking each other; rubbing your cocks against one another; kissing, sucking and licking all over the body; rimming – to name but a few.

If you're finding safe sex difficult, call a helpline or speak to someone you feel you can trust for support. The Terrence Higgins Trust Helpline, which is open from noon to 10pm every day, can be reached on 0171 242 1010.

One

The tall figure in the half-mask made an elaborate bow and the audience, assembled in a cold huddle before him, gave a perfunctory clap.

Behind the mask, coal-black eyes watched the crowd with ill-disguised distaste.

'It is a tragedy,' he announced, placing a hand to his brow, palm outwards. 'I shall never again know the life of pleasure I have so enjoyed.' The voice was low and rich with a faint Spanish accent. 'I am condemned to an . . .' He gave a huge theatrical shudder. '. . . An *ordinary* life!'

The crowd laughed in response and a fat young man in the front row called, 'You should give it a try, mate!'

The figure on the stage, who was dressed in an elaborate but faded Harlequin costume, sighed and put his hands on his hips. The costume clung tightly to the wiry contours of his supple body, to the bones of his hips and the hard, flat pads of his chest muscles.

'Simpletons,' he hissed out of the corner of his mouth.

Another figure bounded on to the stage. He looked exactly like the other, his long black hair bound with a ribbon, swarthy face half-hidden by a mask, but a neat, pointed beard and moustache distinguished him from his twin. Also he wore a curiously old-fashioned costume of doublet and blue hose.

'Never fear, my friend,' he boomed. 'Help is at hand. I can show you a life of pleasure undreamt of in this time.'

Harlequin approached him. 'Explain, stranger,' he said out loud, then, under his breath, 'I told you we should never have come here. They're a humourless lot and no friends to the King.'

The other shushed him by laying a long finger against the Harlequin's lips.

'Come,' he announced grandly, drawing back a curtain and revealing an impressive castle set. 'I will show thee paradise!'

Some distance away from the wind-blown drapes of the travelling theatre, an altogether more solid building lay under a thick blanket of new snow.

Night came quickly at that time of the rolling year and, outside the great walls of Sir Harry Melcombe's house, the snow continued to fall in a thick curtain, caught and illuminated now and then in the glow of a carriage lamp.

Inside, Sir Harry, as dependable-looking as his property, contented himself with a glass of sack and stared broodingly into the fireplace.

Shifting his weight from one ample buttock to the other, Sir Harry contemplated his day. A late start (too much wine the previous evening) followed by a brisk ride across the fields on the fine new mare he had bought at market only the other day. His elder son Thomas had ridden with him and the knight had glowed with pride at the sight of the handsome young fellow, tall and imposing on the back of his jet-black stallion. How his dear Elizabeth would have loved to see Thomas full grown.

Sir Harry's face fell a little as he remembered his late wife and his heavy features pooled into shadow as firelight flickered over them.

Later, he and Thomas had given one of the new grooms a good ticking off over some misdemeanour or other. He couldn't quite remember what. He seemed to forget an awful lot of things these days. Anyway, the lad was insolent and needed to be taught a lesson. He would certainly have been dismissed had not the times been so difficult, so extraordinary.

But the times were extraordinary and Sir Harry had more on

his mind than the misbehaviour of junior grooms. He and Thomas had spent much of the afternoon in heated discussion: England unfairly ruled; a king not worthy of his crown.

The door opened and a servant came in. This was young William who had taken the place of the family's old retainer some two years previously. A fine-looking lad, thought Sir Harry, and, in the soft glow of the fire, almost feminine in his grace.

'Will there be anything more, sir?' he enquired.

Sir Harry shook his head. 'No, William. Get yourself to bed.'

William's pretty face dissolved into an almost imperceptible smile. 'Then I'll bid you good night, sir.'

Sir Harry nodded in response, and William closed the door behind him with a resonant thud.

Outside, the snow piled thick and wet against the house's mullioned windows.

Sir Harry was grateful to be inside. Here, at least, everything was safe and ordered; a known quantity. There was Humbleford, the village over which his family had presided as squires for some three hundred years, set in its quiet Oxfordshire valley. And the house itself. Upstairs, Thomas would be sleeping soundly whilst, in the adjoining room, his younger brother Ned . . .

Sir Harry sighed and raised his eyes to the ceiling. Ah, Ned. He was quite another matter altogether.

Thick blankets lay like a thick woollen drift over the still, sleeping form of Ned Melcombe, outlining the contours of his lithe, graceful body. He lay with one strong arm beneath the pillow, his head deep in its downy embrace.

Moonlight gushed through the window, lending his fragile features an unearthly beauty. And an uncommonly beautiful young man he was. His hair fell in a jet-black mane from a high, pale forehead; smooth as soap-stone. His brows were dark and joined imperceptibly above his small, straight nose. Sleeping, his eyelids were heavy and sensuous. Beneath them, eyes of glittering green darted restlessly, caught in pleasant dreaming. The high cheek-bones of his heart-shaped face cut through the creamy softness of his complexion like skate tracks in ice, leading down to a full-lipped, slightly petulant mouth.

Ned turned over in his sleep, exposing his wiry, finely muscled torso. Snowflake shadows dappled his dark nipples and rounded pectoral muscles. His eyelids flickered.

He groaned and smiled; a funny half-smile. It wasn't winter where Ned's dreams took him. There it was summer, hot and blazing. The water of a mill sparkled like liquid diamond as a great wooden wheel clapped through it. The sun showed as a perfect disc through a haze of fine cloud.

Ned was brushing feverishly at the soft coat of a big, imposing horse. Astride the horse was another figure: tall and muscular, his long legs bare, his feet slipped into stirrups. But, in the strange way of dreams, his face seemed obscured. Ned sensed that his hair was long and blond. His eyes perhaps blue like melting Arctic ice but he could not be sure.

In his dream, Ned seemed to be much younger and he gazed up at the man on the horse, loving and resenting him at the same time.

Smaller and underdeveloped, he felt weak and useless in the horseman's powerful presence. He could see the thickness of the other's cock through the soft leather of his short britches and felt a pang of jealousy.

Looking down Ned saw his own body. Arms and torso too skinny, his face too pretty for a boy and his cock a shy snail, peeping out from the sparse fuzz of his pubic hair. He wanted so much to be like the horseman. To tear across the summer fields with the wind streaming over his hair, pressing his bare legs against the horse's flanks, feeling the pressure of the saddle against his crotch.

He looked up at the horseman again but the sun dazzled him and still he could not see the stranger's face. Instead, the mysterious rider jabbed his heels into the horse and trotted off across the courtyard. The dream-Ned shielded his eyes against the sun's glare and, squinting, watched the horseman disappear in a dusty cloud.

Angrily, he threw the handbrush into a leather bucket and stomped away towards the imposing bulk of the barn. He paused to dip his head into the trough but the water was warm and brackish, providing scant relief from the heat as it coursed through his hair and down the slender length of his neck.

4

Sunlight shone in his eyes and in the droplets which clung to his downy cheeks and full, reddened lips. He pushed at the barn doors and walked suddenly into cool darkness.

For a moment, he could not accustom himself to the change and stumbled, his narrow body, naked except for rough cotton britches, banging against a large wooden prop. He swore, using a word his brother Thomas had taught him but whose meaning he did not know.

Ned lay down in a wall of hay which had been stuffed into the far section of the barn and stretched out, feeling the sharp barbs of the hay prick into his back and calves. He put his hands behind his head and blinked up at the darkened beams of the barn ceiling. He enjoyed the coolness of his surroundings, the deep, secretive shadows of the barn. He felt good here. Secure and in control. Slowly his eyes began to close.

Something stirred in his flat belly; a kind of pleasant, drowsy ache. He smiled to himself, spreading his legs in the warm, tinder-dry hay, enjoying the feel of it between his naked toes. The pleasant ache spread into his loins and he stretched himself, wriggling into a more comfortable position and letting the rough fabric of his britches rub against the bare flesh of his young arse.

He flicked a comma of black hair from his eyes and allowed his hand to steal over his chest. He plucked at his dark nipples, tugging and kneeding them until they stood like berries above the pale smoothness of his chest.

Eyes still closed, he let a confusion of sensations steal over him. He saw the sun, dazzling his shielded gaze, the swaying wheat of the fields, heard the heavy drone of bees, watched the rippling flanks of the horse, saw again the enviable thickness of the horseman's cock, straining with anticipation through the fine, soft leather of his britches . . .

His hand strayed from his chest down to his narrow hips. His fingers stroked the hollow above his groin and he shuddered a little at the delicate thrill of pleasure it gave him.

He felt blood beginning to course into his cock, so that it bobbed and strained at his cotton britches. His slender fingers pushed under the waistline of his garment and closed around the warm shaft of his blood-engorged penis. He felt its juvenile slenderness, the smoothness of its pulsing head. He knew what he wanted. What he yearned for.

Opening his eyes, Ned found himself looking up at a corresponding pair of eyes, peering down at him from the darkness of the barn ceiling. He scrambled to his feet, pulling his trousers close around him, but a warm, soft voice drifted down as though to reassure him.

'Nay, young master,' it said, 'don't you pay no mind to me.' And down from the rafters swung the horseman, dropping from beam to beam with the agility of an ape and stepping into a pool of dusty sunlight.

His blue eyes shone with a light of their own, though his face remained in shadow, and they narrowed as he smiled at the trembling young man before him.

Ned's gaze ranged appreciatively over the horseman's naked torso. His chest was completely smooth and glistening with sweat. It lay in a sheen over his great, firm breast and the hard muscles of his abdomen which jutted out like a turtle shell.

The dream-Ned stepped back a little, his throat unexpectedly dry. He sensed that the horseman was smiling, a lazy, sensuous smile.

'What is it?' the stranger whispered thickly.

Ned found he couldn't meet the stranger's gaze. When he found his voice it cracked with nervousness. 'What do you want here?' he stammered. 'What are you doing on my father's land?'

The horseman's face refused to swim into focus but he seemed to be running his hand through his glossy blond hair. Then, to Ned's astonishment, he let his hand fall to his crotch. His wide, splayed fingers began to trace the outline of his cock through the creaking leather of his britches.

'Well,' he drawled, 'I happen to like it here.'

Ned stepped back further, the dry hay rustling beneath his naked feet. 'I don't think my father would be pleased if he found a stranger in here,' he offered without much enthusiasm. His blood seemed to be boiling in his veins and his heart slammed in his ribs like the firing of a brace of muskets.

The horseman pierced him with his huge blue eyes. 'I won't tell if you won't,' he said, moving closer.

He gestured expansively with his free hand. 'Such a lovely day. Seems a shame to waste it in idle talk.'

Ned swallowed. 'What do you mean?'

The horseman was rubbing his hand over his thickening cock, its outline clear through his britches. 'I've seen you looking at me, young master,' he murmured in a throaty whisper. Ned's gaze jumped to the stranger's crotch. The rounded triangular outline of the head of his cock was clearly discernible. Ned's blood pumped through him like a river of fire. He licked his lips.

'I know what you want,' continued the stranger in his honeyed, sensuous voice.

Ned cleared his throat, hoping this might make him sound a little superior. 'And what's that?'

The horseman pulled at the laces which held together his leather britches, exposing the beginnings of a delta of dark, wiry hair.

'You want me, my young buck.' He continued to unlace his trousers until they hung loose around his hips. 'You want me now, don't you?'

As if of its own volition, the horseman's massive cock slipped from its leather prison, projecting like a great fleshy sword and slapping against the hard, flat plane of his belly.

Ned marvelled at its great, veiny thickness, at the silky beauty of its purple head. As he watched, the stranger's cock pulsed with life, growing ever thicker, ever stiffer.

The horseman gave a little chuckle of satisfaction at Ned's astonished reaction. Ned's mouth fell open in confused desire.

Within the fabric of his own britches, Ned's cock set solid as rock. This was what he wanted. What his muddled desires had coalesced into. This tall, beautiful stranger, standing before him with his tumescent cock raised like a standard of his desire.

Suddenly, though, there was a pounding at the barn door. The dream-Ned tried to ignore it. He reached out for the horseman. Opened his arms wide for the stranger to take him, possess him. But the insistent knocking on the wooden doors continued. *Thrum, thrum, thrum . . .*

Ned woke, watching the pale moonlight stream through his window for several long moments before he connected his real, chilly circumstances with the blazing lustiness of his dream. He shifted beneath the covers and the knock came again.

In reality, it was the softest of rappings against the oak of his bedroom door. The floor beyond the door creaked and his father's voice whispered, 'Ned? Ned, are you awake?'

It was well past one in the morning and Ned was in no mood to talk to anyone. He turned his face away from the door and pulled the blankets over his muscular shoulders. Getting no response, his father stumped off to his own room.

Ned sighed angrily. He hated to be woken, especially from such a rare dream. But, snuggling down under the thick blankets he managed a smile.

Despite the chill, the dream had left him feverishly hot. He was very much aware of his own body, the rough blankets slipping over his naked flesh. He propped himself up on the pillows, leaning his head on one, finely boned hand. His hair fell into his eyes and he tossed it back with cat-like grace.

Lost in thought, his face wore a slight frown, a couple of deep creases marring the millpond smoothness of his forehead.

The nameless horseman seemed to flicker before him now, real as any dream. He groaned with lusty yearning, longing to feel the hard muscles of another man's stomach pressed tight against his sweat-slicked arse.

He found himself smiling his half-smile, his hand drifting to his thickening cock, and summoned up the image of the horseman in his tight, leather britches.

As he saw again the wonderful thickness of the horseman's cock, his own began to lengthen between his fingertips. In contrast to his dream self, Ned's penis was large and strong. He let his fingers caress the swollen head, tugging at the foreskin just as he had wanted his dream lover to do.

Ned stretched out on the bed, enjoying the gorgeous sensations coursing through him. His cock felt slender yet large, its smooth shaft occasionally puckered by blood-engorged veins.

Ned's hand closed into a fist around his cock and he began to pump at it, all the time remembering the beauty of the horseman's body, imagining its weight on his chest, the great cock filling his mouth, then his arse, possessing him utterly.

He got up and stood by the window. He put the flat of one hand against the cold plaster of the wall and leaned forward on tiptoe.

His calf muscles strained pleasantly and he bit his lower lip as the beginnings of a sleepy orgasm rippled through his haunches. In the moonlight, his firm, rounded buttocks clenched and shivered. His cock stood out from his moon-blanched body as he rubbed and tugged at its hot shaft.

He grunted as waves of lazy, gorgeous pleasure drifted through him. Against the wall, his flat hand dug into the crumbly plaster. Eyes closed, Ned again saw the nameless horseman; smelt his musty cock in the warm leather of his britches, imagined his lover's delighted panting as he thrust his huge cock into the yielding arse of his young master . . .

The hair on the back of Ned's neck rose and he gasped and grunted again as orgasm washed over him, his hot semen hitting the bare floorboards in quick jets.

His movements slowed and he opened his eyes, glancing down absently at the engorged purple head of his cock, now white and foamy with his come.

Ned let out a deep sigh, then a shudder of cold and leaped back into the warmth of his bed. He smiled and closed his eyes, drifting back into sleep with the sharp smell of his own semen filling his senses.

The Harlequin, without his mask now, ladled soup into a small pewter bowl and sat down on the edge of his bed.

The caravan in which he sat was pleasantly warm and lit by one solitary candle of enormous proportions. The Harlequin sipped his soup, his quick, dark eyes catching sight of his own reflection in the mottled mirror which filled one whole corner of the room.

The door opened and his twin came inside. He threw down his mask and headed straight for the tureen of steaming soup.

'S'blood!' he cried, rubbing his hands together. 'I thought that performance would never end.'

The Harlequin smiled, his supple features dimpling at the corners of his mouth. His brother sat down next to him and began to unbutton his doublet.

'Where to now, I wonder,' he said.

The Harlequin shrugged. 'Nan has a few places in mind but we'll have to go north if we're to find anywhere really friendly towards His Majesty.'

The other stroked his neat, pointed beard. 'North? 'Tis cold enough in Oxfordshire.'

The Harlequin set his soup aside and began to wriggle out of his costume. He turned down the bedclothes and leant over to blow out the candle.

For a moment, his wiry, dusky body was illuminated, honey-yellow, in the glow of the candle.

'Well,' he murmured. 'Either that or we change our allegiance.'

The bearded one gave a small, tight smile. 'To Mr Pym and his Puritans,' he said.

The other shook his head. Neither could possibly imagine such a thing.

Sir Harry Melcombe struggled out of his clothes and laid them out over the back of a chair. His bed was chilly and unwelcoming and he lay awake long into the night.

He sighed. What vexing times for a gentleman to live through! At least now he could sense there was reckoning coming. And that meant the Melcombes would have to be on their guard, prepared to do their bit for Parliament and country. If there were more like his beloved Thomas out there, then the future of England was in safe hands.

But he sighed again, full of doubt and fear and glanced across the room towards the direction of Ned's room. Thomas he could fathom. Thomas was full of promise. But, aye, to be sure, something would have to be done about Ned.

Two
_____

The next day was Sunday and, through a frost-misted window, Ned watched a solitary robin peck through the thin ice covering a water barrel.

The sky was a bleary white, threatening snow. Ned dressed quickly. William the butler had brought a message from Sir Harry requesting Ned's presence on a matter of some urgency. Ned knew from past experience that it wasn't wise to keep his father waiting but he couldn't resist preening himself just a little before the mottled mirror.

He cut a striking figure in black coat, britches and stockings, a crimson cravat tied loosely about his neck the only splash of colour. In the wintry light, Ned's pale complexion looked fine as china, his lips red as berry juice.

He adjusted his clothing and made his way swiftly downstairs, his buckled shoes ringing off the stone of the stairway.

A large breakfast of porridge, cheese and ham awaited him on the sideboard and a fire was already crackling in the grate. The room itself was wood-panelled and plainly furnished as was Sir Harry's preference.

It was a puritan household but Ned's father was by no means a humourless man. Nevertheless, it was with some apprehension that Ned seated himself by the fire, two plates of food balanced on his knee.

Sir Harry rarely requested such a meeting, preferring the company of his favourite, Thomas. Ned chuckled to himself. Thomas would have been up and out hours before. Off to inspect the lands he would one day inherit or hunting either an unlucky fox or a lucky local girl. Well, Thomas thought them lucky anyway. Ned gave a wry smile.

Turning, Ned rubbed at the mullioned window panes and looked out on to the frost-rimmed gardens. Great God, how glad he was that none of this would ever be his responsibility; that his brother, so naturally suited to be his father's heir, would continue the dreary day-to-day maintenance of the Melcombe estate. But what did Sir Harry have in mind for him? A little knot of anxiety began to worm around Ned's belly at the thought.

Ned stretched out his muscular legs towards the fire and popped a slice of ham into his mouth. He had taken a position as a junior schoolmaster shortly after his twenty-first birthday and now, five years later, was a much-liked and respected local figure.

Privately, he considered his grasp of mathematics and Latin rather shaky but was pleased that his natural talent as a painter could have such a practical application. Under his tutelage, many of the local boys had come to love and appreciate art in all its forms. But it was all just 'doodling' to Sir Harry. England was in turmoil, the old man kept insisting, and no one, including Ned, could be indifferent to it.

But Ned felt distinctly indifferent as he munched at his breakfast, staring into the crackling flames of the fire. His thoughts were entirely elsewhere, with the horseman of his dreams, with the local man he was currently enjoying and perhaps, most of all, with a certain Lewis St John . . .

The door opened and William came in. He was the most adept of the Melcombe small retinue of servants. Slender and tanned, his hair long, straight and parted in the centre, William was indeed a pleasant sight on so frosty a morning. His eyes were almond-shaped and curiously well-defined, as though outlined in dark charcoal.

His appointment had been at Ned's insistence. Sir Harry had been abroad and Thomas sick with fever when old Peel, the Melcombe butler some forty years, had suddenly passed away. The household had been thrown into confusion and Ned had decided to act quickly, asking around the countryside for anyone suitable to take up the position. The candidates had proven a dull bunch until the striking William had slid like an elegant shadow into the house.

Despite his youth, his references were excellent. But Ned had been more interested in the young man's eyes, his bee-stung lips and the way his britches clung to the firm globes of his buttocks.

There was an insolence too, behind the eyes, which Ned noticed and liked, suggesting that William considered himself every bit the equal of his master.

Ned had appointed him on the spot and none in the family had ever had cause to complain, except Ned himself, who had never yet found the youthful butler clambering into his bed as he'd hoped.

'Early this morning, sir,' murmured William, clearing the pewter plates from where Ned had left them.

'Aye,' smiled Ned. 'It's a wonder.' His eyes flickered over the firm, rope-like muscles of William's neck.

'A wonder indeed, sir,' remarked William, stoking the fire.

Ned laughed. There was the lad's insolence again.

William moved past him to open wider the heavy curtains and, despite himself, Ned felt his pulse quicken as the servant brushed past his chair, so close that he could smell the lovely muskiness of William's body.

William glanced at him, as though aware of Ned's thoughts and Ned looked quickly away, his cheeks burning. Within his black britches, his cock suddenly stiffened.

Returning to the fire, William bent low, thrusting the poker deep into the glowing embers. He wore his britches unfashionably tight and Ned's appreciative eye took in every detail of his firm buttocks, as perfect and discernible as two cheeses beneath wet muslin.

Ned longed to stand up and thrust his cock between them, to pull William's insolent face to his and force his tongue between those creamy, sensuous lips.

In his mind's eye, he was already doing it: tearing apart the

13

wooden buttons of William's shirt, letting his hand rub hard against the dark, swollen mounds of the lad's nipples.

There was a shuffling sound from beyond the doorway and Sir Harry entered, all in charcoal-black save for the wide whiteness of his collar.

He looked tired and grumpy, clearly not having slept well. William bade him good morning but the knight ignored him and made straight for the sideboard, shovelling every available food onto a large pewter plate.

'Good morning, father,' said Ned evenly. Sir Harry grunted and moved to the fireplace, stuffing cheese into his mouth without looking up.

Ned watched as William moved to the door and exited. The servant shot him one last, faintly cheeky look before closing the door behind him.

Still very much aware of his own erect cock, Ned settled himself more comfortably into his seat. Carefully, so that his father couldn't see, he managed to push his penis to one side within his britches, making its stiff hugeness slightly less obvious.

'You wanted to speak to me, father?' he said at last. Sir Harry nodded and made a gutteral sound in the back of his throat but it wasn't until he had polished off the ham and the last of the porridge that he spoke, fixing Ned with his most unnerving stare.

'Now then, Ned. I've been thinking. It's time we found you something else to do. Something more befitting a Melcombe.'

Ned set his square jaw firmly. 'I'm happy in what I do, father. I can ask for nothing more.'

Sir Harry coughed in irritation. 'Happy enough, aye, but you don't challenge yourself. Look at Thomas –'

Ned sighed. How many times had they been through this? Ned was not like his brother. It was pointless to think so. In spite of his exasperation with his father, Ned's erection persisted. It was almost as though William's distracting attractiveness lingered in the room. Ned saw again the perfect peaches of the servant's arse, so ripe, so inviting . . .

'Are you listening to me, lad?' barked Sir Harry. Ned nodded. The knight continued. 'Compared to Thomas –'

'Compared to Thomas I am disappointing indeed,' said Ned. 'But you're forgetting. Comparisons are odious.'

'Fine words –' began Sir Harry.

'Not mine, father. Shakespeare's.'

Sir Harry dismissed his son's flippancy with a wave of his thick hand. 'Nevertheless. The time's come for you to get out of that schoolroom and put away your brushes and oils.'

Ned looked around the room. His own canvasses hung on the panelled walls. Landscapes, portraits. All excellent, talented work. He sighed deeply. 'What would you have me do?'

An hour or so later, Ned Melcombe stood before his bedroom mirror once more, ran his hand through his mane of thick black hair and looked steadily at his reflection. His brilliant green eyes were almost feverishly bright and his skin, more ivory pale than ever. When he retied his cravat, his long, slender hands shook and his father's voice seemed to echo in his head.

'I fear we are headed for war, my son,' Sir Harry had said in a low, grave whisper.

Ned had sat forward in his chair. 'War? With whom?'

Sir Harry had sighed at his son's unworldliness. 'With ourselves. Neighbour against neighbour. Family against family.'

'Civil war?'

Sir Harry had nodded solemnly, going on to confess that he saw little chance of avoiding it. The King would not accept a free-thinking parliament.

Ned changed his shirt and stood for a long moment in the cold, snowy daylight, his smooth chest spotted with goose-flesh.

He picked up a fresh shirt and pulled the linen tight over his pectoral muscles. As he did up the blond wooden buttons of the cuffs he heard himself ask the fatal question: 'And what does that have to do with me?'

Sir Harry had almost leapt from his chair, his face red with fury. 'It has everything to do with you, sir! You are an Englishman. And if this King of ours is set on a course of self-destruction, I think you should be concerned about it!'

Ned had regretted his flippancy at once, but he didn't want to think about politics, didn't want to give up the quiet life he so enjoyed. In the warmth of that sitting room he wanted to think of nothing so much as how to get the unattainable William into his bed. To run his tongue over the honey skin of the servant's thighs. To take the great sac of his heavy balls into his mouth and then suck at his stiff cock, drown in the heavy musk of his body.

Standing before the mirror, Ned laid his palm over his breast, stretching the linen tight over his nipples. They were hard with desire. Even remembering the unpleasantness of the recent conversation he couldn't quite erase his desire for William, his need to conquer and control him.

The house seemed big and silent now and Ned threw himself onto the bed, kicking off his shoes as he did so.

There was a while yet before he was expected at church and he needed time to think. He stared up at the beamed ceiling, blinking slowly as he considered his father's closing remarks. 'The time will come when Thomas and I must absent ourselves from here. And someone must take over the running of the estate.'

Although Ned was grateful that his father didn't expect him to fight, the assumption of control of the Melcombe lands represented everything he despised. It meant responsibility. It meant an end to the freedom he so enjoyed, the lovers he was able to take.

Ned pushed his head back onto the pillow and groaned. Then his eyes opened wide as though he had been struck by inspiration. Perhaps the reverse was true. Perhaps, by becoming Squire in his father's absence, there was infinitely more opportunity for him to indulge himself. To achieve control. For there was surely nothing in the world so desirable as control over others. Over other men.

For a moment his mind drifted back to his dream of the strange horseman. The beautiful man who took him and possessed him, controlled *him* the way none ever had. None save one.

It was always at times such as this, Ned reflected, that he thought of Lewis. For as long as he could remember, ever since the last time he had seen his very first lover, he had sworn that no other man would ever have him, that only Lewis – sweet, gentle, wonderful Lewis – would ever be master over him.

Every other lover, every servant or common soldier he had known in the intervening years had been his. His to order, his to punish, his to enslave. There would never be another like Lewis St John.

Lying on the bed, his mind filled with confused thoughts and desires, Ned let himself drift back to an earlier, simpler time when thoughts of grown-up responsibilities were far from his mind.

He had been scarcely eighteen, the skinny, underdeveloped boy of his own dream. The news that Sir Harry was expecting visitors hadn't lifted his young spirits much. He was feeling sulky and unwanted that summer, his desires as yet unfocused, his resentment of all forms of authority as strong as any youth his age.

He spent most of those warm, balmy days in aimless wandering around the estate, lying in the fields and gazing up at the china-blue sky, taking the seemingly constant stiffness of his cock into his hand as much as three times a day.

What he fantasised about back then he could hardly remember. A collage of things, he supposed, from the pert breasts of local girls, the closeness of the boys he played and fought with at school, the weight of the great horse beneath his crotch when he and Thomas went riding.

And that was all he wanted to do that far-away day when the St Johns had arrived, to beat with quick, urgent passion at his cock, to achieve a delirious orgasm under the glaring heat of the sun, not stand like a mannequin on the driveway as his father's undoubtedly tedious visitors arrived.

The St Johns were distant cousins, Sir Harry told him, who had decamped to the north some years before. He promised that he wouldn't insist on Ned and Thomas's constant presence but it would be nice if they could at least show their faces from time to time. Sullenly, Ned had agreed, though secretly promising himself to be off into the woods as soon as possible.

The appointed day duly arrived and a large, dusty coach brought the St Johns to Humbleford. Ned and Thomas had been dressed up in their plain but smart Sunday best and stood at their father's side, uncomfortably hot.

Old Peel (still alive then before cheeky William had taken his place) opened the coach door revealing the rather finely dressed figures of Mr and Mrs St John, all satin and bows.

Trooping after them, as sullen and bored as Sir Harry's two, came the children. Sarah, the eldest with her bright, perky face and carefully braided hair; Silas, the youngest, as plain as she was pretty, and finally Lewis, tumbling from the carriage and dressed in faintly ridiculous blue velvet coat and highly polished shoes.

Ned had perked up at once. He felt his heart begin to pound and his cock set hard as rock within the confines of his britches. It was as if all those confused impulses, all that unfocused passion, leapt suddenly into physical form.

Lewis stepped onto the dusty driveway and gazed miserably at the ground. He was four years older than Ned and elegantly slim with a fine, rather fragile, high-cheek-boned face. His crown of straw-blond hair hung down to his shoulders and, above eyes the blue of cornflowers, his brows were almost unnaturally dark. Ned found the combination of blond hair and near-black eyebrows almost supernaturally beguiling. Lewis's nose was gently snubbed and rose over deliciously soft, perfectly sculpted lips.

Ned stood up straight, hoping to catch the newcomer's gaze. Surely there was something in his manner, some gleam in those lovely blue eyes which betrayed him?

But Lewis didn't look up. When introduced to Ned and Thomas he had hardly given them a second glance. Dismissed until dinner, Ned suddenly found he had little interest in running off into the countryside. Instead, he went straight to his room, listening to the muffled voices of the strangers below and thinking of Lewis.

In the next few days, to Ned's disgust, young Lewis fell into Thomas's circle. They were around the same age, of course, and seemed to have much in common. They would often ride off together to wreak some form of havoc in the village.

Lying in the summer fields as usual, Ned would shudder when he heard their voices raised in ribald shouts or gales of bawdy laughter.

Yet still the youth obsessed him. He could think of nothing but pressing his lips against the delicate rosebud of Lewis's mouth, of caressing his slender neck, of feeling his cock next to Lewis's own, thrusting and rubbing as they both spiralled to orgasm. But nothing happened.

By the end of a week, Ned had resigned himself to being a

background player in the newcomer's life. It wasn't that Lewis was unkind, far from it. Just that his easy friendship with Thomas served to make him seem older and Ned all the more juvenile and foolish for it.

Then, one Saturday, everything had changed. Sir Harry and Thomas had arranged to take the entire St John family to the spectacular Greenacre Falls, a local beauty spot which no visitor was ever allowed to miss.

Ned, in his usual sullen mood, declined the invitation and watched the group depart through his bedroom window. The sun shone down as brightly as it had throughout the summer but Ned was startled to see that the St John family wasn't quite complete. Silas and Sarah dutifully followed their parents into the coach but of Lewis there was no sign.

Excited, but with some trepidation, Ned had made his way down to Lewis's room. Peering through a crack in the door he saw the object of his affection propped up in bed with a cold flannel laid over his forehead.

Ned's throat went suddenly dry at the sight of Lewis, his chest bare in the hot room, his lovely eyes closed. Ned was just manoeuvring himself into a position where he might watch unobserved when Lewis spoke, loud and confidently.

'Are you spying on me?'

He opened one eye and the effect was so comical that Ned couldn't helping laughing. Feeling oddly emboldened, he walked into the room. Motes of dust hung suspended in the light streaming through the heavily curtained windows.

'No,' said Ned. 'Not spying. I didn't realise you were ill.'

Lewis's perfect lips widened into a grin and he tossed the flannel from his forehead.

'I'm not!' he cried brightly. 'I just couldn't bear the thought of a day with my parents and your father. Oh!' His hand flew to his mouth. 'Forgive me. I didn't mean –'

'It's all right,' laughed Ned. 'I couldn't bear it either.'

Ned glanced down at Lewis's chest. He was better developed than Ned with finely outlined muscles in his ribs and shoulders. His arms were long and powerful-looking and his hands wide and large like a grown man's.

Lewis seemed to catch Ned staring at his body and Ned looked quickly away. Lewis smiled in a friendly fashion and patted the bed. 'Come and keep me company,' he said softly.

Heart pounding, Ned sat down on the edge of the coverlet. He didn't seem to be able to meet Lewis's gaze until Lewis took his chin in one hand and lifted up his face.

Ned gazed rapturously into Lewis's icy eyes, took in every detail of his tousled blond hair and soft, peach-fuzzed skin.

Lewis's lips opened imperceptibly and Ned could see a delicate tracery of spit between them.

'You mustn't be jealous of that brother of yours, you know,' said Lewis.

Ned pulled his head from Lewis's hand angrily. He didn't like to think that his moping crush was so obvious.

'Jealous? What do you mean?'

'He's a fine fellow is Thomas. But just good sport.'

Lewis's voice had thickened, his breathing seemed quicker, more excited.

'And what am I, then?' asked Ned, holding up his head defiantly.

Lewis smiled again. 'I've seen you looking, Ned. Looking at me. And I'll tell you what you are.'

Ned swallowed. His heart was slamming against his ribs like an engine.

'What?'

'You're beautiful,' whispered Lewis.

And suddenly he was upon Ned, forcing his warm tongue into the boy's yielding mouth.

Ned frowned, all hot desire and confusion. His lips responded to Lewis's at once and he closed his eyes. He couldn't believe it was finally happening.

Lewis's big hands grabbed his arms and he felt himself thrown back onto the bed. He shivered as he felt Lewis's downy cheek slide over his and opened his eyes to see that Lewis was struggling out from under the bedclothes.

He was naked save for a pair of baggy cloth trousers and his cock made the fabric stand up as though a living creature were trapped within.

Ned lifted his arm urgently and gestured towards the door. Lewis pulled away for an instant and leapt from the bed, turning the heavy key in the lock and jumping back on top of Ned in one swift movement.

The weight of Lewis's body pinned Ned down and he could feel the ram-rod hardness of Lewis's cock against his own, just as he had imagined it.

Ned wanted to sit back and take stock. Or rise out of his own body so he could watch the scene he had so long imagined. All kinds of thoughts mingled through his brain as he kissed Lewis, his heart thumping, his cock straining inside his britches.

His breathing became quick and irregular. Blood pounded in his ears as he let his tongue intertwine with Lewis's.

Warm spit trailed between their mouths and Ned gasped as shivers of pure sensual lust raced through him. He would never have believed something could feel so good. Lewis's lips were so soft and warm, his hot breath streaming on to Ned's flushed face.

Lewis's eyes rolled lustily upwards as he finally transferred his attention to Ned's slender neck.

Ned gave out little groans of pleasure as Lewis kissed and bit and licked at the pale flesh, his tongue lapping around the curve of his ears. Lewis's mouth on his Adam's apple made Ned gasp and a warm, fuzzy delight spread through every part of him.

Now Lewis grabbed him by both wrists and pinioned his arms over his head, keeping Ned at bay whilst he pulled at the loose folds of Ned's britches.

He wriggled out of his own garment in the process and lay above Ned like some sensual angel conjured from the ether. There seemed to be room, too, for splendid wings to develop from the rippling muscles of Lewis's shoulders as he forced Ned's arms down onto the counterpane.

Ned's skinny frame contrasted sharply with the tanned litheness of Lewis's exquisite body but soon they were breast to breast, and their cocks slid and bobbed parallel to each other as heavy droplets of sweat dropped from Lewis's face.

Ned stretched out under his lover like a cat in warm sunshine and Lewis straddled the now naked boy across his chest. Ned struggled to sit up a little. His mouth yearned to close around the great, pounding stiffness of Lewis's erect penis.

Lewis smiled lustily and prodded his cock playfully against Ned's lovely face. It jabbed into his cheek and Ned tried to snap at it, his teeth clicking like the jaws of a pike.

Lewis gave a short laugh and rubbed the huge, engorged head of his penis over the smooth skin of Ned's forehead, over his eyelids and along the ridges of his cheekbones.

Ned could smell the gorgeous musk of Lewis's cock and salivated in anticipation. Inclining his head, he was able to lick at the sac of Lewis's balls, rolling each heavy testicle with the wet point of his tongue.

Lewis moaned and renewed his assault on Ned's body, nibbling and licking at the boy's shoulders and hard, aroused nipples.

Ned manoeuvred so that his lips finally closed around Lewis's cock. It felt wide and huge as it slipped past his teeth, almost touching the back of his eager throat. He panted with desire and began to suck hard at its blood-engorged length, his head bobbing up and down like a Hallowe'en apple.

Lewis let out a long, sustained groan of pleasure, his hands releasing Ned's wrists and slipping down Ned's ribs and onto his nipples which he began to rub and press with his thumbs.

His touch was strong and rough and Ned felt little spasms of desire bursting from his sensitised nipples. Lewis kneaded at their dark points, thumbs rotating, till Ned thought he would go mad with lust.

Then Lewis's hands moved behind his back and grabbed the proud shaft of Ned's cock. With his strong, slightly calloused hands he eased back Ned's foreskin and began, slowly, to pump the boy's cock with practised ease.

Ned's eyes flicked wide open as pleasure coursed through him, his mouth still filled by Lewis's massive cock. He writhed in delight, loving the sensation of Lewis's great hand tugging at his erection.

All of a sudden, Lewis pulled himself out of Ned's mouth and sat back on his haunches, his saliva-covered cock throbbing before him.

Sitting on Ned's legs, his arsehole was wide and exposed and its warm, secret vulnerability excited Ned. He looked up into his lover's face and saw that Lewis was no longer smiling. His face had taken on a kind of lusty blankness, a slightly cruel expression that only served to excite Ned further.

Without a word, Lewis laid his hand on Ned's hip and turned the boy over onto his belly. Ned inhaled the downy smell of the bedclothes and felt its smoothness caress his own stiff cock. He lay there for long moment, blinking in anticipation till his wrists were suddenly pinioned behind his back and strapped together by something. He couldn't see what but presumed Lewis had taken his belt from the pile of clothes.

Lewis pulled the belt taut and Ned gasped for a moment, realising he was completely at the stranger's mercy.

Lewis's hand tunnelled under Ned's stomach and pushed upwards, forcing Ned's arse high into the air. His young buttocks jutted upwards like unripened fruit, the crevice between them opening of its own accord. Ned felt air rush in and a strange, pulsing need beginning to throb within him.

'Beautiful,' hissed Lewis between his teeth.

His heavy hands caressed the smoothness of Ned's arse and he slipped one, then two fingers inside. Ned cried out, pain stabbing briefly through his whole body.

Then he relaxed a little, gradually receiving Lewis's fingers which shunted in and out, in and out.

Lewis then bit savagely at the smooth whiteness of Ned's arse and let his tongue drift slowly towards the forbidden mustiness of the boy's anus.

He worked away with his fingers until Ned felt his passage begin to relax. Then Lewis's tongue was at work in there, lapping and teasing, his breath sending waves of unnameable desire through Ned's being.

And suddenly Lewis was inside him.

Almost without warning, the great, pulsing shaft of the young man's cock slid into his arse, feeling so huge that Ned thought it must surely burst through his panting belly. He cried out in an agony of pleasure.

Lewis filled him entirely and he felt the tight muscles of his anus contract around the wonderful length of his lover's penis. He could feel the hard, rounded pads of Lewis's pectoral muscles skimming over his shoulder-blades as he withdrew then pounded into Ned once more.

Ned opened his eyes wide, seeing only a confusion of hazy sunshine and the snowy whiteness of the bed linen. The world seemed to be exploding around him. He gasped and panted rhythmically, in time to the coarse, animal thrusting of Lewis inside him. He felt his own cock pressed hard against his stomach, beating with blood.

Lewis slammed into Ned's arse again and again, sweat coursing down his face to land in the hollows of Ned's back. Lewis's own buttocks clenched together as he possessed young Ned and pleased them both.

Ned almost wept with delight. His hidden, unfocused desires had been given a name, had taken on substance. There was nothing in his world but the sleek, stark beauty of this beautiful man's body, his massive cock, the pulsing power of his shapely calves and thighs.

. He felt Lewis's feet covering his own and his arms shadowed by his lover's as Lewis locked them together, a mirror image of desire.

They rocked back and forth together as one body, Lewis sliding over Ned's back in a slick of sweat. Lewis kissed and bit at Ned's neck as he moaned in delight.

'Oh Christ!' he gasped. 'Christ, Ned. Open to me!'

Ned mumbled in response, lost in a haze of darkness and pleasure. He tried to relax still further and felt the head of Lewis's cock penetrate further. Still he rammed into Ned's arse till, with a cry of ecstasy he came, sending great jets of hot semen into Ned's yielding tunnel.

Lewis gradually slowed and Ned continued to rock back and forth alone, feeling Lewis's hot seed inside him, his buttocks banging against his lover's thighs as he rubbed himself against the hard mattress.

Ned's head jerked upwards and a smile of pure joy stamped itself across his face. His head buzzed, time stood still and his spirit seemed to soar as orgasm slammed through him.

Wave after wave it came, utterly consuming him. His own

come shot into the warmth of the bed, pooling beneath his sweat-soaked belly and he stopped moving at last, still feeling Lewis's semi-hard cock inside him.

Lying on his bed now, Ned found himself growing hard at the wonderful memory of Lewis St John. He stretched out and yawned, enjoying the dark, erotic warmth of his cock as it prodded at the front of his britches.

God, he had been grateful to Lewis. Grateful that his first taste of another man's sex had not been some schoolboy fumble but union with such a beautiful, experienced young man.

They had spent the remainder of the summer together, their lovemaking growing in intensity. Now it was Thomas's turn to feel jealous as Lewis no longer seemed interested in his rough and tumble lifestyle, preferring to disappear with Ned for long, wonderful, golden afternoons of secret sex. There were life-lessons too, from the experienced Lewis, who told Ned all about his theories of getting on in the world.

Ned pulled his big smooth cock from out of the folds of his britches and began to kneed at its swollen head. The musky scent of it drifted over the bed towards him and he closed his eyes, summoning up, once again, the gilded image of his first lover.

In the distance, church bells peeled brightly. Ned's eyes sprang open and he let out a stream of oaths, pausing only to jam his cock back into his trousers and slip on his shoes before careering down the stairs. He was late!

A short time later, Ned found himself strolling towards the church in the company of his father and brother.

He was still a little out of breath from his hasty run to catch them up and avoided speaking, although Thomas and Sir Harry were so deep in conversation he wondered whether they noticed his presence at all.

He listened to them in a desultory way as the squat tower of the Saxon church came into view. The King must be made accountable to his people, to the properly elected authority of his parliament, thundered Sir Harry. But the King believed his power to come directly from God, bewailed Thomas, and how could they hope to counter an argument like that?

Ned looked about him at the lichen-covered gravestones which projected from the ground at strange angles like loose teeth. His mind was far from kings and politics.

Thoughts of Lewis St John continued to haunt him and he felt a pleasant, dull ache beginning to develop in his balls, the kind of impromptu lustiness which lazy Sundays always seemed to promote in him.

But this was no idle fantasy. Something awaited him at the church. He smiled to himself and felt his cock begin to thicken again beneath the folds of his cloak.

Constricted by his undergarments, it strained against the waistband of his britches, bending like a well-oiled bow, before stretching into its full length to lie in a firm, diagonal bar across his belly.

Sir Harry and Thomas were still talking as the three approached the church. There to greet them was the decrepit but cheerful figure of the Reverend Peters, wearing two off-white cassocks to protect him from the cold. He greeted them by name and nodded to Ned as the young man slipped past him and headed for the rear of the church.

The door to the vestry opened with a soft click and Ned stepped through into total darkness. It was always like this.

Ned smiled as he closed the door behind him. The steady, lovely throb of his stiff cock nestling in his britches almost made him purr with pleasurable anticipation.

He took off his hat and laid it down in its accustomed place, then stood stock still in the musty silence.

Suddenly he felt two hands connect with his face and begin to trace their way over the strong, faintly bristled outline of his jaw.

The hands paused gently on his throat and then continued their journey down the muscled contours of his chest. Ned swallowed, his breathing beginning to quicken.

He could still see nothing in the darkness. The hands found their way to his nipples and rubbed hard at them, the rough cloth of his coat and shirt making them stand up like beads.

Ned shifted his weight and sighed gently. The hands stole down his body and finally came to rest on his crotch. Within the folds of his black britches, Ned's cock pulsed with urgent life. He could almost smell his own sex.

In an instant, the hands had wrenched his britches to his knees and he felt the cool, damp air of the vestry kiss his exposed legs and thighs. His cock stood up firm and proud, an emblem of fiery lust in the musty blackness of the room.

The hands, feeling calloused like Lewis's had, brushed against the marble smoothness of Ned's skin, travelling over his thighs and then gripping him tightly by the base of his cock.

Ned groaned and the hands slid up the shaft of his cock, tugging at his foreskin, back and forth, back and forth.

He could hear breathing in the darkness; excited, nervous breathing and, reaching out his hands, he felt a head of thick hair hovering before him.

With an urgency born of his lust, he pulled the head forward and suddenly felt his cock enclosed in the slick warm tunnel of a mouth. Ned hissed with pleasure and gripped the mane of hair in both hands.

A phantom tongue rolled over the velvet-smooth head of Ned's huge stiff cock, tickling and teasing. The feel of the rough tongue on the underside of his glans made Ned shiver with delight.

He felt smooth cheeks beneath his hands and pulled the head forward and back, thrusting his cock deeper and deeper till it seemed he would lose it in the stranger's throat. Little spasms of desire thrilled through him and he felt his buttocks twitch in response.

He grinned and tugged at the hair, glorying in the spit-drenched baseness of it all, pounding his cock in and out till the mysterious lover almost gagged.

In the aisle of the church, thought Ned distractedly, the congregation would be filing inside. Little did they realise the profane scene being enacted only feet away from their pious faces.

Ned wound lengths of hair around his fists and pushed himself harshly, repeatedly, into the wet mouth. His cock felt like it was about to burst and currents of electric bliss shot up and down his spine.

Suddenly he tensed, his jaw fell slackly open and he cried out as orgasm washed over him. The mouth continued to work away, sucking, sucking, sucking as sperm jetted from Ned's cock deep into the throat.

'Enough!' gasped Ned, pushing the head away.

With practised skill, Ned pulled up his britches, the vestry shutters were opened and pale, milky light flooded the little room. Ned swept up a pile of hymn books and moved out into the church without a word.

Entering the knave, Ned went about his appointed tasks quickly and efficiently.

Sir Harry looked on appreciatively from the family pew. Thomas was staring into space, more than a little bored.

The church was full now and Ned took his place by his father's side just as the ancient Reverend Peters shambled into his accustomed place in the pulpit.

Ned ran a hand through his raven-black hair and bowed his head in prayer. His eyes remained open, however, and he watched as the vestry door opened and a young cleric entered.

Ned lifted his head slightly and gave the cleric a conspiratorial smile. Cornelius Matthew, his pretty face still flushed from the pleasure it had just given Ned, flashed a shy smile back.

By long tradition, the squire's family would assist in the smooth running of the Sunday service. Sir Harry had served in this capacity himself as a young man, eventually giving way to Thomas and finally to Ned. Until some little Melcombes came along, therefore, it remained Ned's duty.

These duties had been perfunctory and dull, until the arrival of the new cleric some three years before. Suddenly, Ned's duties became infinitely more pleasurable.

He and Cornelius had got on at once and, within a short time, had become lovers. This was now a Sunday tradition. The cleric would have arrived early so that all the actual work was done well before the congregation arrived and so that the precious quarter of an hour could be spent in other activities.

Ned watched Cornelius go about his own work as the Reverend Peters droned interminably on. Cornelius had long, coppery hair which hung in scooped strands over dark eyes. His neat, dark brows contrasted with the paleness of his blue eyes and the soft, almost feminine shape of his wide, well-proportioned mouth.

Suddenly Ned noticed something, hanging gossamer-like from Cornelius' fine hair.

He caught Cornelius' eye and gestured as subtly as he could.

The cleric frowned, then rolled his eyes upwards to examine his fringe.

A stringy bead of semen hung there and Cornelius quickly brushed it away with his hand, embarrassed and horrified and amused all at once.

He bowed his head, blushing furiously as the Reverend Peters finally came to the end of his sermon. The congregation got to its feet in order to sing the first hymn and Sir Harry turned to Ned, nodding with satisfaction.

'Good service,' he whispered.

Ned could only agree.

Three

Edward Vane had always been an early riser. As dawn broke over the city of Nottingham, he strode out into freezing morning, dressed in black from head to toe, his long legs carrying him across the cobbles in swift steps.

He was an extraordinarily imposing man of some forty years, ruggedly handsome with a mane of greying black hair and eyes as black as coals. His hawkish nose and thin, cruel mouth struck fear in all who saw him but this was singularly appropriate for the King's own Prosecutor.

It was Vane's task to travel the country in search of those heathen, treacherous men and women who had deviated from the path of Christ and, therefore, threatened the safety of the realm. Some called him a witchfinder but he paid no mind to them. He had the power to cut out the tongue of any dissenter and often took great delight in doing just that.

He had an appointment with the Governor that morning and intended to lecture him on his folly at allowing a band of travelling actors to decamp in the city. Actors always brought bad folk with them and, in such restless times, order had to be maintained.

Vane walked through a large, chilly section of cloistered stone and then stopped suddenly as he heard a bird's song, high and bright on the morning air.

He looked about and saw a tiny robin perched on a nearby

stone buttress. He smiled at it, his chalk-white face folding into deeply etched lines. The bird continued to sing, its throat warbling and its crimson chest puffed out.

Vane crept closer with easy stealth, smiled again, raised his gloved fist above the bird and then smashed it into a bloody pulp.

His smile faded at once and he cocked his head to one side, looking at the gory mess on his glove. He wiped his hand absently on the stonework and then strode away as if nothing had happened.

Cornelius Matthew set down a heavy pewter candlestick at the side of the altar and immediately got to work polishing its twin. Morning light spilled through the stained-glass church windows, bathing Cornelius in red from head to toe like a martyred saint. He smiled to himself as he worked, recalling with excited clarity the previous day's encounter with Ned Melcombe.

Beneath his heavy black gown, Cornelius' body seemed to tingle with remembered sensation. He saw himself kneeling on the cold stone floor, his eager mouth sucking at the great stiff length of Ned's cock, his hair pulled tightly by his lover as he approached his orgasm. Then the hot, salty flood of Ned's sperm as it jetted into Cornelius' throat.

Then, out into the church as though nothing had happened and their games were over for another day.

Cornelius found it hard to remember a time when he and Ned had not been together. Theirs was an intense, if strange relationship, with very specific rules which Ned had laid down the very first time they had made love. It had been years now, three years of wonderful, forbidden union. And yet Cornelius Matthew was not a happy man.

He sat down on the steps leading to the altar and sighed. He knew he was handsome, he knew his body was pleasing and he knew that the profane things he and Ned practised meant everything to him. But never once, in all this time, had Ned spared him a fond word.

When their games were over, there was never a time of lazy, loving sleep, never an affectionate kiss. This was not how Ned wanted it.

Ned was Cornelius' master, the cleric his slave. It was a game with strict rules that never changed.

Yet the more the beautiful Ned abused him, the more harshly he treated him, the cleric seemed to fall ever deeper in love.

Just once, thought Cornelius, he wanted to turn up at the manor in the dead of night and just slip into Ned's bed, feel his strong arms wrapped around him, keeping him safe.

Ned's detachment, however, ruled this out.

Once or twice, he had tried to speak to Ned about their prospects together but he had refused to be drawn. This was how it had to be, Ned insisted. If Cornelius was unhappy with the arrangement, then it would simply cease. And Cornelius would never do anything to jeopardise what he had with Ned.

In the meantime, of course, he was allowed a life of his own.

There was a short, sharp knock at the church door and Cornelius got to his feet to answer it. His shoes clap-clapped over the cold stone aisle as he made his way down.

As he opened the door, a wave of cold January air blew past him, sweeping his copper hair back off his high forehead.

Standing in the porch was a young man of perhaps nineteen. He was poorly dressed in a ragged, rust-coloured coat and ill-fitting britches, his bare toes, poking out of the sides of broken shoes, were white with cold.

He was shivering but, for a moment, Cornelius made no move to let him inside the church. Instead, he spent a long moment letting his gaze wander over the new arrival's face.

Under a crudely cropped head of slick black hair, was a face of saturnine beauty, its darkness exaggerated by the heavy blackness of his brows and deep brown eyes. His complexion was creamy smooth yet obscured by mud and his nose, broken long ago, had the snubbed look of a fist-fighter's. His mouth, his neat, trembling mouth, was as red and petulant as a sulky boy's.

Cornelius let his eyes drink in the details of this exquisite boy on his doorstep and then moved to one side.

'Good day,' said Cornelius simply and the newcomer slipped past him with a nod. Cornelius hovered in the porch a moment to ensure they had not been seen and then closed the door.

For a moment, he could not see the young man but then found

him shivering by the font. Cornelius smiled, beckoned and then led the way back up the aisle of the church, his cloak billowing behind him.

All the way, the stranger clutched at himself as though in fear and cast anxious glances into the shadowed corners of the church. Cornelius led him through the vestry – the vestry where he and Ned shared their Sunday ritual of cock sucking – and on into a small building joined to the main body of the little church.

It was a plain, spartan room, as was only fitting for the lodgings of a cleric but Cornelius had managed to make it pleasant all the same. His bed was wide and fresh linen was stretched tightly over it.

The young man stood by the door once they were inside and Cornelius moved swiftly to the windows, closing the shutters over them. Little chinks of snowy light peeked through the shutters' cracked wooden surfaces.

In the darkness, Cornelius could only just make out the outline of the newcomer but could hear his breathing, quick and agitated as a cornered deer.

Cornelius felt a current of drowsy lust pass through him and shivered with anticipation. He took the boy's hand and led him into the centre of the room.

A sliver of light from the uneven shutters fell in a bar over his huge brown eyes and Cornelius smiled. He ran his hand over the oily quills of the boy's cropped hair and kissed him gently on the mouth.

'Welcome,' he breathed.

The boy said nothing. He merely reached out his own hand and ran it, haltingly, over Cornelius' face. Slowly, with great deliberation, he began to unbutton the cleric's shirt.

The boy's name, Cornelius had discovered to his delight, was Miracle Smith. He had been christened thus after being born so premature that no one believed he would live. But live he had, and had grown, as was obvious to all in Humbleford, into an extraordinarily beautiful creature. Unfortunately, he had also been born dumb and this had set him aside from his fellows to such an extent that his parents despaired of ever finding him a role in life.

That was how Cornelius had come across him, skulking in his

father's farm, gently playing with a lamb. Miracle's family had, according to tradition, decided to put the fool of the family into the Church.

The Reverend Peters had instructed Cornelius to seek the lad out and determine whether he had the right spiritual qualities to be of some use to the parish. It took Cornelius very little time to determine that Miracle Smith had qualities all of his own.

In the hush of the room, Miracle pulled Cornelius' cloak over his head and continued to unbutton the cleric's linen shirt, exposing his broad, well-defined chest and small, erect nipples. Then, laying his arms by his sides, he let Cornelius do the same for him, shrugging off his tawdry coat and slipping his ragged shirt over his cropped head.

A broad expanse of hair, like the image of a pressed butterfly, covered the big, solid peaks of Miracle's chest. Years of labour on the farm had made him extraordinarily fit and his arms and belly were bunched with muscle. A teasing trail of hair led down into his groin.

Cornelius felt his own cock beginning to stiffen within his britches. In the expectant hush of the room, he could feel the blood pounding into it, just as he could feel the racing of his heart.

He grasped Miracle by his arms and kissed him feverishly all over his face and neck.

Miracle shivered with pleasure, then, like an aroused animal, embraced Cornelius and pressed his own lips firmly against those of the young cleric. His tongue was long and warm and Cornelius felt it probe all around his mouth, entwining with his own tongue, reaching to the back of his throat, running around the underside of his moistened lips.

Miracle began to push Cornelius backwards towards the bed and Cornelius let out a little groan of delight. The farmboy's hands were all over him now, pinching at his swollen nipples, running appreciatively over the smooth skin of the cleric's chest and back.

They fell back together onto the bed and Cornelius gasped a little at the weight of the solid young man lying on top of him. He could feel Miracle's cock, straining for release, banging against his own.

Without once ceasing his kissing and biting, Miracle began to pull down Cornelius' britches and stockings. The cleric let his feet dangle over the edge of the bed and heard his shoes slip off and clop to the floor. He felt Miracle's warm, strong arm burrow under him and pull off the remainder of his garments before hurling them into the corner, leaving Cornelius naked.

He lay beneath the beautiful farmboy, enjoying the alternately rough and smooth texture of Miracle's britches and warm chest as they slid over him. Miracle kissed him for the longest time, their mouths locked together in passion, their tongues stabbing deep into the other's throat.

Cornelius placed his hands at the top of Miracle's britches, feeling the marble-smooth hollow at the base of the boy's spine.

Then he let his hands slip inside the britches and run over the already sweaty globes of Miracle's beautiful arse. As they kissed, Cornelius grasped Miracle's buttocks, allowing his fingers to play at the entrance to the boy's arse.

Miracle suddenly broke away and, with the impatience of a frustrated beast, pulled his own shabby trousers down to his ankles and then kicked them off. His thighs, buttocks and legs had an athlete's definition and his impressive, thick cock rose proudly from a forest of wiry black hair.

They both lay naked far a moment, enjoying the warmth of their bodies pressed together, then Miracle slid to Cornelius' side and gathered the cleric up into his arms, laying one long, muscular leg over Cornelius' thigh.

Cornelius gazed lovingly into the boy's big brown eyes.

'You are so very beautiful,' he murmured. The farmboy met his gaze. His lovely face was set into a kind of concentrated frown, as though his desire for Cornelius, the burning sexual passion within him, was an animal instinct he was helpless to resist.

This moment of calm was brief. Miracle slid his leg from Cornelius' thigh and held him tightly in a fevered embrace. He kissed him on the forehead, on the cheek, on his collarbone and chest before running his spit-glistened tongue over the smooth hollows of the cleric's thighs.

Cornelius' head began to move from side to side as though of its own accord. He meshed his fingers into the slick, short tufts of Miracle's hair and began to stroke fondly at them.

Miracle's head bobbed and jerked about as he licked and kissed all over Cornelius' groin. Finally, his tongue found the big, loose sac of his balls and began to lap at them.

His tongue felt warm and rough, like a cat's and Cornelius groaned with pleasure. He felt Miracle's sweet, broken nose jab into the soft flesh of his thighs as he scooped up Cornelius' balls with his mouth and gently sucked at them.

The cleric stretched out on the bed, feeling the cool softness of his pillow swamp and muffle his ears. His breath began to come in short, soft, excited bursts as Miracle let Cornelius' balls slide from his hot mouth and transferred his attentions to the aching, thick rod of his cock.

With one, broad, muddied hand, Miracle placed his own cock between Cornelius' legs and the cleric moved his knees together in response, trapping the big, purple head between his calves. With Miracle leaning over him, he was able to rock a little, pleasuring his lover as Miracle pleasured him.

Miracle grunted in response as he licked at the base of Cornelius' cock. Cornelius kept his thighs pressed together, enjoying the lovely, firm presence of Miracle's cock between his sweaty legs.

The boy's tongue made its way up the shaft of the cleric's cock, lapping and tickling at its veiny length.

Then Miracle's mouth closed over the head of Cornelius' cock and began to slide up and down. Cornelius gasped at the violence of the act, feeling the soft tissue of his cock sliding over Miracle's teeth.

A gorgeous, sensual warmth began to wash over him and he sighed in complete contentment as Miracle's wet mouth sucked at the hot, wide head of his organ. The boy's skilled tongue flicked over the glans so that Cornelius let out little gasps of pleasure, then insinuated itself into the little crack of his urethra.

Cornelius jerked with pleasure and, moving his legs, felt the great thickness of Miracle's cock slip from between them and come to rest by his sweat-soaked arse. As Miracle sucked at him, so his cock banged repeatedly at the cleric's buttocks. It was almost too pleasurable to stand.

Cornelius grasped Miracle's head and began to force it up and down, thrusting his thighs forwards so that his cock penetrated deep into the farmboy's throat. Then Miracle pulled away and kissed him again, his mouth tasting of Cornelius' own sex.

The cleric kissed him in response, bright and alive with passion, his hot tongue rolling and licking over Miracle's flushed, beautiful face.

Then Miracle returned to his work, this time moving himself so that he was able to handle Cornelius' cock and, with his fingers, stretch out the delicate membrane beneath its purple head.

Cornelius cried out with joy as Miracle's tongue began to gently, expertly flick at the glossy surface, sending little currents of electricity through him. He felt a tremendous build-up of pleasure and wrapped his legs around Miracle's body.

Still Miracle continued, his wet lips sliding over the most sensitive part of Cornelius' blood-thickened cock. The cleric gripped him tightly between his legs and then gasped as his climax suddenly powered through him. Light seemed to flood his brain, to illuminate the lids of his closed eyes and he didn't know where he was, who he was any more.

He came and sperm lashed against the warm, hard, tanned body of Miracle as he hovered over Cornelius, yet still he carried on, his mouth sucking hungrily at his lover's penis.

Sensitised beyond endurance, Cornelius banged with his fists at Miracle's broad, muscled back, his body twisting beneath Miracle's lips, his cock slick with come.

'Enough! Please! Please!' he cried, his breath coming in fits and starts.

Finally, Miracle ceased and looked up at Cornelius. He was grinning broadly and there was a wonderful shadow smile of white sperm laced across his beautiful face. Cornelius gently caressed Miracle's cheek and kissed him affectionately on the lips.

'You're a miracle indeed,' he whispered and the farmboy smiled again. Then the same, concentrated frown returned to cloud his face and he sat up on his haunches, exposing the tumescence of his lovely cock.

'Well,' said Cornelius 'What are we to do with that, then?'

Miracle pressed his soft lips against Cornelius' and embraced him lovingly. Cornelius looked up at the low plaster ceiling. If only it could be this way with Ned. If only they could share such intimacy as well as passion.

Cornelius grunted as he felt the air almost knocked out of him by the weight of Miracle on top of him. The farmboy's cock was lying, ram-rod straight, over his belly.

The cleric raised his legs into the air and hooked his feet around Miracle's neck, leaving his arse exposed and prone. The cheeks of his buttocks parted slightly and he felt air rush inside him.

Miracle hovered over him, like a bull awaiting release, then felt under the pillow and retrieved a small, ceramic pot. He pulled out the cork with his teeth, revealing a modest supply of honey. Cornelius smiled up at him and nodded.

Rapidly, his cock pulsing and throbbing before him, Cornelius' legs wrapped around his neck, Miracle scooped out the honey and plastered it liberally around the entrance to the cleric's anus. His slippery fingers found their way inside, making Cornelius' arse a warm, lubricated tunnel, aching to receive him.

Gently, he laid the pot to one side and, steadying himself, slid the great, slick length of his cock inside Cornelius.

The cleric gasped. It was impossible not to. Although they had made love many times before, the physical presence of Miracle's huge cock within him always made Cornelius feel like it was the first time.

It was extraordinary, it was wonderful, to feel that two men could join like this, almost fuse into one being.

Cornelius shut his eyes and concentrated on the sensation of being filled by this beautiful, silent boy. Gradually, Miracle pulled out a little, his honeyed cock enclosed by the constrictive tunnel of Cornelius' arse.

At once, he pushed back in again.

His gentleness was delicious and Cornelius wondered that he could find such pleasure in both a loving union and the violent, wanton lust he enjoyed with Ned.

But his arse was open to Miracle now, filled with him so that the silky walls of his anus shuddered with pleasure. Miracle began to move faster, his hips slamming against Cornelius' bones as his rigid cock moved within him.

Cornelius grabbed at Miracle's hair, shouting and gulping great lungfuls of air as his lover fucked him. It was impossible that anything could feel so good, he decided, somewhere within his buzzing, lust-befuddled mind.

The piercing rod of Miracle's cock would surely split him in two. And perhaps that was what he wanted. To die like this. To die in such ecstasy. He was suddenly consumed by the desire to be flogged, to feel Miracle's hand cracking across the soft flesh of his buttocks, even as the farmboy's great penis slid in and out of him.

And then he thought of Ned, remembered Ned taking him from behind or like this. He saw himself pressed hard against a wall, his wrists tightly chained, his naked, sweat-soaked body rammed against it by the force of Ned's huge cock. And Ned not seeming to care for him, content only with his own pleasure.

Cornelius opened his eyes and saw the beautiful boy above him, his dark features dripping with sweat. But the image of Ned kept returning, overlaying itself onto Miracle's gorgeous, sulky face.

Cornelius shook his head as though to clear it and clamped his eyes shut. He bit into his lower lip and smiled in satisfaction as he heard Miracle begin to grunt rhythmically as he approached orgasm.

Banishing all thoughts of Ned from his mind, Cornelius let waves of pleasure break over him, glorying in the incredible, hot beauty of Miracle's cock jammed into his arse.

He moved his hips back and forth, encouraging Miracle to his climax. It should never end, he thought, but finally, with three long thrusts, Miracle shot his seed into Cornelius' anus and the cleric felt it fill him like jets of warm water.

He let his legs fall from Miracle's neck and grasped the farmboy tightly as he pulled his softening penis out of the honey-drenched hole of Cornelius' arse.

Miracle gazed lovingly into Cornelius' eyes and the cleric smiled. He had to restrain himself from patting the boy on the head.

Cornelius was glad to have the boy, to know his love was unconditional. He closed his eyes.

They lay there, side by side, gripping each other tightly as though sheltering from a storm until both slid into a deep, dreamless sleep.

Ned put in a hard day at the schoolhouse before excusing himself mid-afternoon. He needed to think over the impact of his father's words, especially now Sir Harry had supplied more detail.

After church, they had sat around the dinner table (William serving them with a saucy sly look in his eye the whole time) whilst the elderly knight spoke passionately about the coming war he envisaged. His tired old face seemed infinitely sad. It was not a conflict he sought, but there seemed no way to avoid it.

'And therefore we must be ready. *All* of us,' he declared, fixing Ned with his beady stare.

Ned wandered the frozen grounds of the Melcombe estate in something of a daze, his breath steaming in great clouds as he tramped over the fields which were soon to be his concern.

He hardly felt competent to deal with the day-to-day running of the place, never mind filling his father's formidable boots. He stopped and hugged himself against the freezing cold.

Beneath his feet, a frozen furrow of mud was glazed by a pane of frost. He brought one foot down smartly on to it and it shattered satisfyingly. Ned rolled back his head and gazed up at the darkening sky, suddenly feeling immensely dissatisfied.

Thoughts of Lewis St John, of the happy, simple time they had spent together, had made him look again at his life. Perhaps his father was right. Perhaps he was just wasting his potential shut away in that gloomy little schoolroom. But to become Squire of Humbleford in his father's absence? The leap of imagination required made Ned almost light-headed.

The harsh *caw-caw* of a rook brought Ned back to earth and he continued his graceless stumble over the frozen soil.

Ahead, in a little copse of trees stood a funny, ramshackle building something like a small Greek temple in appearance. Twin columns fronted a dark doorway, thick with briars.

This was the Melcombe Folly, built by Sir Harry's grandfather some hundred years previously. In their childhood, Ned and Thomas had delighted in the place, imagining it a fort one day, a fairy-tale castle the next. Gradually, the sandstone building had fallen into decay and, these days, none but Ned had a use for the place.

Ned approached its crumbling exterior with a wry smile and plonked himself down on the stone steps which led to the entrance. He rested his head on one hand and his black hair fell forwards into his eyes.

He shivered a little and closed his eyes, willing himself away from the cold, back to the glorious summer of his eighteenth year.

What was plain to him now was that he had been in love with Lewis. Ten years of fevered couplings with anonymous men and his strange relationship with Cornelius Matthew had proved that to him. But, when all was said and done, he had only been a boy.

The St Johns visit had drawn to its inevitable end and Ned was bereft. The older boy had taught him things he'd never even dreamt of, opened doorways to the forbidden darkness in his soul. Most of all he had taught Ned the power of control. That he must never let sentiment cloud his ambition. That men were merely sexual objects for him to enslave and use. Ned had found his words thrilling and exciting, longing for a time when he would be old enough to put this ethic into practice.

He and Lewis spent their final, golden afternoon together and Lewis had squeezed his hand tightly before planting a final kiss on his lips.

'Now I'll leave you,' Lewis had said. 'And we'll never see each other again, because that is how it should be.'

Despite Lewis's callous principles, Ned felt his heart ache as he watched the St Johns depart.

Much as Lewis had obviously enjoyed his lips on Ned's mouth, his great cock inside Ned's arse, the warmth of his taut, lithe body pressed against him, Ned knew he was just one of many. Lewis prized his freedom and independence above all and he had found an apt pupil in Ned Melcombe.

In the years that had passed, Ned had efficiently shut down his emotions so that his power over other men was never threatened.

The cold was starting to tickle at Ned's face, sending summer thoughts flying.

Distantly, the church bell tolled five. Ned craned his neck

around the corner of the temple. Cornelius was late. Normally he was here by now.

It was the same every Monday. Another ritual. Ned smiled humourlessly. Would Lewis be proud of him, he wondered. He shook his head as though to clear it. That was a long time ago. It was senseless, dangerous even, to look back.

The snort of a horse signalled, at last, the arrival of the young cleric. He sauntered into view wrapped in a thick black cloak, atop a grey mare.

His coppery hair protruded from under the cowl of the cloak, his pretty features fixed in a boyish grin.

'I know. I'm late!' he called brightly, swinging himself from the saddle. Ned said nothing and scarcely reacted when Cornelius pulled Ned towards him and gave him a hug. The cleric stepped back, his left eyebrow shooting up in a question mark of puzzlement.

'What's the matter?'

Ned shook his head and took Cornelius by the hand, leading him through the temple doorway into the darkened interior of the ruin.

This was their private place. In contrast to the damp decay of the exterior, the inside of the folly was well preserved. Rugs and sacking covered the floor and the broken walls were festooned with candles. Rivulets of wax covered every niche.

But the room could not be made too comfortable. For that would spoil the games that Ned and Cornelius liked to play.

In addition to the drifts of wax, the walls held other adornments. Thick metal bracelets cushioned with velvet hung from two walls, from another, looped ropes.

In one corner, a solid old table had been converted to carry chains at each leg. Bulky braziers were grouped in the shadows along with a variety of flails, whips and birch rods.

Ned looked about at the dark place as he led Cornelius inside. In a moment of inspiration, he had daubed the stones with cabalistic symbols. Should the place be discovered, he hoped it would be taken for a witches' coven rather than a lusty playground.

He closed and locked the temple door then lit four nests of candles, bathing the old room in a lovely, opalescent light.

Cornelius stood before him, his liquid eyes wide with a kind of expectant wonder. Ned took his hand again and led him towards the wall.

'We cannot be too long tonight, Ned,' said the cleric, matter of factly. 'I have to go Nottingham tomorrow on church business and –'

Ned clamped a hand over Cornelius' mouth, cutting him off abruptly. Ned's eyes were bright with lust.

'Not a word,' he whispered, grabbing Cornelius by the arm.

The young cleric gave a little whimper of pleasure as Ned pushed him against the cold stone at the temple wall and pulled off his black cloak in one movement.

Beneath it, Cornelius wore only his big, thigh-high boots. Ned had instructed him to ride naked save for his cloak. It was all part of their game. Ned knew how Cornelius loved the thrill of it, the danger of discovery.

Cornelius stood shivering in the candlelight. His body was fine and freckled with an almost feminine voluptuousness which Ned liked. His thighs were dimpled with goose-flesh above the high sides of his boots.

Silently, Ned lifted Cornelius' arms over his head and clamped his wrists into the manacles set into the wall.

For a long moment, Ned let the cleric stand there, naked and shivering, his cock shrivelled, his balls retracted into their sac.

The candle-flame sputtered a little in the cold. Cornelius bowed his head, his hair falling forward like the patterns of wax which surrounded him.

'What is it . . . master?' he whispered at last.

Ned stepped back, slowly drawing a three-tailed leather flail from the iron stand next to him. 'You were late,' he murmured.

Cornelius breathed in sharply and twisted in the manacles, as though expecting Ned to crack the flail across his naked buttocks. But no blow came.

The young cleric craned his neck in an effort to see Ned but his heavy hair obscured his vision. Still no blow.

'I was late. I'm worthless, I know. Punish me, master. Punish me.'

Ned looked down coolly at the naked globes of Cornelius' arse.

He still held the flail in one gloved hand and, moments later, he began to trace a line with it over Cornelius' flesh. The young cleric shuddered in anticipation. The suspense was exquisite.

Ned thrust his hand into his britches and pulled out the warm, thick rod of his own cock. The sound of this made Cornelius flinch again.

Ned began to rub at his cock, feeling the head grow sticky with pre-come beneath the soft leather of his glove. With the other hand, he swished the flail through the chilly air, just missing Cornelius' arse.

The cleric flinched again and gave a low groan.

'Please, master,' came his thick whisper, 'punish me!'

Ned's face was fixed in a slack, lazy smile of desire. 'You like to be flogged, Cornelius,' he said teasingly. 'If I am to punish you, surely I must refrain from using this instrument.'

Cornelius shook his head urgently. His hair ruffled over his naked, freckled shoulders. 'No. Please,' he murmured, his voice scarcely more than a low grumble of lust.

Ned moved closer, still holding his huge stiff cock in one hand, and let the trailing ends of the flail brush once more over the naked skin of the cleric's arse.

Then he took up position, legs spread wide, and let the head of his cock play around the entrance to Cornelius' anus. He ran his gloved hands over his lover's back and shoulder then, gripping Cornelius' neck, kissed the smooth, exposed flesh with a fierce urgency.

Cornelius groaned with pleasure. Ned opened his mouth wide, twin trails of spit stretching between his jaws, and bit hard into Cornelius' neck. The naked cleric yelled in delight, then tried to evade Ned's vampire-like grip on him.

'No, no, no,' he muttered. 'No more.'

Ned ignored him, biting, sucking and kissing at the muscular length of his lover's neck. Then he stepped back, seizing his own cock again and suddenly lashing the flail over Cornelius' arse.

The cleric cried out in pain, a cry that immediately dissolved into a low mumble of desire.

Ned looked down at Cornelius with a kind of detached passion, enjoying the sight of the naked, manacled man, the candlelight giving his body a painterly beauty, his legs all but hidden by the great leathery enclosures of the boots.

The flail swished through the air again, slapping against Cornelius' buttocks and leaving a bright red weal on the pale skin. At once, Ned brought it to bear again, then again, then again, stinging his lover repeatedly with the three-tongued flail.

Cornelius gasped, biting his lip in undisguised joy. Still Ned rubbed at his own cock with a gloved hand, the soft leather arousing him further.

He beat Cornelius until the cleric writhed in pleasure and pain like a penitent sailor lashed to a ship's wheel. His arms struggled in their manacles, muscles standing firm as his cock, which Ned could just make out as Cornelius twisted in his chains, standing ram-rod erect from its furze of dark pubic hair.

'Now, master,' begged Cornelius. 'Take me now.'

Ned threw the flail aside and grabbed Cornelius by the hair, pulling back his head and biting and licking at his mouth and throat.

He kissed the cleric fiercely, ramming his hot, wet tongue into Cornelius' willing mouth. Then, grasping Cornelius' manacled wrists, he draped himself over his lover's naked form and manoeuvred his cock into the tunnel of Cornelius' arse.

Cornelius cried out as Ned thrust up and then deep inside him. Ned felt the walls of his lover's anus clamp close around the pulsing shaft of his cock and groaned with pleasure.

Already slippery with sweat and pre-come, Ned's cock began to move in and out almost of its own accord.

A gorgeous, formless pleasure began to gush through Ned's body, coupled with a delicious sense of power. The naked, manacled man he was fucking was his to own. His possession. His slave.

Somehow, the anonymity of Cornelius' form, his face hidden by the coppery curtain of his hair, only served to excite Ned further.

An image leapt into his mind of Cornelius bound and hooded, devoid of self-will, merely a toy for Ned's satisfaction.

Ned grunted with pleasure, the image burning itself into his mind, overlaying even the reality of the swaying, sweating, naked man he was entering.

His cock slid easily in and out, slick with moisture, and at each thrust he felt himself grow nearer to his climax.

He gripped Cornelius' buttocks in both hands, forcing the cheeks apart with his gloved thumbs as his cock rammed inside. The room seemed to swim in and out of focus, a pleasure-hued riot of candlelight and sweat, the tinkling of Cornelius' manacles, the staccato groaning of the cleric as Ned pleasured him.

Cornelius clenched his buttocks tightly now, sending wave after wave of delight through Ned's body. Ned ground his teeth and gasped as orgasm ripped through him.

In a frenzy of lust, he bit and chewed at Cornelius' back and slapped his gloved hands repeatedly at his already red-raw arse.

Finally, Ned pulled out, sperm trailing from his cock.

Ned stood for a long moment, his cock hanging limp but still thick outside his britches. He wiped his brow with the back of his hand and then thrust his cock back inside his clothes.

He unlocked the manacles from Cornelius' wrists and the cleric almost fell to the floor. He turned towards Ned, his face burning with pleasure and gorgeous shame, his cock large and proud with arousal.

Ned smiled and threw Cornelius' cloak at him.

'Come,' he said. 'You'll be late for the Reverend Peters.'

The cleric's pretty face fell. He glanced down at his cock as though pleading for satisfaction.

Ned smiled his familiar half-smile and grasped hold of Cornelius' cock in one gloved hand. The cleric gasped as Ned tugged at his penis, pulling him gently into the folds of his cloak.

Skilfully, Ned's fingers jerked at the bulbous head of Cornelius' cock, slipping the foreskin back so that it made a gentle tick-tick rhythm as he was masturbated.

Cornelius closed his eyes and moaned softly to himself. His cock stood firm and upright in the clenched palm of Ned's hand and his fine chest heaved up and down in breathy desire.

The proximity of his lover and the heat of his breath seemed to make Cornelius shiver. He nodded his head slowly, lost in his lustiness.

His eyes flickered slowly open. They were filmy with desire and he grinned broadly. He groaned as the pressure of Ned's hand on his cock increased then nodded again as though incapable of speech.

Ned saw that he was close to coming and increased his pumping of the cleric's cock.

He tossed his head back imperiously and looked down at the writhing, naked man he was bringing to orgasm. Soon, he would be Squire and Lord of the Manor. Anything might be possible then. He would no longer have to hide out in damp ruins like the temple. He could use the house freely. He could . . . Ned laughed quietly at the expression . . . *entertain*.

Cornelius cried out and jerked suddenly within Ned's grasp. His semen shot out of his engorged cock in three or four quick bursts, covering Ned's glove.

Falling to his bare knees, the cleric began to plant fervent kisses on Ned's hands. He seemed scarcely aware of the effect of the rough floor on his skin and scrambled about, giddy with the afterglow of his pleasure.

Ned wiped Cornelius' sperm onto the cleric's own face and then lifted the point of his chin so that he was gazing directly into Ned's eyes.

'I am to be Squire of Humbleford,' said Ned. 'What do you think of that?'

'You are my master,' murmured Cornelius.

'No,' laughed Ned. 'It's true. I am to be Squire whilst my father and brother are away.'

Cornelius was genuinely surprised. He pulled his cloak quickly around his shivering frame. 'Away? Where?'

'They're planning to raise a force of troops,' said Ned, turning for the door. 'My father expects war.'

Cornelius looked troubled. He scurried up to Ned's side as Ned unlocked the heavy old door. 'What will it mean for us?'

Ned opened the door and peered out to make sure they weren't seen then stepped out into the dusk.

'It means fun,' he said with a smile, wiping the last of the cleric's come onto his cloak.

★ ★ ★

47

January brought momentous events. King Charles, enraged at the constant attacks by Parliament upon his authority, ordered the arrest of five of its members. He came to Westminster himself, only to find the five MPs had already disappeared.

To many, the King was showing himself in his true colours, as a tyrant and a rogue. He made his way to Hampton Court, his coach surrounded by a teeming throng. Many carried placards upon which was written the single word: *Liberty*!

The Queen fled abroad in the hope of obtaining help from the Royal houses of Holland and Denmark whilst Charles firmly resisted a militia order from Parliament, transferring power of the armies of England to them. 'By God! Not for an hour!' thundered Charles. 'You have asked that of me which was never asked of any king.'

Sir Harry Melcombe took a grave view of these incidents. He told his sons that battle lines had effectively been drawn. The storm was gathering . . .

Four

The summer was wet and unsettled. A weak, almost wintry sun managed an occasional peak through the clouds above the city of Nottingham, where a circle of wooden caravans was grouped. In the centre of them stood a large, smiling woman with forearms like hams.

Nan Fiennes was florid-faced and in her late forties. She wore her blond hair up in a pile on her head but strands of it kept falling down and irritating her little snub nose and wide, humourous eyes.

She was laughing as she plunged her hands into a wooden tub full to the brim with hot, soapy water and pulled out a bundle of wet clothes. She craned her neck to address a slender, striking young man dressed, incongruously, in a fading Harlequin costume.

'Leicester, you say, Solomon?' said Nan, giggling through her words as was her habit. 'Well, if he comes any nearer he'll feel the toe of my boot up his arse, king or no.'

Solomon threw back his head and gave a short laugh, making the smooth muscles of his neck stand out. His auburn hair was long and tied at the back with a crimson ribbon. He wore a neat moustache and small pointed beard on his pretty, angular features. There was something about his swarthiness and the coal blackness of his eyes that hinted at Spanish ancestry, though no one in Nan's company of players knew anything very much about Solomon's past. Gregarious though he was, he had few confidants save his twin brother, Simeon, who emerged now from the caravan they shared.

'Careful. That's treasonable, Nan,' said Simeon with a sly smile.

Nan was grateful that Simeon was clean-shaven for otherwise she would have found it terribly hard to tell the brothers apart. Like Solomon, Simeon was slender to the point of skinniness but with the wiry poise of a born athlete. The costume of tight blue Elizabethan doublet and hose emphasised the suppleness of his chest and legs and the firm, tangible roundness of his buttocks.

Simeon clapped his brother on the shoulder and Solomon looked round, grinning. He held his Harlequin mask rather feyly in one hand and a small goblet of wine in the other.

'Well, I'm for the King', said Solomon. 'For, I swear, if the Puritans get their head, there'll be no more work for us.'

Simeon pulled a face. 'No more of plays and players!'

He made an elaborate bow, bending at the waist, and Nan couldn't help but notice the long, thick presence of his penis, tucked neatly into one leg of his blue hose. She gazed appreciatively at it and chuckled.

'No, no more work for poor actors like you. Then there'll be nothing for it but for you to join the army.'

Solomon stopped toying with the Harlequin mask and shot a pained look at his brother. 'God. Can you imagine? I could no more go into battle . . .'

Simeon was suddenly serious. He whipped the goblet from his brother's hand and drained the contents. 'The King's in Leicester, then?'

'Aye,' said Nan. 'And heading our way.'

Solomon cast his huge black eyes towards the ground. 'I've heard tell that the King's support is dwindling. Perhaps it will not come to war. Perhaps . . .'

He trailed off dismally. Nan began to squeeze water from the pile of washed clothes.

'Well, my pretties, in the meantime, we must get on with our lives. And on with our show.'

The twins nodded silently. Nan frowned concernedly, anxious

to dispel the mood of gloom. She flicked the wet washing at them and they both squealed in surprise.

'Now get off with you,' chuckled Nan. 'I've work to do.'

Grinning, Solomon and Simeon set off across the field, weaving their way through the circle of caravans towards the city proper.

Neither was much impressed with Nottingham, a town of market traders, silk workers and tanners, but its people seemed an appreciative lot. The last two nights of their show had been well received with money tossed generously into Solomon's Harlequin cap at the end of the night.

The players had erected a large, rather impressive tent in the town square and that was where the twins headed now, in high spirits despite their recent conversation with Nan. They were happy in their chosen life and hoped that all this politicking wouldn't interfere with things too much.

Nan's Company was a unique place, even amongst bands of touring players, for the company was almost exclusively what Nan liked to call of 'the Greek persuasion'. Whether she simply preferred the company of such men, no one could tell, but the fact was, Nan's troupe counted amongst its members some of the fairest and sauciest young men in the kingdom. And every large city or town they visited seemed to swell their ranks further.

As a little sunshine lit up the square, it was all the twins could do to prevent themselves holding hands and running down the unevenly cobbled streets.

Merchants milled around them and Simeon managed to sneak an apple from a fruit stall as they made their way towards the tent. He bit into it, laughing and then stopped dead, gazing into the distance.

'What is it, Sim?' called Solomon.

For answer, Simeon merely arched a black eyebrow cheekily and inclined his head.

Threading his way through the crowd was a man of about twenty-eight years. He was tall and well proportioned with a handsome face and shoulder-length, copper-coloured hair. Though the twins did not know him, the newcomer was none other than Cornelius Matthew, looking about himself eagerly, as though anxious to locate something.

Simeon nodded to his twin and they immediately sat down on the sawdust dais which lay beneath the sweeping canopy of the tent. As the young man approached, Simeon extended a blue-hosed leg and deliberately tripped him up.

The cleric fell forward and Solomon caught him deftly. He could feel the hard, rounded pads of Cornelius' chest muscles through his cloak.

'I'm so sorry, my dear sir,' apologised Simeon, coming to Cornelius' aid.

'That's quite all right,' said Cornelius, dusting himself down.

'Can we be of any help?' offered Solomon with a pleasant smile.

The cleric looked up at the tent and nodded. 'Would you be anything to do with the theatre?' he asked brightly.

The twins both laughed and indicated their bizarre costumes. 'If we were not,' said Simeon, 'I expect they'd haul us off to the physic.'

Cornelius grinned from ear to ear. 'Excellent, excellent!' he cried, a little out of breath. Then his pretty face fell. 'I . . . well . . . I don't quite know how to ask this.'

Simeon laid a wiry arm across the boy's shoulder. 'Ask away. What is your name, by the way?'

'Cornelius . . . er, Prentice,' said the cleric, holding the brim of his hat between his fingers.

Solomon put his arm around Cornelius so that the twins almost carried him between them and said, 'Save all your questions for the inn, dear Cornelius. Whatever it is you have to ask will seem better with ale. Is it not so?'

Cornelius nodded shyly and allowed them to hustle him off towards the lowering pile of a nearby tavern.

The twins exchanged winks as they neared the door and both looked appreciatively at the lines of Cornelius' chest. They could just see a narrow line of exposed flesh at the junction of Cornelius' shirt and britches. Its trim, muscled lines promised much.

Simeon cocked an eyebrow in his familiar gesture and had to restrain himself from giving the newcomer a little pat on the backside.

'Well, Prentice,' he murmured. 'Let's see if you live up to your name.'

The trio ducked down and entered the tavern.

The Governor of Nottingham sat back in his chair and, rubbing the bridge of his nose, let out a long and weary sigh. Before him stood a very old man and a tall, terribly thin woman with a haughty expression. Both were chained and a guard stood by them. The Governor waved his hand airily and the two prisoners were pushed forward.

'What was the charge again?' whispered the Governor.

The guard took a step forward. 'Destruction of church property, sir –' he bellowed.

The Governor held up his hand and shushed the guard into silence. The night before he had imbibed rather more than usual and was feeling the effects.

'Not so loud,' he murmured. 'Go on.'

The guard went on to explain that the man and woman had broken into a church during the service and attempted to smash all the crucifixes and ornamentation in the building.

'Popish trash!' hissed the thin woman.

'Thou shalt not worship graven images,' chimed in the old man.

The Governor held up his hand once again. Really, he could hardly be bothered with these people. The King was on his way and he had other things on his mind. He looked over his shoulder and called to a figure sitting in a window seat.

'What should I do with them, my sweet? Hmm? What should I do?'

The figure got languidly to his feet and strolled over the tiled floor towards the Governor.

He was tall and powerfully built, his triangular torso carefully emphasised by the billowing white shirt he wore. He had on leather britches over his muscular legs and, on one hand, a hawking gauntlet. His blond hair fell in waves over his beautiful face and blue eyes, setting off his straight nose, high cheekbones and full lips. Curiously, his eyebrows were unnaturally dark.

Older now, perhaps thirty, Lewis St John had lost none of the beauty which had so entranced Ned Melcombe ten years before. in the watery August sunlight which flickered through the window he looked like a fallen angel, a sulky pout on his glistening lips.

Lewis sniffed dismissively and let his gaze fall on to the two prisoners.

'Hang them,' he said evenly.

The old man fell at once to his knees and began to beg for forgiveness but the woman stood her ground. She set her mouth into a firm line and hissed at Lewis.

'Hang me and there'll only be another in place. Aye, and we'll go on until this is a proper Protestant country again where we don't live in fear of a knavish King and his Catholic wife.'

Lewis cocked his head to one side. 'A pretty speech,' he said softly. 'I wonder you don't go into Parliament.'

The Governor laughed loudly and slapped his knee. Lewis wandered back to the window seat and sat with his knees under his chin, looking out at the busy street below. The Governor gazed lovingly over at Lewis who gave him a small, secretive smile in return. Licking his lips, the Governor waved impatiently at the prisoners.

'Oh, take them away. Vane will sort it out, I expect,' he snapped.

The guard pushed the strange pair out of the room, the woman squawking anti-Catholic curses all the way.

The Governor was a tall, well-groomed man of fifty. His face was rather reddened from years of drinking but it had a noble quality which even his greying beard could not quite hide.

He got up from his chair and sauntered over towards Lewis who continued to gaze out of the window as he approached.

'Look at them all. Hurrying to and fro like bees in a hive,' said Lewis languidly.

The Governor laid a hand against Lewis's cheek and gently stroked it. 'Aye,' he murmured, 'but none can give honey like you, my sweet.'

Lewis lifted his head up a little and then swung himself around so he was facing the Governor. His leather-clad legs hung over the side of the window seat.

The older man placed both hands on Lewis's knees and gave a little mumble of pleasure. Lewis looked up at him coquettishly, his lovely hair framed in a golden halo by the sunlight.

The Governor's hands moved up Lewis's legs and came together over his crotch. The laces holding his britches together were already straining at the hot pressure of his cock beneath.

Lewis shifted his weight slightly and his britches creaked. The Governor smiled and laid his lips to Lewis's.

At first his kiss was gentle, like a parting lover's, then he pressed more firmly and Lewis could feel the moist warmth of his tongue as he attempted to insinuate it into Lewis's mouth. But Lewis resisted, breaking off and turning his head away.

'No,' he said firmly. 'That's not part of the agreement.'

The Governor nodded a little sadly and turned his attention towards Lewis's cock. With the fingers of one hand, he felt between the laces of Lewis's britches. His fingertips found soft whorls of hair then a large area of smooth flesh before settling on the large, hot, silken head of Lewis's cock.

Lewis stretched out and yawned, a picture of indifference.

The Governor's fingers began to ease back his foreskin and then pulled at the strings of his britches.

At once, Lewis's cock sprang out. Large, yet still only semierect, it projected from a forest of blond pubic hair and the firm, athletic outline of his thighs.

Lewis put his hands behind his head and closed his eyes.

'Suck me,' he ordered.

The Governor nodded and got down on his knees. He pulled Lewis's britches down and began to plant feverish kisses on the soft, white flesh of his thighs. Lewis smiled, his heavy, sensuous eyelids remaining closed. He liked to imagine that any passer-by, looking up, would be able to deduce precisely what was going on.

The Governor began to lick at Lewis's balls and Lewis gasped a little as he felt the warm point of the older man's tongue jab at the sensitive tissue.

His cock began to harden and soon it was poking against the Governor's cheek. The Governor could not ignore this for long and, spreading his hands wide over Lewis's thighs, he began to slide his tongue up the engorged shaft. It rolled around the hot, hairy skin, up towards the head, licking at the entrance to the urethra.

Lewis groaned with pleasure and jerked sensitively as the Governor suddenly took the whole of the head of his cock into his mouth and began to suck. He emitted low moans like a contented child.

Shifting his buttocks on the soft cushions of the window seat, Lewis arched his back, pushing his hips forwards so that his cock went deeper and deeper into the Governor's mouth. He pressed against the leaded windowpanes and could feel the warmth of the sun through his shirt.

The Governor's throat seemed to open still wider and Lewis cried out in delight as his cock slipped ever further inside the Governor. Briefly, he opened his eyes and saw his hairy groin and the very base of his cock rasping against the Governor's beard.

At last, the Governor pulled back, releasing Lewis's massive, stiff cock from his wet mouth. His tongue flickered over the soft, delicate membrane beneath the head and Lewis stiffened.

He stretched out his legs and the muscles bulged with the effort. He unclasped his hands from behind his head and dug them into the soft cushions beneath his arse.

As the Governor licked at his cock, his finger strayed to the entrance to Lewis's anus. The Governor looked up, as though seeking approval. Lewis's eyes were fluttering but he noticed and nodded quickly. His breath was coming in short, excited gasps.

The Governor paused for a second and licked his fingers, then resumed his tonguing of Lewis's cock. He then gently inserted the index finger of one hand into Lewis's arse, pressing deep into the forbidden, satin-soft flesh.

Lewis arched his back again, grunting in delight as the Governor's finger wormed its way inside him. It withdrew a little and then plunged deeper, like a teasing parody of a man's cock. Lewis felt the aching stiffness of his huge penis and screwed his eyes tightly shut. The feel of the Governor's tongue on his cock and finger up his arse was indescribable. His head felt as though it would burst.

'Suck me!' he commanded through gritted teeth. 'Suck me now!'

The Governor clamped his mouth around Lewis's cock and began to suck hungrily at its hot, smooth length.

Lewis cried out, feeling his toes curl almost to the point of cramp within his boots.

'Suck me, you bastard!' he gasped, pulling at the Governor's hair with his long, elegant fingers.

The Governor's mouth was a warm, wet hollow, drinking him in. Lewis cried out once more and suddenly light seemed to explode beneath the canopy of his closed lids. He stretched out full as orgasm came to him and shot a hefty wad of hot semen into the Governor's mouth. The older man snorted with delight as it hit the back of his throat and trickled inside him.

Lewis pulled back, releasing his penis, and the Governor buried his head in Lewis's lap, lapping and licking at his sperm-covered thighs.

Vaguely, Lewis became aware of cheering in the street below. He opened his eyes and looked out of the window. He got an impression of a crowd and horsemen. Somewhere a trumpet sounded. Lewis smiled absently.

'Governor, dear,' he said softly.

The Governor looked up. His face was smeared with Lewis's come and his own cock was clearly discernible through his britches, begging for release.

'Oh, my sweet, sweet Lewis,' said the Governor, planting further kisses on the younger man's groin.

Lewis nodded impatiently. 'It's none of my business I'm sure, Governor,' he said.

'What isn't?'

'Well,' drawled Lewis. 'Don't look now but I think the King's arrived.'

The Governor's flushed face turned suddenly very pale. He jumped to the window and gazed down at the street below.

'God a'mercy!' he cried. 'His Majesty!'

He leapt to his feet and, with an oddly obsequious bow, straightened his clothing and dashed from the room.

Lewis stayed in the window box for a while, his leather britches still pulled down to his ankles, his thick cock, flaccid now, lying over the big, hairy globes of his balls. He ran a hand through his mane of blond hair and toyed idly with his cock.

The King would have to be entertained, of course. That meant work for him. It was what the Governor expected and what, at least at first, he had been paid to provide. His Majesty must have the very best.

Lewis would slip away once the formalities were over and see what he could find to bring to the Court. Edward Vane, the Prosecutor, had been complaining about a troupe of actors that had entered Nottingham some days before. Perhaps they would divert the King from his present troubles.

At any rate, thought Lewis, rising and tucking his already thickening cock into his britches, even if the King could not be satisfied, there was bound to be someone to divert *him*.

Cornelius was enjoying his little game, playing the innocent, all wide eye and stammers. His several days of church business in Nottingham might yet have very pleasant results.

Solomon was sitting up at the window of the tavern, his Harlequin costume, so tight and fitting snugly to the wiry contours of his body, wrinkling at the knees. A crowd of people outside the tavern pressed closely against the bottled panes.

A short time earlier, the inn had completely emptied after an excited girl had delivered a message to the landlord. Word had spread rapidly but not to the newcomers. Perhaps they were not to be privy to this secret. At any rate, they now found themselves apparently alone in the low-ceilinged room.

'What is it, Sol?' asked Simeon from his place at the table.

Solomon shook his head, his handsome, swarthy features crumpling into a puzzled frown. He sat back down at the table and smiled.

'Well, whatever the fuss is, we shouldn't let it spoil our fun, eh, master Cornelius?'

Cornelius sat between the twins, already rather worse for drink. He leant his head on one hand and shook his head slowly.

The twins had regaled him with colourful stories of their life with the troupe and, as the drink flowed, Cornelius had relaxed, and began to make up a story about a fictional fiancée called Sarah. He felt the twins would enjoy a bit of a challenge.

Simeon poured more wine. 'You wanted to ask us something, did you not?' he said, fixing Cornelius with his large, near-black eyes.

'Aye,' murmured Cornelius. He cleared his throat and tried to focus his drink-befuddled brain. 'It's Sarah —'

Solomon sighed. 'Forget the lady for now, Cornelius,' he said. 'Was there not something else you wanted to say?'

Cornelius nodded slowly. He put his hands under the table and was startled to find them immediately grasped by Simeon. Cornelius looked over in surprise but Simeon just gazed levelly at him and then moved closer.

Under the table, Cornelius could feel the warmth of Simeon's leg pressed against his. He swallowed nervously as Simeon lifted one of Cornelius' hands and placed it brazenly on the soft sheen of his blue hose. Simeon's hand closed over Cornelius' and began to rub it up and down his leg.

Cornelius felt a shiver run through him.

'Well, sweetheart?' said Solomon. 'Come. You mustn't be shy with us.'

'No,' breathed Simeon. 'You mustn't be shy.'

Excited, Cornelius felt his hand moving up Simeon's thigh, enjoying the feel of the actor's muscled limb through the fabric of his old-fashioned hose.

'Well . . .' stammered Cornelius. 'It may seem foolish but . . .'

Solomon stroked his dark, pointed beard. 'Go on.'

'You see, Sarah wants me to become apprenticed to a tailor . . .'

Solomon exchanged glances with his twin. Simeon winked in response. Slowly Solomon moved so that he was sitting right next to Cornelius, buttock to buttock.

'It's a good trade,' he drawled. 'We'll always have tailors.'

Simeon smiled. 'Aye. We'll always have them. Given half a chance.'

The twins laughed and Cornelius swallowed hard. He found the proximity of the twins' bodies to his own exciting beyond words. He could sense the litheness of their flesh through the tight constriction of their costumes, Solomon in his Harlequin, Simeon in his Tudor doublet and hose.

Both men were strikingly handsome, their skin soft and honey-coloured, their eyes bewitchingly dark. And now it was Solomon who took Cornelius' free hand and guided it straight to the diamond-patterned crotch of his Harlequin costume.

Cornelius could feel the solid knot of Solomon's cock beneath the cloth.

'And you don't want to be a tailor? Is that it, Cornelius?' asked Solomon.

Cornelius smiled inwardly. If they only knew . . .

He shook his head. Simeon pushed Cornelius' hand further up his thigh until it came to rest on his cock, which was stretched out fully in the soft enclosure of his hose. Cornelius could feel every contour of its veiny thickness, the soft curve of the velvety head.

Now Cornelius sat pressed between the twins, both hands on their cocks, his heart slamming in his chest.

'Don't tell me,' said Simeon softly. 'You'd like to become an actor.'

'Yes!' cried Cornelius. 'That's it!'

He wanted to laugh. What a perfect scheme. In his delight, he let both hands jerk away from their warm hiding places.

'Oh,' he said. The twins both laughed.

Solomon looked around the tavern to check it was still empty and then kissed Cornelius gently on the cheek. Cornelius felt his hair stand on end.

'Well, my friend. If that's what you want, you realise you'll have to be trained.'

Cornelius cleared his throat. He found that he was already missing the feel of the brothers' cocks beneath his warm hands. 'And what . . . what does that entail?'

Simeon snuggled closer and kissed Cornelius himself. 'You'll see,' he breathed.

Emboldened by drink, his mind whirling with dark, forbidden possibilities, Cornelius asked what he knew to be a leading question. He looked at each twin in turn, his pretty face wreathed in smiles.

'But you think I have possibilities?' he said quietly.

Solomon and Simeon looked at each other and laughed.

'Oh, definite possibilities,' they chorused together.

In their lusty stupor, all three failed to notice that the inn was not quite empty. A tall, powerfully built man clothed entirely in black was watching them carefully from behind a wooden partition. Edward Vane bent forwards, trying to catch their conversation.

A little later, the actors and the cleric were making their way through the bustling streets of Nottingham, swaying slightly under the influence of the wine. The twins half-carried Cornelius between them and he just giggled and grinned at everything they said until he found himself being pushed up the ladder and into the brothers' caravan.

Solomon led the way and Cornelius found himself admiring the neat lines of his rump, outlined by the Harlequin costume as the bearded brother bent down to open the door.

Suddenly Cornelius felt a small shove in the small at his back and fell forwards on the ladder. For a brief, enticing moment, his face was squashed against the pert globes of Solomon's arse, his nose connecting with the crease of his buttocks.

Cornelius could smell a delicious muskiness combined with fresh sweat. He imagined peeling the Harlequin costume from Solomon, exposing the firm, elegant muscles of his calves and thighs.

Solomon looked round and giggled as Cornelius righted himself on the ladder. Simeon was behind him, grinning all over his face. He gestured for his brother and Cornelius to hurry up and then, glancing around, entered the caravan himself, locking the door securely behind him.

Inside, the room was dark despite the weak sunshine. Cornelius caught a vague impression of shutters and a chaos of trunks, costumes and cooking pots.

There was only one bed and it was so large that it swamped the little room. A patchwork quilt covered it and there was a single, fat bolster pillow at one end.

For a long moment, the three men stood in silence, Solomon stroking his beard in his familiar fashion, Simeon by the door with hand on hip and Cornelius simply gazing at the floor in a feigned rigour fright.

Then Simeon moved towards Cornelius and, lifting up his face, kissed him gently on the lips. Cornelius felt the same shudder of pleasure ripple through him. This was so wonderful and unexpected. Whoever would have thought that a dreary church mission could turn out like this?

But all he could feel now, all he could think about, was the hot, wet tongue forcing his lips apart and thrusting deep into his willing mouth. Simeon's smooth cheek brushed over his as they kissed, their tongues connecting and twisting in their passion.

Suddenly Simeon pulled away and turned Cornelius smartly about to face his brother. Cornelius looked at Solomon who had not moved, still languidly stroking the dark point of his beard. He blinked slowly, his long, feminine lashes closing over his impossibly dark eyes.

As Cornelius looked at Solomon, he felt Simeon come up behind him and begin to kiss his neck. He groaned and closed his eyes, his head rolling back to meet Simeon's lips. Simeon nibbled and licked at the cable-like muscles of Cornelius' neck and he ran his hands through the long, shining strands of the cleric's coppery hair.

Cornelius bowed his head as Simeon's lips fluttered over his neck and collarbone. Then he felt his face lifted again and he gasped as he realised Solomon had crossed the room and was kissing him. The twins embraced him so he was sandwiched between them.

With practised skill, Simeon pulled down Cornelius' trousers and stockings and Solomon whipped off the cleric's shoes. Both brothers grabbed at Cornelius' coat and shirt and within seconds he was stark naked between them.

His muscles, sculpted into firm contours, were revealed along with his long, powerful cock. Simeon arched his eyebrow appreciatively as he saw it.

Cornelius could feel the animal warmth of their bodies as they pressed against him, Simeon behind, Solomon in front.

He kept his eyes clamped shut, almost afraid to look at the beautiful men who so desired him. After a time, he was conscious of a different kind of sound and opened his eyes to find that, though the brothers still held him between them, they were now kissing each other. The sight of the twins; so alike, so gorgeous, sent a further thrill of forbidden desire rocketing through Cornelius.

He felt his cock grow stiff upon the instant and Solomon murmured as it poked into his diamond-patterned belly. Jammed between them, Cornelius let out an involuntary moan as the twins explored each other's mouths, Solomon's neat beard brushing over the smooth lines of Simeon's jaw.

They parted at last, their dark eyes twinkling, and returned their attentions to Cornelius.

Simeon's hips were right against the taut hemispheres of Cornelius' buttocks and he could feel the delicious poker-hardness of Simeon's cock poking through the soft material and probing at his flesh.

Cornelius felt so absolutely naked in the company of these strange twins; vulnerable yet liberated. Simeon's hands reached around him and, as his cock pressed against Cornelius' arse, his thumbs rubbed hard at the rounded pads of the boy's pectoral muscles.

Solomon pulled himself closer too, his stiff cock in his Harlequin costume pushing against Cornelius' naked one. They kissed fiercely, and Cornelius felt desire thumping through his system.

Outside, a lamb began to bleat. The room was still silent save for the men's breathing. Then, as though acting on an unspoken cue, the twins separated and guided Cornelius to the broad bed. He padded across the floor and lay down on top of the quilt, his cock standing straight up and hard against the flat plane of his belly.

Still making no attempt to undress, Solomon and Simeon clambered onto the bed, taking their places either side of him.

As usual, Simeon took the lead, kissing Cornelius passionately and then letting his lips trail all over Cornelius' neck and shoulder. Although clean-shaven, the feel of Simeon's face on his soft skin made Cornelius shiver. As Simeon moved to suck at his small, dark nipples, Solomon kissed Cornelius on the forehead, the nose, the eyelids and his open, hungry mouth.

Cornelius writhed in pleasure as Simeon's tongue licked at his nipples, leaving a trail of saliva over his hard, taut muscles. The feel of Simeon's tongue against his naked sides was wonderful. And Solomon's kiss was so deep, so penetrating, Cornelius thought his jaw must surely break. He forced his tongue back down Solomon's throat and, almost without thinking, moved to lie on top of the bearded twin.

He had never taken such an active role before, always preferring to be the passive partner. But now a powerful passion surged through him and, in a moment, his naked body was pressing Solomon onto the bed.

Solomon's breath was forced out of him like the last exhalation of a dying man.

Cornelius began to bite and lick at Solomon's face, chewing at his strong jawline with animal ferocity. Solomon twisted to and fro, moaning and shuddering with pleasure.

Cornelius pinioned Solomon's arms to the bed and began to rub his cock against the smooth fabric of the twin's Harlequin costume. Much as he wanted to see Solomon naked, the tightness of the diamond-patterned design seemed to excite him. He could see the gorgeous contours of Solomon's belly pressed against the material and it clung equally tightly to his muscular arms and legs.

All this time, Simeon continued to kiss, lick and bite at Cornelius' naked body and suddenly Cornelius cried out as he felt the hot point of Simeon's tongue delve into the entrance to his anus. Simeon lapped and licked, sending waves of pleasure shuddering up and down Cornelius' spine.

Again, as if at an unspoken signal, Solomon wriggled out from under Cornelius and began to undress. Cornelius rolled off him and then thrust his arse lasciviously into the air so that Simeon's tongue might probe deeper into his anus. Simeon responded at once, his warm, slick tongue thrusting into the secret, satiny cleft.

Cornelius moaned and looked down excitedly as Solomon began to pull of his Harlequin costume. It seemed to button at the back but Solomon made short work of it and was soon rolling the tight, one-piece costume down his trunk and over his legs.

Cornelius was not disappointed at the body which was revealed. As he'd expected, Solomon was wiry and athletic, every muscle group compact and taut. His nipples stood out, erect and aroused as his long, slender penis. Cornelius was faintly shocked to see that Solomon had shaved every vestige of hair from his body, leaving his cock sexily exposed.

Solomon seemed to be ready now. He spat on his hands and rubbed copious amounts of saliva into his own arse.

His own anus still being serviced by Simeon's tongue, Cornelius grabbed Solomon's discarded costume and rammed it under his own nose. He inhaled deeply of the gorgeous, sweaty smell of the actor's body, feeling his breathing quicken.

Solomon lay down on his belly and then reached behind himself to pull Cornelius on top of him.

Cornelius felt his cock grow yet more stiff as he lay down on Solomon, the strong globes of the twin's buttocks pressing into the warm concave of Cornelius' thighs. Almost of its own volition, Cornelius' cock slipped inside Solomon's warm and willing arse.

Cornelius reared over Solomon and pushed his cock deep inside the twin. Solomon gasped in pleasure and grunted at the weight of the cleric on his back.

Then, almost before he knew what was happening, he felt Simeon's hand moving over to the entrance to his anus, daubing it with saliva. Simeon's wet fingers moved swiftly and Cornelius shuddered with pleasure as he felt them move inside him.

He looked up and noticed, for the first time, a large mirror in the corner of the caravan. Unaccustomed to the darkness he must have missed it but now he could see everything it revealed.

Solomon's face, flushed and fixed in a frown of passion, was just visible over the pillow. Cornelius saw himself, his hard, muscular torso rising over Solomon's back, the shaft of his cock disappearing into Solomon's arse. And, finally, Simeon leaning over him. The smooth-faced twin was stripped to the waist now and clad only in his antique blue hose, his slender cock straining to be released, visible through the fine material.

Cornelius reached behind himself and pulled Simeon towards him. Blood pounded in his ears and he grabbed hold of Simeon's hose, ripping them apart at the crotch and releasing the twin's cock from its prison.

At once, Simeon thrust it into Cornelius' spit-lubricated anus and Cornelius felt it fill him utterly. He couldn't believe the joy he was experiencing, one beautiful twin below him, impaled on his rigid cock, the other fucking him so that the three of them lay piled on the bed like some impossible geometric puzzle.

As Cornelius thrust into Solomon, so Simeon thrust into him and Cornelius felt he would catch fire with desire. Solomon's breath rasped as Cornelius' cock slid in and out of him and Cornelius found he had completely lost control of himself as the wonderful slenderness of Simeon's cock thudded into him.

Sweat fell from his forehead in great, heavy drops, splashing off Solomon's smooth, naked back.

Cornelius felt Simeon's teeth sink into the flesh of his shoulder and gasped in pain and delight. He felt like the three of them had fused into one, sweating, delirious engine of desire, pumping each other like pistons.

'Oh, Cornelius,' murmured Simeon, his hot breath streaming over Cornelius' back. 'Let me take you, let me take you.'

Cornelius thrust his hips backwards so that Simeon's cock entered him even deeper and thrust forwards to spear Solomon with his own, engorged member.

'My beauty, oh my beauty,' Cornelius began to murmur, over and over, not quite knowing what he was saying. In that moment he felt he loved both twins, loved the pleasure he was able to give and receive from both. If only he could take Ned Melcombe this way, be master over him yet be gentle and loving.

He thrust backwards, feeling the shaft of Simeon's cock utterly fill him and then went down again into Solomon's wonderfully yielding arse. He thrust and thrust, feeling tiny pinpricks of electricity running over his skin.

Behind him, Simeon was gasping and gulping air, moaning insensibly to himself as he forced his cock inside Cornelius. Beneath them both, Solomon was biting at his lower lip, battered by double thrusts from his lover and his twin.

Cornelius knew he was about to come and held back as long as he could. He shot quick glances at the mirror, hoping to gauge when Simeon's own climax was approaching. By the smile of pure joy across the twin's face he reckoned it would be soon.

Letting go of his every sense and concentrating solely on the beautiful, heaving arse before him, Cornelius plunged his cock into Solomon and virtually screamed as his orgasm pummelled his system. Semen sprang from his stiff cock and he felt it fill Solomon's arse. At the same instant, he heard Simeon cry out and a wonderful warmth fill him as the twin's come flooded into him.

Simeon gradually ceased his thrusting and rapidly pulled out. Cornelius let his cock slide from Solomon's anus and the bearded twin was up in a second. Simeon and Cornelius lay down on the bed, dripping with sweat and Solomon reared over them, squatting on his haunches.

His cock was long and hard, but, aroused beyond reason, it took only a few swift strokes for him to come and, panting, he let his seed jet in hot showers over the naked forms of Simeon and Cornelius.

Then he crashed down onto the bed with a long, exhausted sigh.

For a long time, the three men lay curled in each other arms, gently kissing and stroking each other as the day wore on.

Finally, Cornelius hitched himself up on one elbow and smiled. 'Did I pass?' he murmured.

The twins laughed and looked at each other. 'Well, Cornelius,' said Simeon. 'You have to understand. Training to be an actor is a very long and involved process.'

'Oh,' said Cornelius with mock seriousness. 'So it could take some time?'

Solomon began to giggle.

Five

A squat, square-headed colonel on horseback cleared his throat and made an expansive gesture with a gauntleted hand. A group of some twenty soldiers, dressed in a variety of splendidly coloured coats and hefty, segmented armour, were struggling to drag a huge red pole into a field. The colonel signalled again, this time to indicate they should get a move on and the dispirited group pulled and heaved at the pole.

Nearby, at the head of a small knot of horsemen, a small, grave-looking figure looked up mournfully at the dismal grey sky. A curtain of fine rain was sweeping over the field, gradually soaking the assembled army.

The sad-looking man had huge brown eyes like a spaniel and a small, neat beard and elegant moustache. He was dressed in black, from his richly patterned coat and buckled shoes to the splendid, feathered hat on his curly hair.

'Not v-very prepossessing weather you offer us, G-Governor,' he stammered in a gentle Scots lilt.

The Governor of Nottingham shifted uneasily in his saddle. 'No, Your Majesty. Such things are, I regret, beyond the powers of we burghers.'

King Charles scratched at his moustache and watched as the sweating gang of soldiers struggled to erect the red pole into a shallow hole which had been dug into the ground using daggers.

The Governor turned to look at Lewis St John whose horse stood by his, quietly munching at the wet grass. It was difficult for the Governor to avoid looking at him. Fully dressed, he cut a splendid, dashing figure, his finely cut red coat and britches flattering his shapely body. Under his hat, his blond hair and dark brows were smeared with drizzle and his lips were sulkily pouted. The Governor licked his lips, remembering the taste of Lewis's cock within his mouth.

'I trust tonight's entertainment will please His Majesty?' he whispered at last.

Lewis, who was bored and cold, rubbed a trickle of cold rain from his face and nodded.

'It's all in hand. Don't fuss,' he said testily.

The Governor's face flushed with anger. He hoped the King had been unable to hear Lewis's impudence. It would not do for him to be so undermined. And if any gossip about his relationship with Lewis were to reach the ears of His Majesty . . .

Shaking his head as though to dismiss such an unpleasant thought, the Governor refocused his attention on the flagpole.

A herald began to read a proclamation, denouncing the House of Commons and its troops as traitors. It was a fine piece of writing which the King had unfortunately chosen to alter at the last minute. The herald could scarcely read His Majesty's spidery hand and his delivery was halting and poor. Several soldiers coughed embarrassedly.

Finally, the soldiers had the pole in position and the Royal standard was raised. There was a desultory cheer and King Charles nodded, then turned his horse and left the field.

The Governor followed, shooting a venomous look at Lewis as he did so.

Lewis remained in the field, staring at the standard, a blank look fixed on his beautiful face. After a time, the colonel's horse came trotting towards him and the soldier tipped his hat in greeting.

'Anything ail you, sir'?' he asked kindly.

Lewis smiled and shook his head. 'Just the preparations for His Majesty's entertainment, Colonel. So much to organise . . .'

He trailed off and the colonel frowned, as though sensing there was more to be said. Finally Lewis gestured at the flagpole.

'Well,' he murmured, 'the standard's been raised. It's war now.'

The colonel nodded and sighed. 'Aye. A war without an enemy, save our fellow Englishmen.'

The two men turned their horses and drifted back towards Nottingham. The rain continued to fall and a strong wind blew up, scouring the wet grass and setting the standard flapping. A few hours later, the pole and the elegant flag fell down.

Ned Melcombe threw open the window and let a blast of sharp, unseasonably cold air flood into the dining room. He closed his eyes and breathed in deeply. It was the taste of freedom.

Only hours before, Sir Harry and Thomas had finally departed, taking with them a substantial body of men to fight for Parliament's cause.

Ned kicked off his shoes and, throwing himself into a chair, warmed his toes by the fire. He sighed contentedly. Finally, he was Master of the house.

The last few days had been agonising. Once he had reconciled himself to the responsibilities thrust upon him and the opportunities for sport they might well present, Ned had been anxious for his father and brother to leave. But Sir Harry was fastidious in the extreme and delayed endlessly over the smallest detail.

Finally, they had gone, Thomas as impatient as Ned to see them quit the place. But whilst his brother longed for action on the battlefield, Ned's thoughts were on altogether different engagements.

A filigree of desire coursed through Ned's loins. He had no idea where to start, what to do. He would have to manage the estates, of course, the family affairs could never be allowed to run to ruin under his care. But the rest of the time he could indulge himself freely. How to start, though?

Seized by a sudden impulse, he reached above the fireplace and pulled sharply on the bell, then settled back into his chair with a smug smile on his face. He folded his arms and stretched out his legs, feeling a warm sensuality bubbling inside him.

There were footsteps in the corridor and William knocked and entered.

'Yes, sir?' he said quietly.

For a long moment, Ned said nothing, merely drinking in the loveliness of William's face. His long, straight hair was parted in the middle, and hung like curtains over his chiselled features and brown, almond-shaped eyes. When he spoke, his soft lips pulled back to expose even, white teeth.

At last Ned cleared his throat and looked away. 'Well, William, I find myself Master of Humbleford and all I survey.'

'Yes, sir,' said William flatly.

'I am Squire and at liberty to order what I choose.'

William nodded. 'Indeed, sir.'

'And what would you do in my position?'

William frowned, his lovely face wrinkling at the corners of his eyes. 'In your position, sir?'

He looked Ned up and down the length of his prone body as though calculating exactly what could be achieved in such a position. Ned found the servant's intense scrutiny exciting. Finally, William looked away.

'Well,' he said, 'I suppose I might try to raise funds for Parliament.'

Ned was disappointed. He shook his head and his raven-black hair swung over his creamy complexion.

'No, no, no. Take all that as a given. The estates will prosper under my watchful eye. What I mean is . . .' He gestured broadly with his open hands. 'What I mean is, William, how is a young man like me to amuse himself? You know my father's ways. There's not been a lot of fun within these walls for many a year.'

William shrugged. 'A game of cards, sir?'

Ned's eyes flashed with anger. What he wouldn't give to take the insolent servant over his knee and beat his lovely, pert backside. 'Are you being deliberately obtuse, William?'

William shook his head, almost smiling. 'Oh no, sir.'

Ned got out of the chair and walked over to the fire, his stockinged feet padding on the cold floor. He lifted up the tail of his coat and began to warm himself.

'You must watch your tongue, my fine fellow,' said Ned. 'I am your master. I appointed you and I can just as easily dismiss you.'

William held his gaze. 'Good staff is hard to come by these days, sir.'

Ned grunted. 'Yes. It is, isn't it?'

He looked at William, wondering what on earth was going on behind those lovely eyes. His gaze travelled the length of William's slender body, taking in the details of his fine hands and swan-like neck. His tunic was sufficiently short to show the thick, curled form of his penis tucked neatly into his tight britches.

Ned found himself utterly bewitched by the servant, probably, he had to confess, because he wasn't used to rejection. Why did William hold out on him? He could hardly make it any plainer that he wanted to lie with him, make love to him.

Turning his back on William, Ned looked into the fire. When he spoke it was with a coldness which he felt he had to assume in order to re-assert his authority.

'I'm expecting guests,' he said at last. 'Make up three or four rooms, would you?'

'Certainly, sir,' said William softly. 'Will that be all?'

Ned looked round and nodded in silent anger. He would break that boy, by God he would.

Ned heard the door close. He rubbed the back of his neck, surprised at how tense he suddenly felt. He shook his arms out. It was time to enjoy himself. Cornelius was expected back from Nottingham and he had promised Ned a few surprises.

Standing by the fireplace, Ned let the warmth from the hearth wash over him. He closed his eyes, imagining what the cleric's surprises might be, or, rather, whom. Cornelius had long promised to bring more young men into Ned's circle. Now, as Squire of Humbleford, the opportunity had come at last.

Images flickered through Ned's mind. Images of strong, beautiful men, their naked haunches pumping into warm, oiled backsides. He saw their limbs writhing, knotted together as youth after youth tumbled over him. He saw their red, red mouths, clamping onto his, felt their tongues entwining with his, the insistent hardness of their cocks rubbing against his belly.

The light of the fire made Ned's beautiful face seem almost ethereal. His heavy lids remained closed but his delicate, fluted nostrils moved gently as imagined couplings ran through his mind. His lips retained their startling redness, as though he had bitten deep into a succulent blood-orange. Long shadows pooled under his cheekbones and the strong line of his jaw.

He opened his eyes and moved with sudden swiftness to the door, locking it with a heavy, iron key. Bleak white daylight flooded the room and, for a moment, Ned considered drawing the floor-length curtains which hung over the leaded windows. But the wet summer meant the gardens were deserted and, naturally, the threat of discovery only added spice to his game.

Ned smiled and took a large wooden box from the mantelpiece. The box was usually hidden in the floorboards beneath his bed but the house was his now and he felt brazen enough to bring it downstairs. Carefully, he opened the lid.

Inside, inset in dark, crimson velvet, was a wooden phallus. It was made of the softest, blond willow and had been carved with great skill and attention to detail. Whorls of grain covered the smooth surface like the perfect, moist curves of a conker.

Ned ran his hand along its eight-inch length, feeling the sculpted ridges, the gorgeously smooth wooden head. Then he felt about inside his coat and produced a small pot of some greasy lubricant which he began to slap generously onto the phallus. The sweet, sticky stuff glistened in the light of the fire and Ned felt his own cock turning hard as his daubed hand moved up and down the length of the toy.

Finally, he got down on all fours on the rug before the fire and, putting the phallus to one side, hauled off his britches and stockings. Rapidly, he unbuttoned his coat and threw it to one side, leaving him only in his capacious muslin shirt, his strong, muscular arms showing through the translucency of its baggy sleeves.

He sat back on his haunches, feeling his warm feet beneath his firm, defined arse and looked down at his cock which was sticking straight upwards, its steely hardness covered by the length of his shirt.

Ned flattened the gossamer muslin over and around his cock and enjoyed the feel of the soft material on its throbbing hardness. Wrapped like that, his cock looked as though it were encased in spider's web.

He let his head fall back, exposing the smooth, naked beauty of his throat and, through the tight muslin, began to pull his foreskin back and forth.

As he did so, he picked up the slippery wooden phallus and, reaching round, stroked its rounded end against the entrance to his anus.

The toy slipped easily into his sphincter and Ned adjusted himself so that he was able to sit backwards on it. Still pumping at his own rock-hard cock in its muslin sheath, he eased back his buttocks and felt the slick wooden phallus slide inside him.

Ned groaned as the walls of his anus stretched to accommodate the soft willow. He felt the thing fill him and pushed it gently further until only its knobbly base protruded from his tight, shuddering arse.

He let go of his own cock for a moment, letting it bob and pulse under his shirt, and, placing his hands behind his back, began to slide the phallus slowly in and out of himself.

Stretching further backwards on his haunches, he moaned delightedly at the gorgeous sensations which flowed through him. Finally, he felt sufficiently comfortable to resume masturbating his cock whilst using one hand to fuck himself with the toy.

A ragged, unexpected lustiness overpowered him, as though the feelings from his cock and the sharper sensations from his arse had merged into some new form of desire. He slipped his hand under his shirt and felt the delicious, smooth warmth of his cock as his fingertips moved over its surface.

His buttocks slapped against the arched soles of his feet as he sat back on the phallus, feeling its lovely wooden hardness thrusting into his most private sanctum.

Sweat began to trickle down Ned's face and he could feel his hair getting progressively wetter as he pounded at his cock. He ran his hand through it and then peeled back his foreskin to fully expose the huge purple knob of the end of his penis. He felt its smoothness and remembered the shiny wooden surface of the phallus which was now slipping in and out of his lubricated hole.

Ned opened his eyes and looked around. His clothing was slung all about him, coat and trousers in a heap, stockings lying like cast-off snakeskins. He could see the gardens through the window but there was still no one about.

He uncurled himself and lay down on his back so that he was able to thrust the phallus in and out of himself from the front. With one hand on his pulsing cock and the other on the base of the toy, he rocked gently back and forth, biting his lip at the currents of pure, sensual pleasure which flowed through him.

Unbidden, the image of Lewis St John flashed into his mind. The beautiful, hard phallus inside Ned was Lewis's, he imagined, pumping into his insides, no longer willow but real flesh, powerful in its veiny, sweaty greatness.

And that was not Ned's hand on his cock, it was Lewis's, his broad, manly fingers teasing Ned expertly to his orgasm. Ned could almost feel the soft, trailing ends of Lewis's blond hair brushing over his face, seizing him and kissing him with a brute force born of his lust.

Ned swivelled on the wooden cock, panting with desire as he pushed it with ever more violence in and out of his slippery anus. It felt all of a piece with his real penis, as though a great, hard rod extended through his body from his buttocks to the tip of his cock.

He wanted to feel Lewis moving inside him, to push him over the brink of ecstasy with the massive, glossy length of his wonderful cock.

Ned gasped, his whole body shaking, his muscles became rigid and the whole room swirled into darkness as a massive orgasm ripped through him. The feel of the toy up his arse and the semen rushing up his cock combined to batter his senses.

Sperm thudded on to his chest and right into his face and he felt its salty heat dripping down into his mouth. He let it slip over his lips and then licked them, enjoying the taste of his own come.

Ned let go of his cock and sat up, carefully removing the wooden phallus from his arse. He twitched sensitively as it came out and he felt its every inch as it slid from his lubricant-drenched passage. Finally, he laid it to one side and lay back on the rug, his sperm trickling over his pectoral muscles and down the muscled contours of his sides.

He opened his eyes and looked up at the ceiling. Little plaster birds were inlaid under the beams and he smiled, noticing them for the first time.

There was a noise close by and Ned sat up. To his astonishment, he saw William come out from behind the curtain where he had obviously concealed himself the whole time. Ned's mind reeled. Of course, he had heard the door close but had not seen William leave!

Ned lay on the rug, naked and prone, his still-hard cock dribbling sperm, the shameful wooden phallus glistening by his side.

William allowed himself a tiny smile and moved to the door. He unlocked it and turned in the doorway. 'Will *that* be all, sir?' he asked gently.

Ned found he couldn't think of a thing to say. He swallowed nervously and felt his hand flutter towards his genitals.

Without waiting for a reply, William smiled again and went out, shutting the door behind him with a gentle click.

The sun was setting over Nottingham as Lewis rode towards the theatre. The city looked fresh and re-invigorated. It was a warm night, though still far short of the usual balminess of summer.

Lewis was dressed splendidly in the same rich, red coat he had worn that morning but his riding boots were new as was his plumed black hat which had replaced one now lying in a rain-sodden heap back in his rooms. He was freshly bathed and shaved, his dark brows and brilliant blue eyes emphasised by the creamy smoothness of his complexion.

He banged his shins gently against the horse's sides and it trotted a little more swiftly down the narrow lane.

Lewis sighed. It had been almost two years now since he had joined the Governor's service. He had little cause for complaint, of course. Once he had become the older man's favourite, he had been relieved of all onerous tasks and set himself up as something of a kept man. Arranging banquets and festivities was not the most taxing job in the world, even when it was the King he had to cater for. Tonight, he had ordered a band of musicians to keep His Majesty from boredom whilst he set out to examine the new theatricals.

Privately, Lewis was troubled. He remained an ambitious man and was frustrated that he hadn't risen further. He had great experience soldiering on the Continent in the service of the King of Sweden but he was in no hurry to get himself killed in this wretched civil war.

It was all bound to have terrible repercussions, even if the King were triumphant, as Lewis was sure he would be. Nottingham was already showing signs of the coming conflict. Families were set against each other, some siding with the King, others with Parliament. And with the King rumoured to be establishing something of a headquarters here in the city, Lewis's rather cosy lifestyle was bound to come into question. What he wanted most was a favoured position at the King's court, perhaps an ambassadorial role. But first, he must prove himself worthy and, much as it annoyed him, the likeliest way to do it was on the battlefield.

He sighed. Best to enjoy things whilst he could.

He approached the centre of town and reined in his horse as the elaborate awning of the portable theatre came into view. In the dying rays of the sun, it looked truly magical, all golden filigree and dusky purple. There were already people milling around, taking their places on the sawdust floor, laughing and arguing as they did so.

On the tiny stage, a rather sweet wooden castle set had been erected. Behind it, rows of gaily painted wooden trees had been cut out to resemble a forest. Flickering braziers had been placed all around and the tent glowed with festive light.

Lewis tethered his horse. Several passers-by tipped their hats respectfully but he ignored them, as was his custom. He sauntered under the awning and was quietly pleased at the whispering which his appearance immediately started up.

He took off his gloves and stood with hand on hip, waiting to be seated. Within moments, a small, obsequious man trotted to his side and gave orders for a chair to be fetched. Lewis stood in silence until it arrived and then sat down without a word. He was the only properly seated person in the whole tented area. Everyone else either stood or sat on the dirty sawdust floor.

From her vantage point behind the curtains, Nan Fiennes watched the new arrival. She sniffed dismissively and turned to the troupe of actors getting changed behind her.

'There's a knob in tonight, boys,' said Nan.

Simeon looked up from pulling on his boots. He wore the same tunic but had replaced the blue hose ripped from his groin by Cornelius. His muscular calves were now clad in purest white.

'Is he bonny?' asked Simeon.

Solomon, in his Harlequin costume, raced to the curtain and peeked through. His eye fell on the pleasing form of the newcomer in his high, elegant chair. He gazed appreciatively at his soft, blond hair, black eyebrows and petulant, kissable lips.

'Bonny indeed,' he breathed.

Simeon came to join him and parted the curtains imperceptibly in order to look.

Around them, the other actors giggled and chatted as they changed. There were ten in the current company, including the twins, and another dozen workers of various descriptions. Only three others were performing tonight and all were strikingly handsome. Nan gazed at each in turn.

There was Piotor, the Hungarian who specialised in acrobatic stunts as well as dramatic monologues. Imposingly tall with the musculature of a born gymnast, he stood bare-chested, his huge, firm torso shaking with laughter. He had the fine, flexible looks typical of an eastern European, wide, pale lips that creased as he laughed, eyes of a peculiar amber colour that burned like coals in the soft backstage light. He wore his hair scraped back from his forehead so that it curled under his ears.

Piotor was sharing a joke with a much smaller young man, stockier but still broad-chested who was clambering into over-sized Puritan garb. This was Jeremiah, an Irish blacksmith who had joined the company after they had visited his village. His collar was huge and white, his britches ridiculously large. Yet, despite the comedy outfit, the exceptional condition of his body was plain for all to see. His hair was shaved off completely and he had three dimples, one in the cleft of his chin and two others which only appeared when he smiled, which was often.

Piotor clapped him on the shoulder and moved to the curtain to see what all the fuss was about. He towered over Nan and the twins and was able to put both arms around them all as he peeked through into the sawdust-strewn auditorium.

'Mmmm,' he purred appreciatively as he saw Lewis. 'Come to give us the once-over.'

'He can give me the once-over anytime he likes,' laughed Simeon.

Jeremiah came to join them, leaving one actor remaining who was getting changed in silence.

Alexander was an enigma, even in this company of enigmas. Brought over from the West Indies as some kind of trophy he had spent his formative years exhibited almost as a freak. Rescued by a kindly parson, he had been brought up a good Christian until the lure of the stage brought him into Nan's company.

Dressed in white robes, he looked extraordinarily exotic, his black skin glistening, his fathomless black eyes deep in thought. His nose was long and straight and his eyebrows arched, giving him a permanently sultry expression.

Despite her principle of never becoming involved with her actors, Nan found him incredibly, almost dangerously attractive. But, alone amongst the company, Alexander remained almost permanently aloof. Nan found him rather frightening.

As the others clustered around the curtain, she watched as Alexander slipped into his baggy Turkish trousers and wrapped a gold sash around his robe.

Suddenly, Alexander looked round and fixed Nan with a steely stare. She froze, gulped and felt her saggy throat constrict.

Alexander's gaze ranged over Nan, as if sizing her up, then, unexpectedly, the imposing actor broke into a broad grin.

Nan felt immediately cheered and smiled back.

The moment broke as the rest of the company moved back from the curtain. Solomon gave Nan a little kiss on the lips and patted her head affectionately. 'It is time, my dear,' he said. 'Time for the magic to begin.'

Lewis St John, blithely unaware of the interest he was arousing backstage, yawned and examined his fingernails. He looked up as a drum-roll sounded, the curtains parted and an actor bounded on stage.

The sight of the huge, beautiful man cheered up Lewis at once. He watched in genuine awe as he skipped and tumbled over the little stage, jumping around in front of the castle set like a man possessed.

His gymnastic skill was truly remarkable but Lewis was more interested in the sight of his bare, oiled chest and the amazing pertness of his arse showing through the flimsy cotton britches he wore.

The actor rolled forward and sprang into the audience, eliciting a squeal of delight, before landing right by Lewis's chair.

'My lord,' he said in a rich, heavily accented voice. He bowed low and Lewis noticed how his taut belly scarcely rippled as he did so. When he stood up again, his blazing amber eyes fixed on Lewis's. Despite himself, Lewis blushed.

The beautiful man smiled and pushed a lock of rogue hair back behind his ear. Then, flashing a wide, wonderful grin, he turned to the rest of the crowd.

'For your delight and entertainment, my friends!' he cried. 'Pray indulge, The Tragedy of the Common Man!'

The audience stamped and cheered as he bounded off and a smaller, darker man came on. He wore a half-mask over his lovely, swarthy face and struck a strange, artificial pose as though lost in thought.

Lewis felt his breath quicken as he took in the details of the actor's fine figure revealed by the cut of his tunic. His eyes lingered long on the actor's shapely legs and round, enticing arse, encased in their white tights.

Laying a long, boney finger against his cheek, Lewis settled back to enjoy the spectacle. He paid little attention to the mechanics of the plot which seemed, in any case, rather perfunctory.

The masked man was playing some kind of loafer, a ne'er-do-well, coaxed from his life of pleasure by a call to arms from the Puritans. Unwilling to give up his carousing and womanising, the ne'er-do-well is eventually press-ganged into service against the King. What the Puritans fail to realise is that they have mistakenly kidnapped his twin, a loyal subject of the Crown, who then acts against them as a spy.

Lewis found himself smiling throughout, not at the crude Royalist sentiments, but at the extraordinary beauty of the cast.

He admired both twins and found his mind reeling with the possibilities of what he might do with them. The Puritan, an Irishman, he guessed by his accent, had a lovely, rough charm and a boyishness emphasised by his dimpled face. Then there was the big acrobat, who never lost an opportunity throughout the evening, to cast a sly look in Lewis's direction.

Finally, as the twins' adventures took them to every corner of the globe, a tall, graceful black man strode onto the stage. His movements were stately, and as convincingly regal as his role as some exotic potentate.

All in all, Lewis had never seen such a troupe of actors. Each dazzlingly erotic in their respective costumes, yet all different. He found his tongue moving slowly and unconsciously over his lips as the company assembled to take their bows before the cheering, stamping crowd.

As the acrobat rose from his bow, his taut belly wrinkling, he once again shot a look of pure, saucy enticement at Lewis, who was clapping his gloved hands in a perfunctory fashion.

Lewis stared back at him and allowed a tiny smile to creep over his features.

He gestured to the small, sweating man who had brought his chair and whispered a few words in his ear. Within moments, he was being ushered through the crowd and behind the little stage.

Lewis found the troupe arranged in a semicircle to greet him. They were all soaked with sweat, which only served to make their costumes cling even more tightly to their muscular frames.

'My heartiest congratulations to you all,' he said in his warm, mellifluous voice.

They bowed to him and Lewis let his gaze range over them all. In addition to the cast, there was a fat woman, who seemed to be in overall charge.

Lewis cleared his throat. 'As Deputy-Governor of Nottingham . . .' He let the impact of his title settle over them. 'It falls upon me to choose and favour those who would provide entertainment for His Majesty. Having seen and greatly enjoyed your revels tonight and having admired all of your . . . performances, I have no hesitation in selecting you for this great honour.'

The fat woman came forward and kissed Lewis's hand.

'Thank you,' she said simply.

Lewis waved her away. 'You may talk terms with this fellow here.'

He indicated the small sweaty man who took her to one side. Lewis was not yet finished. 'However, I have certain terms.'

The actors.looked at him. All seemed a little troubled at this remark, save the acrobat, who wore the same, cheeky smile.

'Terms?' said the woman.

Lewis rubbed the back of his slender neck. 'Aye. I should like to consult each of your company in turn so that I may judge how each may best serve His Majesty.'

He watched as a murmur of understanding passed through the actors and each smiled as though an electrical charge were passing through them.

'Tonight,' stated Lewis, rising to his full, imposing height, 'I choose . . . you.'

He stretched a finger out and pointed at the massive acrobat. The man's wide smile made creases in his cheeks like ripples in a pool. His amber eyes flashed lustily.

'An honour, sir.' he murmured.

Lewis looked around at the others. 'There will be time for you all to . . . er . . . consult me,' he said. He looked with particular earnestness at Alexander, who was staring imperiously back at him. 'All of you,' he said.

Alexander held his gaze and didn't smile.

Lewis waved a gloved hand airily. 'Once again, congratulations. Good night to you all.'

He turned on his heel and beckoned to the acrobat, who followed behind him.

Nan turned to her company and suddenly let out a peal of throaty laughter. 'Well, my beauties. It seems we are Royal favourites at last!'

A small, measly light was burning in Edward Vane's quarters as he sat poring over a thick, brittle-paged ledger. He licked his fingers and turned the pages one by one, his jet-black eyes glinting in the light of the candle.

There was a gentle rap at the door and Vane swung round in his chair.

'Yes?' he barked.

The door opened and a thick-set, bald man with the squashed face of a prize-fighter came inside.

'The papers you wanted, sir,' he said in a thick Nottingham accent.

Vane snatched them from him and rapidly scanned their contents.

'And he has returned to Humbleford now?'

The servant nodded.

Vane put the papers on his desk and grinned devilishly. 'Well, well, Mr Matthew. A priest, I'll be damned.'

He dismissed the servant and extinguished the candle. He didn't wet his fingers but enjoyed the sharp pain which the burning flame caused as it touched his skin.

He spoke to himself in the darkness. 'Let us see what we shall see.'

Lewis's horse clopped gently through the quiet Nottingham streets towards the Governor's residence. Behind him, on a borrowed and far less imposing mount, came the actor whom he now knew to be called Piotor. In spite of his build and presence, he seemed a little shy in Lewis's company and hardly uttered a word.

Lewis smiled to himself and concentrated on the way ahead. It was good to play these games of rank. He was Deputy-Governor, after all, and able to throw his weight around a little.

In truth, he found the beautiful actor a little intimidating, even with his extraordinary body now disguised under a heavy tunic and cloak.

Occasional glances behind gave Lewis a glimpse of Piotor's thick, hairy arms and broad, splayed fingers as he gripped the reins of his horse. Under the cowl of the cloak, Piotor's smooth face with its high, hollowed cheekbones was just visible in the moonlight.

The two men guided their horses through the grand archway of the Governor's residence and into a cobbled courtyard. Drunken shouts and gales of laughter were coming from inside.

Lewis dismounted at once. He turned to Piotor as grooms appeared from nowhere and fussed around the horses. He scarcely looked at the Hungarian, retaining the imperious front which was so important to him.

'We'll conduct the interview in my quarters,' he said matter-of-factly. 'If that suits you?'

Piotor swung from the horse in one easy movement. He towered over Lewis as he said, 'Indeed, sir.'

'Good,' muttered Lewis. 'Then let us away.'

He led the way across the cobbles, each round and bright with moonlight, and began to ascend a narrow flight of stone steps which twisted like a corkscrew through the centre of the building. Piotor followed dutifully behind him.

The noise of the King's carousing was dying away and Lewis could hear Piotor's gentle breathing close by. He began to grow hard, aware of the Hungarian's powerful presence on the pitch-black stair behind him.

Lewis suddenly stopped and he felt Piotor gently collide with him. He put out his hands behind him and felt the warm, rough cloth of the actor's britches meet his fingertips. He didn't turn round, but let his hands explore and felt the massively powerful thighs and webs of muscle discernible even through the fabric.

His fingers suddenly alighted on the pouch of Piotor's balls and Lewis felt his breath quicken discernibly. They were huge. Hard, hard globes that hung in Piotor's britches like oranges.

Excitedly, Lewis let his hands stray upwards to find the massive, thick length of Piotor's cock. It was already fully erect and projecting straight upwards like a lightning rod. Lewis's fingers travelled up and down its length and he let out a little groan of desire.

He had guessed from the actor's build that he must be well equipped but this was beyond all expectation. He layed the palms of both hands over Piotor's whole genital area, feeling the great stiff cock and solid balls beneath his warm skin.

Still without turning, he shivered as he felt Piotor's lips brush over the skin of his neck. He let his head fall to one side, exposing the smooth skin of his throat and, at once, Piotor began to kiss and nibble there.

Lewis heard Piotor's teeth clack slightly as he did so, his wide lips sending shudders through every part of Lewis's body. His own cock was pressing against the constriction of his britches.

Without warning, Lewis continued his ascent of the stairs and Piotor hurried after him.

Lewis smiled to himself. This was going to be fun.

Finally, the two men reached a door inset in the wall which Lewis unlocked. He stepped to one side and ushered Piotor through into his bedchamber.

It was a large, high-ceilinged room of great opulence. Red velvet hung over the walls and, as Lewis lit the candelabrum, its colour seemed to saturate the rest of the place. A large fire was already burning fiercely in the grate.

In the centre of the room was a curtained, four-poster bed, firelight shadows flickering over its elegant fabric.

Lewis moved to the bed and pulled off the blankets and pillows which he threw down on to the floor. Without a word, he arranged them into a comfortable heap in front of the fire.

He caught Piotor's eye and smiled slightly.

'The bed is so formal, don't you think?'

Piotor nodded, a little bewildered, and, kicking off his buckled shoes, sat down cross-legged on the rug. Behind him, Lewis poured two goblets of wine. He crossed the room and, flinging off his cloak, sat down next to Piotor.

He raised the goblet in a toast. 'His Majesty King Charles,' he announced. 'God preserve him and death to his enemies.'

Piotor clashed his goblet against Lewis's and nodded.

'King Charles,' he murmured. Then, looking about, he said, 'The King is here?'

Lewis nodded. 'Within these four walls even as we speak.'

He laid the goblet down and placed a fingertip on Piotor's wide, pale lips. 'Even as we speak. Even as we kiss.'

He moved forwards and kissed the Hungarian full on the mouth. Piotor tasted good, a combination of wine and spice, like a Christmas dish. Their tongues found one another and slid into a knot of passion. Lewis's skimmed the ridged roof of Piotor's mouth and felt the smoothness of his teeth.

Piotor's rough chin scraped over Lewis's face and he shivered with pleasure. They kissed for a long time and then pulled away, looking each other in the eye. Piotor grinned like a child, Lewis kept the same mask of studied indifference.

Piotor took off his cloak and began to unbutton his tunic. Lewis shook his head and began to do it for him, the cheap, theatrical costume flimsy in his hands.

Lewis pulled the tunic from around Piotor's broad shoulders, exposing another, thinner garment which deliniated the firm hardness of the actor's chest. Its square, embroidered neck just revealed a suggestion of collarbone and a few whorls of blond hair.

Lewis had already seen Piotor's chest and knew that the tightness of the undergarment hid exceptional muscles. In the firelight, they were visible as shadowed crescents, on Piotor's upper arms and on his breast.

He put his finger where he supposed the nipple to be and rubbed gently. The flesh beneath responded and hardened at once.

Lewis rapidly unbuttoned his own tunic. He was naked beneath and sat there, his chest moving rapidly up and down, his heated blood pulsing excitedly through his body.

He looked up at Piotor. Strands of his long hair had fallen forwards and hung over his lovely face. He was still grinning and Lewis could see his enormous cock bulging through his britches.

Lewis indicated that he should remove his undershirt and the actor did so without a word, finally exposing the chest which Lewis had so admired back at the theatre.

In the glow of the fire, Piotor's body seemed almost too perfect, as though a Grecian statue had fallen from its plinth and come to rest on the rug. Lewis stared at the glossy hair which covered the actor's chest, at the flat, hard pads of muscle and the neat, dark points of his gently erect nipples.

Lewis laid his head on Piotor's chest, his ear connecting with the warm skin and listened to the actor's steady breathing. He closed his eyes and set his lips on to Piotor's right nipple, gently chewing at the soft tissue and rubbing his tongue over the sensitive surface. It felt warm and delightful beneath his tongue and he mumbled to himself as he took the nipple between his teeth and gently bit at it.

Piotor gasped and made a low grumble in his muscular throat.

Lewis's hands moved over Piotor's chest and stroked gently at his pectoral muscles, making the downy hair stand on end. Then his hands trailed over Piotor's ribs and down his sides, his nails almost scratching the yielding flesh.

Lewis's touch made Piotor cry out in little, injured gasps but he never lost his smile as Lewis's hands ranged over his body and Lewis's mouth suckled at his nipples.

Finally, Lewis lay back on the cushions, his blond hair spreading like seaweed and Piotor took his cue to begin pleasuring the Deputy-Governor.

Lewis looked up at the astonishingly beautiful man above him and felt his own cock throb with desire. Piotor leant forward and more of his hair fell into his eyes as he gazed down at Lewis's fine chest. His head nuzzled into Lewis's breast and he repeated the process Lewis had enacted upon him.

Lewis drew in a sharp breath and bit into his lower lip as he felt Piotor's mouth clamp around his nipple. He jerked and dug his fingers into the cushions as he felt the actor's teeth nip at the agonisingly sensitive skin.

He let his hands fall on to Piotor's head and he dug his nails into the actor's scalp, feeling thick, glossy hair between his fingers. His cock was lying across his belly like a poker and he pushed Piotor's head hard against his chest.

Piotor's mouth moved to Lewis's other nipple, leaving the original wet and exposed. Lewis groaned as the actor's hot mouth sucked at him, pulling at the whole area of skin around the nipple. Lewis could almost feel it bruising and, as Piotor pushed at him, he felt his head bury deeper into the pillows in response.

Finally, with some difficulty, he pushed Piotor away and held the actor's face between his hands. Lewis looked up, eye to eye, blue to amber, and ran his fingers over Piotor's beautiful face.

'Strip me,' he said at last.

Piotor nodded dumbly and sat back on his haunches. Then he reached out with his large, hairy forearms and began to tug at Lewis's britches.

Slowly, he unlaced them, exposing the bones of Lewis's hips and the dark, engorged head of his cock. It seemed almost to have a life of its own, beating a delicate tattoo against the flat plane of Lewis's belly as blood surged into its veiny thickness.

Piotor's huge hands pulled at the rich velvet of Lewis's britches and hitched them down to his knees, fully exposing the Deputy-Governor's cock.

The actor paused a moment, staring intently at the sight of Lewis's penis and then wrenched off the britches.

Lewis's heart fluttered wildly. Despite all his show, despite all his display of grandeur, he wanted only to be taken by this great, sublime man. He sighed as Piotor's hands roamed over his thighs, just brushing the tip of his cock, and began to peel down his black cloth stockings.

'I want you to take me,' Lewis breathed. 'Possess me. Abase me.'

His head writhed from side to side in expectation as he felt Piotor's strong hands stripping him. In a few moments, his shoes and stockings lay in a heap by the fire and Piotor was stroking Lewis's muscled legs with both hands.

Then Piotor sat back on the pillows and lifted Lewis's legs towards his face. At once, he pressed Lewis's strong, boney feet into his face and began to suck on his toes, just as he had Lewis's nipples some time before.

Lewis grunted in delight as he felt Piotor's warm, slippery tongue lick at the ticklish skin between his toes and then his mouth closed around them, bunching them together, as he sucked and sucked.

Piotor inhaled deeply of the scent of Lewis's feet and let his teeth play teasingly over their sensitive surfaces.

Unused to such attention, Lewis found the experience delightful and quivered as new sensations stole up his spine.

Piotor seemed to recognise that he was now in command and spread Lewis's legs wide before him, forcing them down with his strong arms. His great, protuberant biceps were crazed with taut veins, like wicks lost in spheres of wax.

Naked and vulnerable, Lewis stretched out on his improvised bed of blankets and pillows and groaned as Piotor laid his head to Lewis's arse and began to lick at the entrance.

He felt the wet tip of the actor's tongue penetrate him and

gasped as shudders of desire washed over him. He could feel Piotor's long hair brushing against the sweaty cheeks of his arse as the Hungarian pleasured him, still holding his legs wide apart with his hands.

Looking up, Lewis could see only Piotor's broad back, his shoulderblades projecting from his rippling muscles, as his head bobbed up and down at the entrance to Lewis's anus.

The warm tongue inside him made Lewis purr with pleasure. He felt his own long, blond hair spill over his face but made no effort to sweep it aside as his sweat soaked into it. The pressure of Piotor's hands on his thighs was wonderful. Lewis loved the feeling of compulsion which it engendered in him. He was so used to getting things his way, for his every whim to be indulged by the Governor, that being in the power of this colossal stranger was a gorgeously erotic novelty.

Piotor's fingers closed over the muscles of Lewis's thighs, as though he were tempted to squeeze the life out of them and his tongue flashed in and out of Lewis's arse like a dagger.

Suddenly, the actor rose over Lewis and kissed him full on the mouth. Lewis responded instantly, craning his neck to force his tongue down Piotor's throat.

Then Piotor stood up, towering over Lewis's recumbent form, the line of britches bent by the huge form of his enclosed penis.

Lewis looked up at the huge stranger, feeling his chest heaving up and down with desire. His arse was still tingling from the attentions of Piotor's tongue and his mouth hung open in slack lustiness.

With knowing theatricality, Piotor began to slowly unlace his own britches; like his tunic, they were of far cheaper, courser quality than Lewis's. They fell to his feet almost as soon as he touched them.

Lewis gasped at the sight of the man before him, naked save for the plum-coloured stockings fastened tightly around his huge, thick thighs.

Piotor's cock stood upright at an almost inconceivably straight angle, hard and rigid as a sword. Its head was as wide as Lewis's slender wrist. Veins pulsed all along its twelve-inch length and there was a little isthmus of hair running up the base of the shaft.

Beneath a thick nest of dark blond pubic hair hung the great, loose balls which Lewis had fondled on the stairway. In proportion to Piotor's enormous cock, they seemed impossibly large and Lewis imagined them swinging against his buttocks as Piotor slid his cock inside him.

His face unsmiling now, Piotor set his hands on to his thighs and began to roll the stockings from his legs. For a moment, they peeled like the skin of a fruit, then, once past his knees, flopped to his shins. He dragged them over his feet and tossed them across the room.

Now he was entirely naked, standing over Lewis like an erect behemoth, the firelight throwing huge shadows over his ridged abdomen and perfect, peach-like buttocks.

Lewis suddenly felt like curling into a ball. An unfamiliar feeling of vulnerability coupled with excitement was gnawing at his insides. His legs and arms were still stretched fully out on the rug and he gazed up at the fantastic penis above him. What would the giant do next?

Piotor picked up the edge of a blanket and strode across the room, dragging it behind him. Lewis lay on the blanket, feeling like a child in some Arabian fairytale as he slid over the wooden floor.

Piotor stopped at the bed and Lewis found himself in a pile of blankets and pillows at the side of the mattress. In spite of the heat from the fire, he shivered slightly.

Looking about, Piotor made a couple of rapid darts into the shadows and returned with his plum-coloured stockings. He bent down, his hard stomach-ridges rippling like a concertina, and rapidly tied Lewis's hands to the bedpost with the stockings.

Lewis now lay with his upper body on the cool sheets of the bed, his genitals and legs suspended below as he knelt on the carpet of blankets.

He could no longer see Piotor but could sense the huge actor moving behind him. If he looked out of the corner of his eye, he could catch an occasional glimpse of Piotor's big, broad, naked feet padding over the floor.

Lewis tugged at his restraints and was oddly pleased to find them so securely fastened. There would be no play-acting required. He was Piotor's prisoner.

He gasped as he felt something close over his mouth. It was oddly familiar and Lewis recognised the scent of his own body. Piotor was tying Lewis's own stocking over the Deputy-Governor's mouth.

A flash of panic surged through Lewis. What if the actor intended him harm? What if he were an enemy of the Crown, in league with Parliament?

But, deep inside him, he knew these thoughts to be wild and foolish and, as he felt Piotor's huge arms wrap around his body, he relaxed, feeling only the warmth and comfort of the actor's embrace, the rock-hard massiveness of Piotor's cock pressed against his back.

Piotor sat back and manoeuvred Lewis into a kneeling position so that his rump stuck up into the air.

Gently, he pushed Lewis's head down on to the counterpane of the bed and stroked his blond hair. Lewis sighed, adoring the feel of the actor's calloused fingers brushing over his head. He swallowed, feeling the tight gag of the stocking restraining his tongue. The sharp taste of his own sweat excited his senses and he could feel his cock spring into renewed life and jab against the side of the bed.

Suddenly he could feel Piotor's breath on the back of his neck and he cried out as the Hungarian's massive cock began to penetrate him.

It was too much, surely it was too much. He would be split in two. He would perish in seconds. But all Lewis knew was the craving he felt for Piotor's body, his need to have the huge weapon within him and, as he felt the broad purple head slip into his anus, he allowed waves of relaxation to surge through him.

He opened his body fully to the insistent thrust of Piotor's cock and almost screamed as its full, twelve-inch length pierced him.

Lewis's eyes flashed open and shut repeatedly, his jaw hanging open in amazement and desire. He had been taken, utterly possessed by the beautiful actor. He felt that this was all he ever desired and that Piotor should never pull his great dick from out of him.

'You're inside me,' he gasped. 'Inside me.'

He felt Piotor's breath on his back and shivered.

Very, very slowly, the actor began to withdraw, sending bolts of pure, electric excitement shooting through Lewis. He wanted to press the flat of his palm to his belly, irrationally expecting to feel the head of Piotor's cock protruding through his flesh, but the stocking-restraints prevented him from moving.

Instead, he sighed as Piotor's hands wandered down to his groin and took hold of the shaft of his hard cock. Clamping both hands around it, he began to pump at Lewis's cock, even as he eased himself further into the Deputy-Governor's arse.

Lewis scowled, sweat pouring down his face, as Piotor held his cock between his hands, feeling its slick, membranous length slide through his fingers. He buried his gagged face into the mattress as Piotor pulled back and surged into him again, his huge balls, as expected, banging against the globes of Lewis's arse.

Still Piotor's huge arms encircled his cock, and then, suddenly, he let go and began to massage Lewis's nipples with his fingers. Already sensitised by the actor's suckling, they felt like little fires of sensation and Lewis twitched and grunted in response.

Now Lewis was rocking back and forth on his knees. He had taken the full length of Piotor's cock inside him and was furiously rubbing his own against the side of the bed, his breath coming in a hoarse rasp.

He bit into the stocking gag, now soaked with saliva, and felt his bound wrists pull at their restraints. Then, as though tiny messages were being sent by every part of his body to the boiling centre, he began to feel orgasm approach.

Throwing back his head, he thrashed his cock against the hard side of the bed, feeling his foreskin slide back and forth, and thrust his arse backwards to impale himself totally on Piotor's enormous length.

The actor began to draw in great whoops of breath and pressed his hands hard on to Lewis's nipples. Lewis could feel Piotor's cock twitching within him and knew the actor was about to come too.

Piotor let out a long, husky breath and slammed his thighs repeatedly against Lewis's buttocks.

Lewis felt hot seed pump into his anus. It continued for what seemed an age, filling him completely even as his own climax shattered his senses. He lost himself utterly, the room plunged into blackness and he was only dimly aware of the river of warm sperm shooting from his cock and pooling over on the carpet at his feet.

Piotor stayed inside him, panting, for a long minute, before carefully withdrawing. His great cock, lubricated with its own come slid swiftly out, but Lewis still gasped as its enormous length left him.

He fell back to his knees and sank down against the bed. He felt Piotor untie his hands and then sat down and turned to face his lover.

Piotor was standing over him again, with the goblet of wine in his hand. Lewis pulled the stocking gag from his mouth. He was panting with desire and satisfaction.

The actor smiled his great, wide smile and his face dimpled into ripples.

'God save the King,' he said in his deep, throaty voice.

Six

————

All through that strange summer, Cornelius watched as Ned Melcombe settled into his new role as Squire of Humbleford.

He was a popular figure, not least amongst the local girls, who much preferred the visits of the handsome young man to the gruff appearances put in by his father. And, true to his promise, the estates prospered.

Cornelius heard little of Ned's father and brother and, to him, the war seemed a very long way off indeed. There were reports of skirmishes, that the King had established his power-base in Nottingham and that his nephew, the handsome Prince Rupert, had come over to command his forces. But, despite most of Humbleford's menfolk having been press-ganged into Parliamentarian service by Sir Harry Melcombe, the quiet Oxfordshire valley seemed to amble on much as before.

On one of the rare, truly hot days that August of 1642, Cornelius steered his horse up the long, verdant road towards the manor house. Miracle Smith, his arms clasped tightly around Cornelius' waist, was balanced precariously on the horse's rump.

The sky was awesomely blue with only a few wisps of fluffy cloud towards the horizon. Everywhere there seemed a sense that it was good to be alive. The grass along the road, the bees in the flowers, all seemed to hum with pleasure.

Cornelius craned his neck and gave Miracle a reassuring smile. This was to be the boy's first visit to the manor.

Once Cornelius had grown used to the idea that Ned was acting Squire he had become quite excited at the possibilities. Would this mean Ned might finally begin to court him properly? Surely, with the house and the estates to himself, there was less need for secrecy.

But it had been a long, lonely week before Ned had finally invited the cleric to the house. Padding up the stairs towards Ned's room, knowing that they could cavort as they chose, gave Cornelius a little thrill of pleasure.

Ned certainly seemed to enjoy their new-found freedom, taking Cornelius up the arse with complete abandon. He had even moved some of their toys inside from the temple and it was strange for Cornelius to find himself bound and flogged within the confines of Sir Harry's venerable old house.

However, just as Cornelius had feared, Ned had never once thought of allowing him to stay. Each time, after surrendering his yielding arse and mouth to Ned's hot, stiff cock he had found himself wandering home in the early hours of the morning, like a vampire rushing back to its unquiet grave before sunrise.

But Cornelius never complained and, as Ned settled in, he was allowed to come more often. He had brought other young men of his acquaintance, including the actor twins who had come over from Nottingham for what they gigglingly called a 'command performance', other men that he found were charmingly rough, others merely dangerous-looking, but Ned welcomed them all and seemed to enjoy playing Master of all he surveyed. His guests were appropriately humble.

Miracle Smith, however, was Cornelius' private matter. Once, in an unguarded moment, he had mentioned that the boy was his lover and Ned had been immediately intrigued. It was as though he could not stand Cornelius having something that he had no power over. He never insisted, never ordered Cornelius to bring the dumb beauty to the manor but Cornelius was very much aware that Ned wanted to see and taste the boy.

As the horse plodded towards the manor, Cornelius looked up

and saw Ned, standing in the grand porch of the house with his eyes closed, letting the sunshine bathe his face.

The cleric felt a little knot of confused desire grip his belly. The mere sight of that lovely face, the dark brows drawn together, the heart-shaped face slightly burred with stubble, made his heart race.

Cornelius tried to put his emotions aside. Ned had promised that this day would be special. That was why he had finally agreed to bring Miracle along. And it would not do for Cornelius to spoil things by letting his doting love for his master show.

Hands on hips, Ned was stretching his neck in the warm sun. Cornelius shifted on the saddle, feeling a delicious sensuality flood through him. He moved his hips and felt his genitals press against the hard lines of the saddle.

He manoeuvred the horse so that it was right by Ned but the squire remained as he was, eyes shut. Cornelius reined in his horse and it stood snuffling and whinnying in the August heat.

For a long moment, nothing moved and Cornelius felt himself gazing with undisguised lust at the sight of his master.

Ned was dressed in a loose muslin shirt that exposed the pale, perfect hemispheres of his chest. He had on a pair of ragged short britches of the type normally worn by stablelads. His legs and feet were bare and Cornelius' gaze took in the details of Ned's shapely calves and high-arched, noble feet.

It was unusual indeed for one of Ned's position to be so commonly dressed, but the young squire had promised this was to be an unusual day.

At last he opened his eyes and glanced quickly at Cornelius, Miracle bunched tightly behind him.

The cleric beamed and Ned allowed him a small smile in return. Miracle looked slightly afraid, his thick, unkempt black hair hanging in an ill-cut fringe over his forehead.

'Welcome,' said Ned softly.

'Is everything arranged?' Cornelius said excitedly.

Ned nodded. 'No one will bother us. I've seen to it.'

Cornelius looked at him quizzically.

Ned's face was impassive. 'The adventure begins,' he said.

Ignoring Cornelius, Ned helped Miracle down from the back

of the horse. He looked at the boy, his expression betraying the lust and longing he was obviously feeling.

'So this is your Miracle,' he said softly. 'Indeed, you have not exaggerated, Cornelius. He is miraculous indeed.'

Cornelius felt a twinge of jealousy and immediately admonished himself. This was how it had to be. Ned had told him over and over.

He watched Ned and could see what was going through his mind. He was imagining licking the beautiful boy all over his hard, athletic body, forcing his mouth over those petulant lips and finally taking him up the arse, the boy perhaps crying out in a hoarse croak as he came.

Still the jealous thoughts overtook him. Miracle was his and his alone. The boy was something that Ned could never take from him. And there was something else too.

Deep in the back of his mind, Cornelius feared one thing above all. That every new lover he introduced to Ned would push him further and further towards the margins of the young squire's desire. If he allowed Miracle to become part of Ned's circle, perhaps he would soon be favoured over Cornelius and then, one day, the expected summons would fail to come and Cornelius would know he was no longer wanted.

He shook his head, his coppery hair swaying, and took hold of Miracle firmly by the wrist. Ned seemed to notice this gesture and gave a small, cruel smile.

'If you're ready, gentle sirs, there is a coach awaiting us.'

Cornelius watched him lead the way, a miasma of confused emotions trammelling through him. He felt lust mixed with anger, love bound almost imperceptibly with resentment and hatred. Why could Ned never see what he truly meant to him?

Tugging Miracle a little abruptly by the arm, Cornelius set off behind his master, the dumb boy's battered shoes sending little puffs of dust into the still summer air.

As promised, a coach was waiting for them. Small and elegant, it was liveried in black with the Melcombe family crest in gold on its side. Two chestnut horses stamped impatiently at its front.

Ned opened the door and ushered Cornelius and Miracle inside.

Cornelius paused on the threshold. 'Where –'

Ned shook his head. 'Don't ask,' he said quietly, patting Cornelius on the backside.

Inside it was pitch black and stultifyingly hot. Cornelius could hardly see a thing and poked his head out of the window to watch Ned take the reins.

The coach lurched and they were on their way.

Cornelius sighed and relaxed a little into the hard leather upholstery. Across the way, Miracle was sitting, his bright eyes just visible in the gloom.

As Cornelius grew accustomed to the darkness, he began to relax somewhat and found the motion of the coach quite restful. The bright outside world was only visible as a blur of green, sunlight-dappled foliage as they sped through the estate.

He put his hands on his lap and allowed himself to rock from side to side.

Glancing up at the dark space where he knew Miracle to be sitting, he smiled. 'Are you all right?' he said.

There was a motion in the darkness which he took to be a nod. He could just hear Miracle's breathing above the rattle of the coach.

Cornelius had found the strange boy to be not only quick-witted but educated, despite his handicap. They exchanged long written messages as well as passionate hours of love-making.

He was surprised by the power the boy seemed to exert over him. It was Ned to whom Cornelius was slavishly devoted, Ned whose side he wanted to stand by for all time. But the dumb boy's simple, trusting love was a thing of beauty in itself and the cleric found himself strangely moved.

No, he would not risk Miracle's pollution at the hands of Ned Melcombe.

Cornelius sighed and let himself be jostled by the movement of the coach. Above him, he knew Ned was sitting, his hard, pert buttocks resting on the driver's seat.

Closing his eyes, Cornelius tried to imagine what it would be like for him to take Ned, for *him*, not Ned, to be master for once. He thought of his fingers pulling at Ned's long, jet-black hair, of chaining him to the wall of the temple and flogging his milk-white muscly back. And then he saw himself ramming his stiff cock up inside Ned and the young squire crying out in pain and pleasure.

The movement of the coach was almost soporific but Cornelius began to find it more than a little arousing. Vibrations hummed up his body and he could feel his cock thickening and uncurling within his britches.

He let his head hang low and felt it rock frown side to side. He was dimly aware of Miracle's ill-shod feet directly below his gaze. If he looked up he could make out the boy's sun-baked hands stretched out on the upholstery of the opposite seat.

Cornelius kept his eyes fixed on Miracle's feet as a vague desire began to lick at the edge of his senses. Something about the darkness of the interior, the proximity of Miracle and the rhythmic movement of the coach made Cornelius feel an almost drunken lustiness.

Without a word, he moved down so that he was kneeling in the gap between the two seats and placed both hands on Miracle's knees.

The dumb boy immediately bent forward to kiss Cornelius, his beautiful face with its broken nose moving into the light from the carriage window. But Cornelius pushed him gently back into his seat. Wherever they were heading, it was clearly going to take some time.

Cornelius let his hands move over Miracle's legs, stroking his knees and calves and then moving back up to squeeze his muscular thighs. He laid his head in the boy's lap and then trailed his mouth over Miracle's knees, digging his teeth into the fabric of his meagre britches so that he was half-biting, half-teasing.

The cleric felt Miracle react, soundlessly, and grab at Cornelius' hair.

Cornelius smiled, his mouth still half-open as he bit into Miracle's clothed skin. Then, without a second thought, he plunged his face right into the boy's crotch, murmuring excitedly as he felt Miracle's thighs close around him, shutting off all sound as they squeezed over his ears.

He could smell the heady muskiness of Miracles cock through the material of his britches. Of course, as a farmer's boy he knew little of washing but Cornelius didn't mind. He drank in the earthy perfume of his silent lover, feeling the boy's cock pressing against his lips. Sucking through Miracle's britches, he could feel the penis solidifying beneath his wet mouth.

Lifting his hands over his still-smothered head, Cornelius felt his way under Miracle's thin shirt and began to squeeze and knead the boy's nipples. His hands fanned over every inch of the taut, rugged torso, feeling the ridges of muscle next to Miracle's ribs and the contours of his flat belly, solid as fossilised sand-ripples.

Miracle made the familiar throaty sound which meant he was pleased and Cornelius managed to pull his head from between the boy's thighs.

Worming his way upwards, Cornelius leant over Miracle and kissed him brutally. Their tongues connected and slid over one another and Cornelius let his hands ruffle the short, oily quills of Miracle's hair. He pushed the boy sideways and lay down on top of him so that both lay on the one long seat, their feet jammed against the rocking wall of the coach.

Cornelius nuzzled at Miracle's neck, letting his tongue trail over the muscles and Adam's apple. His kissed the boy's cheek and then bit gently into the soft flesh of his strong chin.

Miracle cried out and moaned with delight. Cornelius held him tight, feeling his own cock grow poker hard inside his trousers. He jammed his booted feet against the side of the coach and began to push himself up and down over Miracle's prostrate form.

In the hot darkness of the coach he could see little or nothing of his lover and, as he moved over Miracle's body, his mind began to picture someone else lying sweating and panting beneath him.

He could feel Miracle's lovely, slender cock jabbing at his belly but he thought of it as Ned Melcombe's. Yes, surely it was Ned lying there, squashed below him inside the swaying, rattling coach. It was Ned who had finally submitted to him, was speechless with lust. It was Ned's mouth which opened to him, warm and wide, tongue glistening.

Cornelius' hands roamed about under Miracle's shirt, tugging at his erect nipples, massaging the muscles at his strong arms. As he did so, he continued to rub himself rapidly against the rough fabric of Miracle's britches.

He pulled open the boy's shirt and pressed his face tight against the warm, musty hollows of Miracle's armpits. The odour of days-old sweat hit him full in the face but left him strangely excited. Miracle was a creature of the earth, elemental almost. In his beautiful, brooding, silent way he was like some shy deer, pressed into service for Cornelius' sport.

The cleric felt curiously torn, wanting to imagine Ned beneath him yet incredibly attracted to the lovely youth against whom he was rubbing his erect prick.

Cornelius could feel that he was soaking with sweat within his clothes. He pinioned Miracle's arms to the upholstery with his hands and began to nibble at the skin behind the boy's ear.

This sent Miracle into a frenzy and he gasped dumbly, resisting Cornelius' grip with a lusty fury. Clearly, he wanted to be master, as usual. He wanted to pull Cornelius under him and slide his great cock inside the cleric's unresisting arse.

But Cornelius held firm and the power he had over Miracle made him suddenly grin. If he could not have Ned then he would certainly have Miracle Smith and no one was going to take the boy away from him.

Redoubling his efforts, Cornelius pulled at his own britches, releasing his tumescent cock which throbbed before Miracle's face in the darkness.

At once, the dumb boy's mouth closed around the engorged purple head of Cornelius' cock, sucking it as though his life depended on it.

Cornelius groaned and cried out, the sensation of Miracle's tongue licking at every vein, every sinew of his cock sending him into raptures.

Again, he dug his fingers into the boy's cropped hair and shifted his hips forward so that his cock was in perfect position to slip into Miracle's passive mouth.

Miracle sat up a little. Cornelius ran a hand through his own, sweat-soaked hair and breathed deeply.

'Now,' he said in a thick, hoarse whisper. 'Now, take me in your mouth. I . . .'

He hesitated, the movement of the coach rocking him from

side to side. He could feel Miracle's heart pumping beneath his hands.

'I command you,' Cornelius said at last.

Miracle needed no such command. He grabbed the cleric's buttocks in his big, broad hands and pulled him forward so that his thick cock entered his saliva-lubricated mouth. His fingers clenched at the hollow globes of Cornelius' arse and pulled him further forward still so that Cornelius' cock penetrated right to the back of Miracle's throat.

Cornelius could feel the sensitive tip of his penis brushing against the warm, membranous interior of his lover's mouth and he shuddered with pleasure.

'Lovely . . .' he murmured, his head crowding with sensations. 'Lovely.'

Miracle's tongue was at work again, wrapping itself around the shaft of the cleric's cock as he sucked upon it.

Cornelius pulled back his hips a little way and then shunted forwards in a series of quick, excited movements. Miracle's mouth had formed into a tight, glossy hole and he was rutting it like a beast on heat. The faster he moved, the more the farmboy's firm lips excited the delicate flesh of his cock.

He grasped the boy by the sides of his head, his splayed fingers tugging and pinching and nipping at Miracle's skin. Then, as he fucked the boy's mouth, he pulled at Miracle's head so that the movement shadowed the thrusting of his hips.

The movement of the coach now seemed to tally with the action of Cornelius' body as he pumped his cock in and out of Miracle's mouth. He whimpered with pure pleasure as a crescendo of tingling sensations burst over him. He felt the heat of the carriage, felt Miracle's heartbeat, saw the blurred square that looked out on to the outside world.

'So good,' he cried, throwing back his head. 'My sweet. Let me fuck your mouth. Let me fuck your mouth.'

With a long, rasping sob he came, shooting his sperm deep into Miracle's yielding throat. So tight was the boy's mouth around the shaft of his cock, that Cornelius could feel his come dribbling out of the corners.

He pulled out and immediately let his hand slide under the hem of Miracle's britches. He grabbed hold of the boy's large, stiff penis and rubbed his palm over it. The pulsing head was already slick with pre-come and Miracle groaned as Cornelius' fingertips slipped over it.

Without releasing the boy's cock from his britches, Cornelius began to jerk his thumb and forefinger back and forth over its head, all the time allowing Miracle to kiss his neck and face.

He felt lazy and happy and sated all at once and pumped rapidly at the youth's cock till he felt him begin to strain and moan. A few seconds later, Miracle came, his semen soaking his cheap britches and running over Cornelius' hand.

For a while, they lay like that, Cornelius still with his hand closed around the softening length of Miracle's cock. Then, at last, the coach began to slow. Cornelius kissed Miracle tenderly on the lips and then moved back to his own seat, tucking his cock back into his britches just as the vehicle ground to a halt and the door was thrown open.

Ned was framed in the entrance, a halo of sunlight around his body. He looked from Cornelius to Miracle and smiled.

'Really, gentlemen,' he said. 'Patience is a virtue.'

The carriage had pulled up in a lush green glade, bound on all sides by oak trees. A huge, glittering waterfall dominated the glade and, stepping out into the brilliant sunshine, Cornelius realised this must be the famous Greenacre Falls which he had heard so much about. It was the most cherished part of Sir Harry's estate and Cornelius had long wanted to see it. He had hoped that perhaps Ned would bring him out there some time, alone. But today there were other things afoot.

Miracle clambered out behind him and they stood on the soft, springy grass, the rushing of the fall merging with the chirruping of bird-song.

Ned was standing by the sweat-glossed horses, stroking the mane of one and peering into the middle distance. He turned his head languidly as Cornelius approached and nodded towards Miracle.

'Is he a betting man?' he said.

'Pardon?' said Cornelius in surprise.

'Miracle. Does he wager at all?'

Cornelius laughed. 'I fear he has neither the funds nor the inclination.'

Ned moved towards the shy farmboy and caressed his downy cheek with the back of his hand. He then turned his hand over and let his fingertips glide over the soft fullness of the boy's lips.

'No. I suppose not.'

He glanced down. There was a large wet stain on the front of Miracle's thin britches. He smiled and the boy smiled back, his eyes bright with passion.

'But perhaps he could pay me. In kind.'

He moved his right hand around Miracle's body and squeezed one of his taut buttocks.

Cornelius almost stepped forward to strike Ned. He had not agreed to this. Ned could not just take Miracle from him . . .

The tramp of approaching feet made Cornelius and Ned turn. To Cornelius' astonishment, two soldiers were making their way through the foliage towards them. Dressed in russet-coloured coats and the heavy, dull armour of the Parliamentarian army they were a fearsome sight indeed. Both were tall and well-built and wore segmented helmets which obscured their faces.

Cornelius felt fear wash over him. His first thought was that they had somehow been discovered, that their ungodly behaviour had been witnessed and the authorities had come to hunt them down. The penalty for such acts of sodomy was bound to be death. Was this the way Ned's great adventure was to end?

But the young squire walked boldly up to the soldiers and stood, hand on hip as they came to a halt before him.

In one swift movement, they took off their heavy helmets, revealing them to be young men of perhaps twenty-one. Their hair was closely cropped, one a sun-kissed blond, the other almost as dark as Ned. The reflection from the falls sent light playing over their handsome features.

The blond one had icy grey eyes that narrowed as he looked over at Cornelius and Miracle. His nose was slightly snubbed, his mouth generously wide. His darker comrade's face was shadowed with stubble which extended over his cheeks towards his deep brown eyes. There was a fine pink scar which travelled in a crazed line like lightning from his crown to his left temple.

'Welcome,' said Ned simply, holding out his hands to relieve them of their helmets.

Both soldiers handed them over and began to remove their armour.

Ned pointed to them and turned to face Cornelius and Miracle.

'May I present Christopher and Hal,' he announced. 'Two gentlemen of our gracious Parliament's army who have become my acquaintances. They have kindly consented to a pugilistic display for our entertainment on this lovely day.'

The blond one, whom Cornelius took to be Christopher, gave a low bow, his eyes twinkling as he looked at Cornelius. The cleric felt himself blush and shifted his attention to Hal who was slowly unbuttoning his tunic.

'Pugilism?' queried Cornelius. 'You mean they're –'

'Aye, my boy,' smiled Ned, holding up his arms in a boxing attitude. 'They're here to knock seven bells out of each other. We shall lay bets on them and . . .' He grinned from ear to ear. 'Winner takes all.'

Cornelius looked round at Miracle. The boy was staring at the soldiers, his Adam's apple bobbing up and down as he nervously swallowed.

Sidling up to him, Cornelius gave Miracle's hand a reassuring squeeze and encouraged him to sit down on the grass.

Ned took a step back and they all watched as Christopher and Hal began to strip.

Both soldiers were exceptional specimens, their arms and chests bunched with muscle, their bellies hard and solid as rock. In a few moments they were naked to their waists and turned to Ned as though for further instructions.

He nodded to them and then turned to Cornelius.

'I will wager ten pounds,' he announced.

Miracle looked up, amazed. Ned chuckled.

'Such a princely sum, I know, my little beauty. But ten pounds I'll bet on . . . Christopher'.

He swung round and pointed at the blond soldier who was standing with his hips thrust provocatively forward and his thick arms behind his back.

Ned looked back at Cornelius. 'What will you wager, lover?'

To one of Cornelius' means, ten pounds was a fantastic sum. He shrugged. 'What have I to offer?'

Ned cocked a dark eyebrow and smiled cruelly. 'What indeed?'

Cornelius felt his words cut him to the quick. Tears sprang to his eyes and he looked down at the brilliant green grass at his feet. He only looked up as he saw Ned's bare feet approach.

'I have an idea,' said Ned. 'You brought this little beauty to me.' He nodded at Miracle. 'He is, if you like, your discovery. Wager *him*.'

Cornelius frowned. 'What do you mean?'

Ned cleared his throat. 'Well, you have a . . . shall we say, controlling interest in the boy. If your champion loses the fight then Miracle becomes mine. Body and soul.'

Cornelius felt every instinct in him rise against Ned's cruel game. Miracle was the one certainty in his life, the one thing that Ned was unable to control. If he lost the boy . . .

But there was something else stirring inside Cornelius. A curious, heart-quickening desire. A feeling of forbidden pleasure. He did not know why, but the idea of these handsome soldiers battling for control over the beautiful farmboy made him excited. As Ned spoke, he felt his cock once again grow warm and hard inside his britches. He decided to fight back a little.

'What?' he barked. 'And a mere ten pounds if he wins?' He jerked his head in the direction of Hal who was intended to be his champion.

Ned laughed, his dark eyes blazing with impish delight. 'You would raise the stakes?'

'No. But I think the bargain a poor one. You wish to take Miracle from me. I want more than mere money should Hal be victorious.'

Ned seemed to find this exchange highly amusing. He looked to the two soldiers who stood, impassively gorgeous, at his side.

'Name your price, Cornelius,' he cried.

Cornelius took a deep breath. This was going to be difficult.

'If Hal defeats Christopher,' he said, rising to his feet, 'I demand that, for a period of my choosing, I, Cornelius Matthew, shall be master over you.'

Ned's face fell. His smooth features creased in consternation. 'What did you say?'

Cornelius strolled over towards the soldiers, gazing at their muscular chests, bound by the waistbands of their black britches. He came to a halt by Hal's side, clapped the soldier on the back, then let his hand slide down the sweat-slicked hollow of his spine.

'My terms are clear,' he said. 'To the victor, the spoils.'

He turned to look at Ned whose face was a picture of indecision. Eventually, the young squire shook his head.

'I cannot consent to it,' he muttered. 'I have sworn that no man . . .' He hesitated. Cornelius looked at him closely. 'No man shall be master over me.'

Cornelius had noticed something in that hesitation. There was some secret Ned was keeping from him. Some history to which he had never been privy.

Finally, the cleric shrugged. 'Then the match is off. Come, Miracle.'

He took the hand of the bemused farmboy and headed back towards the coach.

'Wait!' called Ned.

Cornelius and Miracle stopped in their tracks but kept their backs towards Ned and the soldiers.

'What if I were to . . . command you to obey me?' said Ned.

Cornelius didn't look round. 'This time, Ned, I do not think I could do it.'

It was the first time Cornelius had ever called his master by his Christian name but the cleric felt oddly emboldened. He squeezed Miracle's hand again and the boy smiled shyly over at him.

Ned sighed and bit his lip. He looked the soldiers over, thinking hard, then lifted Christopher's chin with his hand. He gazed into the soldier's narrow grey eyes. 'You had better win,' he said levelly.

He turned back towards Cornelius. 'Very well. The wager is on.'

The three spectators sat down on the warm summer grass whilst Christopher and Hal began to limber up.

Both men were in superb condition and Cornelius thought them so well matched that the outcome was genuinely uncertain.

He watched as Christopher bent over and touched his toes, his hip bones visible through the tight material of his britches. His cock and balls formed one solid bulge at their front.

Hal was slightly stockier and perhaps, thought Cornelius, this would give him some advantage. His pectorals were big and curved, their nipples dark, pronounced and hard as musket balls.

Ned rubbed his pointed chin and looked about, deep in thought.

What was going on inside that beautiful head?

Cornelius shook himself out of his reverie as the combatants squared up to each other, arms extended in the classic boxing pose.

Ned's bright eyes blinked and he looked up. 'Begin.'

The two soldiers began to circle each other warily. Christopher rotated his fists in front of Hal's nose and swung an experimental punch which Hal neatly side-stepped and immediately riposted. Christopher ducked and easily avoided it.

Cornelius watched as they moved to and fro across the glade, sweat already coursing over their steely torsos.

Shielding his head, Hal thrust his fist upwards and caught Christopher neatly on the jaw. The blond stepped back in surprise and lashed out wildly with his left hand. Hal bobbed low and the blow hit nothing but air. Seizing his advantage, Hal struck again, catching Christopher over the eye. Christopher grunted and managed to land a low punch which caught Hal on his ribs.

Cornelius felt excitement and lust pump through him. The sight of these delicious, sweat-soaked fighters was arousing enough, but the idea that Hal's victory would bring him his most cherished desire was intoxicating beyond reason.

He glanced at Miracle and Ned and saw that they, too, were completely gripped by the bout. Ned's cock was erect and pressing against the flimsy material of his ragged britches. Cornelius began to imagine what it would be like to have Ned begging at his feet, servicing *him* for a change.

Hal let out a great whoop of air as Christopher landed a blow in his gut. He responded at once, ducking down and jabbing twice in rapid succession at Christopher's jaw, knocking him backwards so that he fell flat on his backside on the soft grass.

Unexpectedly, Hal laughed and grasped hold of the belt which held up Christopher's britches. He gave it a mighty tug and pulled it off.

Christopher scrambled to his feet but his britches immediately fell down and he stumbled, his big, thick cock and pendulous balls flopping before him.

Snarling in frustration, Christopher pulled off his shoes and trousers, leaving him quite naked. He circled Hal and managed to rain several effective punches on the dark soldier's flank.

His bare feet sank into the ground, which was softened by the constant spray from the waterfall, and were soon covered in mud.

Hal, still wearing his britches and buckled shoes, caught Christopher over the eye again and a trickle of bright blood sprang from his flesh. It merged with droplets of sweat and fell into Christopher's eye.

He wiped it away with the back of his hand, but Hal pressed his advantage and cracked him under the chin once again, sending him back to the earth.

For a few long seconds, he lay there, his genitals plainly visible in his muscular lap.

Cornelius stared at them in delight for Christopher's cock was clearly hardening as the fight hotted up.

Hal spotted this and, with a roar of amused bravado, sank to his knees on the ground and clamped his mouth over Christopher's cock.

Ned clapped his hands delightedly. 'Unfair!' he called. ''Tis an unfair move!'

Hal gave Christopher's cock a few playful sucks and then sprang back to his feet.

Christopher, his legs and chest now as muddy as his feet, jumped up at once and smashed Hal in the nose with his big left fist.

Cornelius gasped involuntarily, feeling desire growing within him. Almost unconsciously, he let his hand move down into the warm confines of his britches and take hold of the rapidly thickening shaft of his own cock.

Spurred on by the successful blow, Christopher punched again, knocking Hal to his knees. He stood over the dark soldier, his cock semi-erect, jutting from the wiry bush of his loins. Then, planting one muddy foot in the centre of Hal's chest, he sent him crashing back on the grass.

Laughing heartily, he thrust his hand into Hal's britches and tore them from the young soldier's body.

Hal looked faintly shocked as his short, thick, veiny penis was revealed. Christopher seized his advantage and, pressing his hand around Hal's throat, kissed him full on the lips.

At once, Hal's cock grew erect and Christopher allowed his other hand to close around its head.

Ned shouted something at Christopher and Hal immediately lashed out, catching the blond in the belly and winding him.

Hal leapt to his feet and cracked Christopher on the side of the head. Ned's champion fell to his knees and dazedly shook his head.

Cornelius looked over at Ned and saw the look of anxiety on his face. He felt a rush of adrenalin race through him and quickened the action of his thumb and forefinger over his cock. Hal Looked like he would win and that meant Ned would belong to Cornelius for as long as he chose!

Hal ripped off the remnants of his britches and kicked off his shoes. He grabbed Christopher around the shoulders and pulled him to the ground. It seemed that the boxing match was now to include a wrestling bout.

Christopher responded at once, flinging a muddied arm around Hal's neck and under his chin. Hal gasped and beat his fist against Christopher's thick forearm.

Cornelius watched in undisguised pleasure, beating rapidly at his cock inside his britches.

The soldiers rolled around on the grass before him, both their naked forms plastered with wet mud. This only emphasised their well-defined bodies and perfect, round arses as though life had been breathed into two idealised clay figures.

Hal seized hold of Christopher's arm, twisted it and threw his opponent over his head to land in a naked heap. The blond's cock was fully erect now and jabbing into the muscles of his abdomen.

His pretty face was all but obscured by mud and his hair was matted with blood and sweat but his fierce grey eyes blazed with lust and fury.

Struggling to his feet, his own cock sticking up at right angles to his big, hairy balls, Hal ran at Christopher. The blond stuck his foot into the air and propelled Hal right over him.

Cornelius moaned with pleasure as he stroked the length of his penis. He unbuttoned the top of his britches and let the warm air flow over his loins. Both Miracle and Ned were too concerned with the fight to notice that Cornelius was sitting with his cock out, rubbing furiously at its large, engorged head.

The two fighters crashed into a tight embrace, their cocks slapping together as though engaged in a contest all of their own. Christopher pinioned Hal's arms behind the dark soldier's back and pushed his face down into the mud with his foot.

'Submit!' cried Ned.

Cornelius whimpered as he watched the soldiers. A warm, tingling rush was coursing through him and he slowed the movement of his fingers over his cock into long, measured tugs.

'Fight!' he found himself shouting. 'Fight him, Hal!'

With a supreme effort, Hal manoeuvred his neck out from under Christopher's bare foot and, turning on his back, landed a terrific punch right on the point of the blond's square jaw.

Christopher seemed to hover over Hal for an eternal moment, his long, slender cock still stiff and hard against the muscles of his stomach, then he crashed to the ground, unconscious, just as Cornelius came, orgasm powering through his every sinew.

Ned looked around and caught Cornelius' gaze as semen pumped from the creamy purple end of the cleric's penis and into the grass. Ned had an oddly confused look about him, as though the bottom had fallen out of his world.

Hal stood up, his erection diminishing, and immediately set about reviving his prostrate friend.

Ned wandered over and dropped a purse of coins on to Christopher's chest. The small, leather bag opened and the coins spilled out, rolling off the muddied contours of his body.

Hal looked up and smiled, his teeth showing whitely through the mud which caked his face. 'Thank'ee, my lord', he said, his thick west-country accent rich as wine.

He slapped Christopher gently a few times and the blond opened his eyes. He smiled up at Hal and they kissed fondly.

'A good fight, Hal,' he murmured, then looked up at Ned. 'I'm sorry, sir.'

Ned shook his head. ''Tis no matter.'

He moved off and approached Cornelius and Miracle who were standing hand in hand.

'Well,' said Ned. 'To the victor, the spoils, Cornelius.'

His eyes ranged over Miracle's beautiful face and he shook his head. 'A pity. I should have enjoyed you.'

Cornelius felt almost delirious with new power. He cocked his head to one side. 'So then, what's to do?'

Ned shrugged. 'By your leave ... master,' he said with difficulty, 'I'd like to ask for one day's grace to let me get used to the idea. Then you may ask of me what you wish.'

Cornelius considered this, then nodded. 'Very well.'

Ned turned away, but Cornelius was not quite finished. 'On one condition,' he said.

'And what is that?'

Cornelius looked over his shoulder at Hal and Christopher who were watching this exchange with some amusement. 'We want them. Both of them. Now.'

Ned looked startled. 'I've paid for their pugilism. Anything else must be up to them.'

Hal laughed and stroked his muddied cock with his hand. 'I have no objection to such bonny lads.'

'Nor I,' said Christopher quickly, shooting Cornelius the same, sexy look.

Ned ground his teeth angrily. 'That's settled, then. I'll bid you good day.'

'Oh, and one more thing,' said Cornelius, enjoying the moment.

Ned glared at him. Cornelius gave him his most winning smile.

'Kiss my feet,' he said evenly.

Ned let out a snort of derisive laughter.

Cornelius tutted. 'The wager was agreed before witnesses. Therefore ... slave ... kiss my feet.'

Ned sighed furiously, then got to his knees on the grass and gently laid his lips to Cornelius' toes.

The cleric shuddered with pleasure. He could get rather used to this.

Ned got slowly to his feet and then clambered on board the carriage. Without looking back he whipped at the horses and called over his shoulder, 'I'll send the carriage back for you before sundown.'

With that, he sat down and steered the coach out of the glade in a haze of dust. In a few moments, he was gone.

Cornelius marched happily towards the soldiers and clapped Hal on his naked shoulder.

'Well fought, Hal. You don't know what this means to me.'

Hal laughed. 'I can guess, sir. I can guess.'

Cornelius turned to Christopher. The boy was certainly lovely, and his pale grey eyes narrowed as he smiled at the cleric.

'And Christopher,' said Cornelius, 'I feel it only fair that you be compensated for your loss.'

Christopher put out his hand and touched Cornelius' britches.

The cleric let out a little gasp of delight as Christopher's fingers closed around the sperm-covered head of his cock and gently squeezed at it. At once, blood began to pump back into its length and Cornelius felt renewed desire shiver through him.

Christopher kissed him on the neck and then chewed sensuously at his ear.

Cornelius could feel the soldier's hot breath roaring in his ear and shuddered with delight.

He put out both hands and pushed at Christopher's muddied chest. 'Wait, wait,' he muttered.

Miracle was standing back, fiddling with the strings of his britches, not knowing what to do. Cornelius beckoned to him.

'Miracle. Would you like him?'

He pointed at Hal and the handsome soldier flashed Miracle a devastating smile.

The dumb boy nodded shyly.

Cornelius turned to Hal. 'And you, sir?'

Hal nodded vigorously. 'Indeed.'

'Then let's waste no more time,' declared Cornelius with an authority he didn't know he possessed.

Hal took Miracle's hand and led him off into the glade. The boy looked over at Cornelius, still a little shy, but the cleric knew he would be all right.

Then, to Cornelius' surprise, Christopher let out a great whoop of joy, ran across the grass and jumped into the river.

He emerged seconds later, water sparkling over his fine torso and neck. He laughed and rubbed at his cropped hair, sending a spray of droplets shooting off in every direction.

Cornelius stripped off in seconds and threw himself into the water.

Shockingly cold, the water felt wonderful on his hot, naked skin. He was vaguely aware of Christopher's legs before him and then raced to the surface.

The soldier embraced him and rammed his cool tongue into the cleric's mouth.

Cornelius felt desire course through his body. He moaned as he pressed his lips against Christopher's and felt the soldier's tongue probe around his yielding mouth. Under the water, Cornelius could feel his cock stiffening.

They pulled apart and Christopher took his hand.

'Come,' said the blond soldier.

Cornelius allowed himself to be led through the water towards the sparkling rush of the waterfall.

Christopher paused before the curtain of crashing water and then backed into it, holding Cornelius by both hands. The cleric felt himself drenched in cold, cold water and shivered with pleasure. He could only dimly make out the soldier in the confusion of shimmering light and suddenly felt Christopher's mouth on his again as the handsome stranger pressed close to his body.

He could feel Christopher's cock thrusting against his own and mumbled throatily as waves of sheer lust rippled through him.

As the water soaked his long hair, he pressed his lips against Christopher's nipples and sucked at each in turn, chewing the pink discs until they stood proud from the goose-flesh of his chest.

Christopher rolled back his head and groaned. Cornelius looked

114

at him, taking in every detail of his lovely body: the hollows of his collarbone, the solid, almost square pads of his pectorals, the fuzzy line of wet hair which ran down into his dark navel. And his cock, his ram-rod straight cock, dappled with water droplets and pressed tightly against the soft skin of Cornelius' loins.

The cleric ran his hand over the wet, blond bristles of Christopher's cropped hair and embraced him ever tighter, revelling in the heat of the soldier's body and the incredible feel of that great cock against his own.

He cupped Christopher's balls in one hand and gently massaged them. The soldier let out a hiss of pleasure through his clenched teeth and kissed Cornelius full on the mouth.

Cornelius then pulled back and gazed into Christopher's lively grey eyes. There was something he had to do. Something that he needed to be well-versed in if he were, indeed, to become master of his beloved Ned Melcombe. Something that his experience with the twins had taught him he liked very much.

Taking Christopher by the hand, he waded through the water, out from under the falls and clambered out onto the riverbank. Christopher followed and, as soon as they were on the grass, they curled together in a tight embrace.

Cornelius looked Christopher in the eye again. 'I must have you,' he murmured.

The soldier smiled seductively. 'Then take me,' he breathed, kissing Cornelius again, his tongue flicking over the cleric's teeth and lips.

Cornelius found himself glowing with confidence. It was as though all the years of taking the passive part, allowing Ned, Miracle and all those who had preceded them to be master over him, had melted away.

Now things were to be different and if, as Ned had promised, Cornelius would soon be sliding his cock deep inside the young squire, he was ready.

Gently, he turned Christopher onto his stomach. The soldier sighed contentedly and thrust his arse into the air, exposing the dark cleft of his anus to the warm, summer air.

At once, Cornelius sank his face in between the cheeks of the soldier's arse and pushed his wet tongue up inside him.

Christopher gasped and almost giggled with delight. Cornelius let his tongue move rapidly in and out, exploring the smooth flesh. Then he relaxed so that his tongue broadened into a wide, warm shape that lapped at Christopher's arse. The taste of the soldier's musky, sweaty flesh sent little sparks of lust through him.

Christopher groaned again and dug his fists into the soft soil.

'Take me, my lord,' he whimpered. 'Take me. I want to feel you inside me. Take me.'

Cornelius sat back on his haunches, his own cock, red with exertion already, standing large and firm. He paused. This was how he would first take Ned, he decided, the squire's beautiful face rammed into a pillow as Cornelius thrust his cock straight up into his perfect, taut arse.

Without another thought, Cornelius pushed his hips against the globes of Christopher's arse and guided his cock into the hollow entrance to the soldier's anus. He slid inside without difficulty and rasped hoarsely in pure, animal lust as he felt Christopher's flesh enclose him.

The soldier rested his head on the ground and began to mumble incomprehensibly as Cornelius' cock moved inside him.

The cleric moaned himself, finding the experience pleasurable beyond all expectation. He was glad he had so recently come because he felt so aroused he was sure he would have spilled his seed inside Christopher as soon as he entered him.

Now he pulled back, feeling his own buttocks rest upon his shins and then thrust rapidly forward into the soldier's soft flesh.

Christopher cried out but nodded his head as though to reassure Cornelius. 'No,' he gasped. 'Don't stop. Never stop.'

Cornelius pushed inside him again, a smile of pure bliss widening across his face. It was beautiful beyond words. To have this man pierced by his cock, to pleasure this man just as the soldier's ripe arse gave pleasure to him.

A sound close by momentarily distracted Cornelius and he looked over the soft, white curve of Christopher's shoulders towards the foliage which ringed the glade.

To his delight, he saw Miracle, crouched in just the same attitude as him, powering his great cock into Hal's arse. The sight of his beloved boy's tanned buttocks, his balls dangling beneath, aroused him further still and he bit into his lower lip as he forced his cock in and out of Christopher's arse.

He began to breathe rhythmically, as though willing away the moment of his orgasm. The feel of Christopher's tight arse around his cock made his hair stand on end. A soft, shapeless tingle began to rise from the base of his spine and he pumped rapidly into Christopher's arse, his cock impaling the boy like a hot arrow.

So yielding and wet was the soldier's bare arse that Cornelius was able to fuck him like a girl, his cock slamming in and out of the soft hole.

Cornelius struggled to hold back but a dark curtain of pleasure swept over him, blacking out all sensation except the filthy, wonderfully base feel of his cock inside the young soldier's arse. As he came, he heard Miracle's familiar cry as he too pumped his soldier full of come.

Cornelius kept on thrusting forward and back, unwilling ever to end such pleasure, then gradually pulled out, his cock slick with his own semen.

Christopher let out a long, satisfied moan and threw himself on to his back, panting with exhaustion.

Cornelius kissed him on the wound above his eye and the soldier smiled back. The cleric sank down on to the grass, his breath coming in shuddering gasps, then looked up as Miracle and Hal approached. Both were flushed and grinning but Cornelius noticed that Hal's cock was still fully erect.

He glanced at Christopher to see that, he too, was proud with desire.

Miracle came and sat by Cornelius, kissing him fondly on the lips. the two soldiers, without a word, immediately lay down side by side and began to kiss passionately. In moments, their hands were moving rapidly over each other's cocks. Aroused by each other as much as by the fucking they had just received, Hal and Christopher came together, great jets of milky sperm splashing over their hard naked chests.

When it was over, they came to be with Cornelius and Miracle and all four men fell asleep in a sweat-soaked muddy circle under the beating heat of the August sun.

★ ★ ★

Ned drove the horses furiously back towards the manor. The sun was still high in the sky and he felt uncomfortably hot on top of the carriage. He tore open his shirt, exposing the silky-smooth pads of his chest muscles and cracked a whip over the horses' backs.

There had to be a way out of this dilemma. He had promised himself that none save Lewis St John would ever be his master. None save Lewis would ever take him in his most sacred place, driving him into delirium with their huge, stiff cock.

Cornelius could never be his master. It was a joke, surely the cleric would see that. He seemed perfectly happy with things the way they always were and would soon see the folly of this idea. It was Ned's role to control *him*, to order him about, to take him up the arse or wherever he chose. It was agreed. Cornelius, Cornelius, Cornelius. Why did the boy vex him so?

Besides, what value was a wager sworn before two solider whores and a poor farmboy who couldn't even speak?

The more Ned thought about it, the more amused he became. It would come to nothing and Cornelius would be back to his old servile ways by the time they next met. And then Ned could set about getting Miracle Smith after all.

He relaxed a little and sat back in the driver's seat. As the carriage came over the crest of a hill and approached the manor house, Ned was already thinking what he would do with the dumb boy. He imagined kissing that petulant mouth, running his tongue over the boy's sweet, broken nose, thrusting his cock deep into Miracle's throat. And the boy sucking at him, sucking every drop of sperm from him as Ned held his head firmly down . . .

As Ned approached the house he was so lost in imagining that he almost failed to notice the soldier standing by the porch, his horse tethered to its oak beams.

Ned pulled the carriage to a halt and jumped down from it.

The soldier, a hefty, grey-haired man of forty, marched straight up to him.

'I take it you are the squire, sir. Your servant said you were away for the day.'

'So I was,' said Ned, frowning. 'What is your business?'

The soldier sighed. 'I bring grave news, my lord.'

'My father?'

The soldier nodded. 'There was an engagement between your father's forces and the King's. I fear the Lord did not smile on us.'

'My father –' said Ned again, grabbing the soldier by the scruff of the neck.

The soldier shook his head, his greasy grey hair fluttering over the filthy collar of his coat. 'Sir Harry lives, sir. It is your brother, Thomas.'

Ned felt the hot sun beat down on his head like a lead weight.

'Thomas,' he murmured flatly.

The soldier looked down at the ground. 'I'm sorry. Your brother is dead.'

Seven

One arm dangling over the side of his bed, Lewis St John opened his eyes and stared at the pile of clothes littering the floor.

Late summer sunlight glittered through the windows of his apartments. The room felt warm and fresh. Lewis let a long, grumbling, contented sigh slip past his lips and turned over, his long blond hair brushing the muscular smoothness of his shoulders.

The previous night had seen such an orgy of drinking and carousing that he wasn't at all sure whom he had invited to his bed.

There had been good reason to celebrate. After a miserable month during which the King's closest advisers had confessed that his forces were so depleted they might not be able to safeguard his person, volunteers had suddenly flooded into Nottingham. This was partly due to the mystique of royalty but mostly down to Parliament's decision to seize the lands of anyone who did not declare in its favour. No one was to remain indifferent to this war any longer. Opinion had polarised and the King suddenly found himself with two thousand horsemen and almost fifteen thousand infantrymen.

With his morale greatly improved, the King was now to march for Chester, hoping to gain more support from Wales and Ireland.

As usual, Lewis had been in charge of keeping His Majesty

entertained and had pulled out all the stops to make this last evening very special.

Nan Fiennes' troupe had put on a spectacular masque which even the grave, reserved King seemed to enjoy and then there had been much feasting and far too much drinking.

Lewis lifted his head from the pillow and felt it throb painfully. He laid his palm across his forehead and groaned.

There was a man-sized shape curled up in the sheets next to him but it wasn't clear whose bones he had dragged into his bed. Could it be the Irishman or one of those charming Spanish twins? Perhaps even the wonderful Piotor?

Lewis grinned. The actors had certainly proven a versatile lot. Over the past few weeks he had entertained almost all of them, sometimes dominating them, sometimes playing passive as with Piotor. He had particularly enjoyed the twins who seemed well versed in pleasing a man in collaboration.

Carefully, Lewis peeled back the sheets to reveal the shining, ebony-black skin of Alexander.

Lewis murmured in delight. The one member of the company who had eluded him, the mysterious taciturn Negro, had finally succumbed to his charms.

He cursed himself for being so drunk he couldn't even remember what they had got up to.

Looking over the fantastically smooth contours of the actor's flesh, the curve of his round buttocks, the teasing glimpse of the sac of his huge balls, he knew it must have been special.

But what of his own performance? What if he had been so embarrassingly drunk that he had passed out – or worse?

Well, he thought, the hour was still early and, despite his aching head, there was time to put things to rights.

Pulling the sheets right back, he exposed the whole of Alexander's sleeping form. The young man was long in almost every respect, from his tightly muscled legs and arms to his torso and heavy, slack penis.

His hands were tucked up under his cheek like those of a sleeping child and Lewis smiled a little as he gazed down at him.

Taking care not to wake the actor, Lewis crept down the bed, his own genitals swinging between his legs, and crouched at Alexander's feet.

He leant on his hands and began, ever so gently, to lick the hard, white soles of Alexander's feet.

The actor did not react, even as Lewis's tongue found its way into the little niches between his spatulate toes and over his high, hairless arches.

Lewis murmured to himself. The boy was simply too gorgeous to exist, he concluded. There was a lovely, gnawing lust bursting within his belly and he felt an almost overwhelming desire to eat Alexander.

He smiled at the thought as his mouth closed around Alexander's toes and quietly sucked them. This was almost like eating him, anyway.

Lewis shuffled up the bed a little, his teeth closing around Alexander's knees. Carefully, with exquisite gentleness, he let his teeth sink into the man's flesh and rolled his wet tongue over the surface.

Alexander stirred and groaned but did not wake. Lewis leaned out of the way as the actor turned over on to his belly.

Returning to Alexander's feet, Lewis trailed his tongue up his body from his toes to the base of his buttocks, then, parting the cheeks with two fingers, began to lick at the soft, warm entrance to his arse.

Again consumed by a desire to have Alexander whole, Lewis squeezed at the man's buttocks and let his hands stroke the backs of his firm thighs and calves, as though mapping out territory.

As he licked and teased, Lewis felt his cock begin to grow stiff. In seconds it had swung upright and he felt his balls tingling with anticipation.

Lifting his face from Alexander's buttocks, Lewis peeked around the actor's side. To his delight, he could see the tip of Alexander's big, dark penis squashed under his belly against the mattress.

He crouched down and set his tongue to the small shape of sensitive flesh projecting from under the hard shell of Alexander's belly.

There was a distinctive taste of sperm and Lewis felt his cock respond at the thought. They had enjoyed each other the previous night and Alexander had come. It was too precious an experience to forget and it was time they repeated it.

Placing one hand on Alexander's buttocks, Lewis pushed the actor slightly away from him so that more of his cock was revealed. In the brief time before he let go, Lewis snuggled down so that his face was pressed against the warm, smooth skin of the actor's muscular flank, his mouth enclosing and sucking the exposed portion of Alexander's long, flaccid penis.

Alexander moaned again and turned onto his side, unconsciously responding to Lewis's mouth around his cock.

Lewis pulled up his own legs so that he was lying in a tight, curled ball by the actor's side, sucking the man's long black cock, feeling it grow hard within his mouth.

Casting the occasional glance up the bed to see if Alexander was yet stirring, Lewis pushed himself nearer, feeling Alexander's cock stuff itself into his mouth and nudge the back of his throat.

He let his tongue curl around its great head and teased his way into the dark, hollow urethra.

Summoning up more spit, he began to beat his tongue back and forth over the rapidly expanding head of the actor's cock, tasting its scent, pleasuring the sensitive membrane beneath.

Still Alexander did not wake and Lewis let his hands steal up the actor's broad chest and over his dark nipples. His fingers began to stroke delicately at the little hollow at the base of Alexander's strong, smooth throat and then fluttered over the lines of his collarbone.

There were small tufts of black, knotted hair studding the actor's chest like cloves in a Christmas orange and Lewis stroked these too, his hands forming wide fans over Alexander's tautly muscled pectorals.

Lewis looked up again at Alexander's beautiful, perfectly composed visage. His heavy, sensuous eyelids remained closed, his delicate nose gently expanding as he breathed, his soft, moist lips slightly open as though inviting Lewis inside.

Laying his fingertips to the curve of Alexander's ear, Lewis tickled and stroked till his hand lay over Alexander's mouth. Then, still sucking on the now rock-hard length of the actor's cock, he pushed his fingers inside Alexander's mouth.

It was a strange angle indeed, to lie at, but Lewis felt safe and warm, curled by the side of this exquisite man, sucking at his stiff cock, forcing his fingers into the warm, yielding hole of his mouth.

There was still no response from Alexander but Lewis didn't mind. He wrapped his tongue around the length of his cock and pulled back his head in order to enjoy it.

With his other hand, he cupped Alexander's balls and squeezed them as though gauging the ripeness of fruit in a market.

He felt Alexander stiffen and so retracted his fingers from the actor's mouth to grasp his buttocks instead.

Alexander moaned and thrust his hips forward so that his great cock stretched deep into Lewis's throat.

Lewis's hand curled over the sweaty globes of the actor's arse as Alexander came, grunting and hissing, his semen pouring into Lewis's mouth.

Lewis let it trickle down his throat, loving the sensation, and continued to suck at Alexander's penis until he felt a strong hand close around his wrist.

He pulled his wet mouth from around the actor's cock and looked up.

Alexander's eyes were open and he was grinning broadly. He pulled Lewis up the bed so they were eye to eye.

'Thank you,' he murmured.

Lewis laughed. 'How long have you been awake?'

Alexander shrugged. 'Long enough.'

Without another word he kissed Lewis on the lips, his tongue frantically exploring every corner of his warm mouth. Then he withdrew and began to nuzzle at Lewis's neck, sending shivers of pleasure through Lewis as his teeth and lips whispered over the downy skin of his throat.

Lewis let his hand trail down to Alexander's thighs and was astonished to find that the actor's cock, still creamy with come, was already hard again.

Looking up into Alexander's eyes, Lewis's face hardened with desire. His head was still throbbing but this only seemed to concentrate his passion. He felt the blood pounding in his temples and in his heart as desire for the lovely, exotic Alexander coursed through him.

'I want you to take me,' he hissed into the actor's ear. 'Take my cock in your mouth.'

Alexander nodded and slid down the bed, rumpling the sheets with his strong, athletic legs.

He clamped his mouth around Lewis's cock and Lewis purred with pleasure. Alexander sighed gently and then proceeded to execute a series of the most delicate, sensual actions on the bare, throbbing head of Lewis's cock.

Lewis gasped and jerked spasmodically as rivers of carnal desire swept over him, tingling his skin, crashing over his consciousness.

The feel of Alexander's mouth on his cock was so good, so beautiful that Lewis wanted to lie there for ever.

He closed his arms around the warm body that hovered over him and let his hands squeeze at the exquisite lines of Alexander's chest.

Looking hazily down, he could see Alexander's cropped head swaying as he licked and sucked at the smooth, pulsing head of Lewis's cock.

The actor flashed him a devastating smile but Lewis was too far gone, too sunk in his own lustiness to respond. He felt his cheeks flush and pushed his head back into the pillows as Alexander's tongue moved along the stiff length of his cock, back and forth, back and forth, tickling and teasing at the warm, hard flesh and spit-slicked glans.

Then Alexander shifted his position so he was by Lewis's side. As he bent to lick at Lewis's penis once again, he reached up with one hand to tug at Lewis's nipples.

Lewis mumbled throatily, adoring the pressure of the actor's fingers on the sensitive, pink mounds of his erect nipples.

Alexander looked up, smiling again, and licked the fingers of his other hand. Still teasing Lewis's nipples, he then moved his wet hand over the length of Lewis's cock, over the sac of his balls and, forcing Lewis's hips into the air, pushed his finger up into Lewis's arse.

The Deputy-Governor let out a short, surprised cry which

turned into a grumbling sigh as Alexander began to move his finger about.

Lewis tightened his anus so that it gripped the big, masculine finger. In response, Alexander pushed deeper inside him and Lewis could feel the actor touching the silk-soft lining of his arse with exquisite tenderness.

There was a sudden warmth on Lewis's groin and he knew, dimly, that Alexander was at work on his cock once more.

Twin sources of luxurious pleasure stabbed at his senses. There was the strong, urgent pulsing of his cock which caused his hips to thrust licentiously up in almost animalistic lust. Then there was the aching, glorious torment of Alexander's finger deep within his arse, probing his most secret place.

Lewis gasped as he felt the feelings merge. His body was alive with desire, like a bolt of lightning waiting to be earthed.

His breathing came in great, rasping gulps as Alexander pleasured him, chewing and licking at the glans of his penis, ramming his finger in and out of the hollow entrance to his anus.

Lewis felt his feet spontaneously stretch, almost to the point of cramp, as orgasm swamped his feelings, bombarding his aching head till his ears buzzed and ribbons of hot sperm flew from his cock, slapping into Alexander's face so that they hung, dripping like candlewax, from his heavy brows and soft lips.

Lewis let his sweat-glistened head sink back into the pillows and sighed contentedly.

Alexander pulled his finger from Lewis's arse and let it trail over Lewis's thighs.

Lewis shivered and shook his head. 'No. I can't bear it.'

He smiled and was just about to kiss Alexander when a heavy double knock came at the door.

'Go away!' called Lewis, without taking his eyes from Alexander.

'My lord,' came a voice from beyond the door. 'I have urgent news.'

Lewis grinned at Alexander and then laid his lips to the actor's soft, warm mouth.

'My lord –'

Lewis tutted angrily. 'Whatever it is can wait –'

126

'It is the King, my lord,' came the voice again. 'He has summoned you.'

Lewis shot out of bed, his semi-erect penis swinging like a pendulum between his legs. Alexander laughed to see him so distracted. As Lewis began to pull on his clothes, Alexander sat up on his haunches, his beautiful body glowing with sweat in the morning sun.

'Will I see you again?' he asked.

'You will all see me again,' said Lewis, reaching down for his boots.

'All of us?' queried Alexander.

'Aye. Your troupe. All you players.'

Alexander's face dropped disappointedly. Lewis looked up and saw his expression. 'I have no favourites,' he said dispassionately. 'It spoils the game, don't you think?'

He finished dressing and moved swiftly to the door. 'It would be better if you were not here when I returned.'

Giving Alexander a small smile, he opened the door.

The actor looked at him so reproachfully that Lewis felt himself blush with shame.

Lewis sighed, angry at himself for feeling such emotion. 'Did you not hear? The King wants me.'

And with that he ducked out into the corridor and was gone.

Ned Melcombe pushed open the door of his bedchamber with one broad hand, whilst running the other through his hair.

The warm amber glow of half a dozen lamps sent shadows dancing over his sharp cheekbones and smooth, unfurrowed forehead. He stumbled inside, exhausted, and began to pull off the heavy breastplate which had been his chief defence in the training he had just endured.

Beneath, his tunic was sweat-soaked, clinging tightly to the contours of his finely muscled chest. His stomach, taut and defined, pushed at the wet cloth of his shirt.

He sat down heavily on the bed and dragged off his boots, revealing white cloth stockings blackened by mud and leather-stains. He fell back on to the bed, his head enveloped by the fresh linen of the plump pillow, and closed his eyes.

It had been two weeks, my God, only two weeks since the news of Thomas's death had come to him and turned his world upside down. Sir Harry had returned to Humbleford a broken man, his beloved son lost to him.

Ned had been distraught too, having never quite realised how much his brother had meant to him. They had always been different, always pulling in opposite directions. But Thomas had been family and Ned felt his loss more profoundly than he would have believed possible.

Ned had, of course, expected his brief assumption of the Squireship to cease as soon as Sir Harry returned but this was not quite the case. Though his power to do as he chose was, of course, circumscribed, Ned found that he still had to maintain the day-to-day running of the estate, so out of sorts and grief-stricken was his father.

This was exactly what Ned didn't want. All of the responsibility with none of the compensations. But he was even less prepared for the news awaiting him.

Sir Harry had clomped down to breakfast, hours after his usual time, his eyes red-rimmed, his face pale and sallow. Then, in an echo of his previous interview with Ned, he had stated in simple terms that, with Thomas gone, it was up to Ned to ride at his side in the conflict against the Crown.

'You cannot mean it, father?' an astonished Ned had riposted.

'Certainly I mean it.'

'But I am not a soldier. We spoke of my shortcomings often enough!'

Sir Harry had shaken his great head slowly, implacably. 'Then you will learn, my boy. And, perhaps, come close to the example shown by dear Thomas, God rest his bones.'

And that was that. All thoughts of his life of pleasure had evaporated on the instant. There would be no more of his treasured couplings with the local lads, no more attempts to get William into bed, no more yearning after the dumb beauty of Miracle Smith. He was to be an officer.

Two weeks later, Ned found himself miles from Humbleford, training what felt like night and day to be worthy of his family name and to convince himself that sticking a sword into another human being was something worth doing.

In spite of his fatigue, the exhilaration of battle, even pretended battle, still surged through him. He stretched out, feeling the sinews of his arms and legs strain pleasantly.

In his mind's eye he saw again the rush of colour, the sea of faces, the sun glinting on pike shaft and sword.

The smells of the battlefield – powder and blood and the incongruous beauty of summer flowers – drifted again into his nose. And with them came the other sensation he'd come to associate with the aftermath of training: a bone-deep lustiness as powerful as the rush he'd felt leading a cavalry charge into an imagined Royalist flank.

The feeling washed over him now as he lay back on the bed, sinking deep into his every sense. The smell of his own sweat excited him and, almost unconsciously, his hand stole to the mud-spattered cloth of his britches.

He ran his hand over the surface, feeling his cock swell in response, the long shaft still encased in the wet cloth of his garment.

He eased his hand under the belted waistline, enjoying the hot pressure of his constrained cock. It felt big and smooth and almost noble, this great silky spearhead of his desire.

To his surprise, he suddenly thought of Cornelius Matthew. It was an odd thing, indeed, but Ned missed him. And, though grateful that his unexpected new career as a soldier had, at least, removed him from his promise to be the cleric's slave, he often thought of their times together.

Ned brushed these thoughts aside as misplaced nostalgia and closed his eyes, trying to think, instead, of Lewis St John. He saw him now as he had been that glorious summer, a delicate, desirable fly caught in the amber of time.

Ned remembered a hot July day when they'd enjoyed each other near to the brook which ranged lazily through his father's land. The hazy sun glinting in Lewis's hair, water from the brook hanging in tiny droplets on his tanned skin.

Ned recalled the hot strength of his own cock as he'd sat up on his haunches, pressing the creamy purple head against the hard, smooth muscles of Lewis's chest.

For what seemed like an age, he'd rubbed and thrusted, gasping at the raw desire which coursed through him. Then Lewis had grabbed Ned's cock and jammed it into his mouth, his tongue licking and rolling the head and the smooth shaft; biting and teasing till Ned could feel his blood-engorged penis touching the very back of his lover's throat.

Then, all at once, he had burst into orgasm, jets of sperm spurting down, down into Lewis's open throat. Emerging from the waves of pleasure which threatened to overwhelm him, Ned had been delighted to see Lewis's face smiling up at him, decorated with the creamy whiteness of his come.

Ned smiled himself now, in memory of that blazing summer day and the young man who had taken him with a lust, a force he scarcely thought possible.

He pulled at the sticky membrane of his foreskin, feeling his cock beat beneath his warm hand like a second pulse.

A sharp tap at the door made Ned's eyes snap open like pistol shots. He glanced quickly around him, his lust abating only a fraction at the prospect of discovery. But he was still almost fully dressed and pulled his hand from his trousers as he sat up.

His fingers, mud-soiled but heavy with the smell of his sex, splayed before him. He gave them a lick, as though to keep them happy, and smiled as he shouted, 'Come!'

The door opened and Ned felt his smile broaden at once. A young trooper of no more than nineteen years hovered at the doorway, a crumpled paper in his hands.

'A message, sir,' stammered the trooper.

Ned nodded. 'What is it?'

The trooper passed the paper nervously from one gloved hand to the other. 'It's from the Colonel, sir. I'm to wait on your answer.'

Ned held out his hand, the hand still reeking of his cock, and the young man pressed the parchment into the palm.

Ned scarcely glanced at the thing, some dreary order which could wait until morning and cast, instead, his gaze at the young trooper.

His name was Baines and Ned had long admired him. Ever since the day, in fact, that Ned had arrived at the sprawling training camp. He had noticed Baines, plunging a rusty old sword into a crude straw effigy of a Cavalier.

Ned and Sir Harry had been riding past, inspecting the men, but the raven-haired, slender John Baines had caught Ned's attention at once.

Baines had looked over at his new, young commander and a knowingness, a fluid attraction, had shot between them like a bolt of lightning. Baines had even allowed himself a sly little smile. Perhaps there were ways to get advanced in this army after all . . .

But much of Baines' swagger seemed to have deserted him as he stood before Ned like a virgin bride, his big, liquid eyes cast down to the floor.

'Don't look so glum, John Baines,' said Ned with a smile.

Baines looked up, delighted that his captain knew his name.

'I shan't bite you,' continued Ned. 'Unless you want me to.'

Baines looked down to the floor again. Ned sighed and got off the bed. 'What do you find so fascinating in the rug, Mr Baines? Would you not like to spend your time in other pursuits?'

'Aye, sir,' stammered Baines. 'But the message, sir.'

Ned waved the paper aside. 'It can wait. And as you are to attend me till I give a reply, you must wait also.' Ned cocked his head and shot a saucy look deep into the boy's eyes. 'Is that not so?'

Baines nodded and this time he didn't look away. Instead, his gaze seemed to stray to Ned's trousers and the tumescence of his cock, lying like a diagonal bar in the folds of the cloth.

Ned took the boy's face in his hand and angled it to the lamplight. Baines was a beauty all right, his black hair falling in commas over a forehead as smooth as marble, his face finely chiselled, his mouth, large, red and inviting.

Ned resisted the urge to kiss him right there and decided, instead, to enjoy some of the priviliges of his rank.

After ordering Baines to lock the door, Ned walked slowly back to the bed and lay back, one arm behind his head, spreading his legs wide over the heavy, embroidered blankets.

'I am weary, John,' he murmured, a film of lust rising in his eyes. 'Would you help me with my clothes?'

Baines hesitated a moment, glancing around as though in fear of discovery, then took off his gloves and laid down his helmet.

He had seen less of the recent training than his commander and the leathery newness of his tunic filtered over to Ned as the young man advanced towards the bed.

At first he sat awkwardly down on the very edge of the coverlet. Ned looked at him, smiled, and then grabbed him firmly by the wrist. He guided the trooper's hand to his chest, his torso made pale and ghostly by the still wet shirt, and pushed the boy's fingers over his nipples. At once they grew hard.

Ned looked up at the boy, no longer smiling, his mouth set into a thin, lusty, almost cruel line. He grabbed Baines by the scruff of the neck and kissed him, his tongue ramming into the boy's soft, warm mouth.

Baines didn't resist but dragged himself further up the bed to better enjoy the sensation.

At once, Ned pushed him away and the boy was left gasping, mouth agape, his dark eyes searching his master's face for an explanation.

'You are very forward, John Baines,' laughed Ned. 'I only asked for help with my clothes.'

Baines' face fell and he looked so injured that Ned let out a short laugh.

'Take off my shirt, little trooper,' he said.

Baines leant across and rolled up Ned's shirt from just above his trousers. Ned lifted his arms and pulled the shirt over his head, leaving him in only his britches and stockings, his tanned torso set off by the snowdrift whiteness of the surrounding pillows.

Baines looked at his master and swallowed nervously, his eyes drinking in the details of Ned's fine chest. Ned nodded towards his britches and Baines began to undo Ned's belt, never taking his eyes from the ramrod hardness of the cock before him.

In one movement, Baines pulled his captain's britches off, leaving Ned stetched out on the bed, one arm still behind his head, naked except for the sweat-soaked stockings which covered his muscly calves and came to a stop just above his knees.

Ned opened his legs, the stiff spire of his cock bobbing against his stomach. He lifted one leg and jammed his toes into Baines' mouth. The trooper chewed greedily at Ned's stockinged toes. Ned smiled cruelly and forced the young man's face down towards the counterpane with his leg.

Baines ran his hands excitedly up and down the length of Ned's thighs, pulling Ned's feet hard against his face. Ned looked down at his own, almost naked body and laughed the sight of his stockings.

'I look quite the whore, do I not, John Baines?'

Baines looked up, his eyes locking with Ned's but his awareness quite lost in the power of his lust.

'If I am to be like a lady,' said Ned, grabbing the boy by his collar and pulling him up the bed, 'then suckle me.'

He rammed Baines' face on to his chest and the boy kissed and sucked at Ned's hard nipples. Ned laid back his head, luxuriating in the sensations rippling through him.

He liked the feel of Trooper Baines, heavy in his uniform, as he lay on the throbbing shaft of his cock. He stretched his legs wide across the bed as Baines hovered over him.

Ned raised one leg and, jamming his foot under the boy's ribs, suddenly kicked him off the bed. Baines landed with a crash on to the wooden floor and looked up. His expression was noticeably less bewildered. He was starting to understand his master's ways.

'Mister Baines,' murmured Ned. 'Take off your clothes.'

Baines pulled at his tunic and stripped to his britches in seconds. His body was taut and compact, his belly hard and slightly rounded.

Ned's gaze fell to the boy's cock which was poking through his loosened trousers. Long and thick, it veered slightly to the left which made Ned smile.

'You're a little crooked, John,' he said gently. 'Let me take care of that.'

Baines practically ran at the bed and Ned caught the boy in his embrace, swinging him round and under in one action.

He pushed the boy's face down on to the pillows and wrenched the britches and stockings from the lad's body, exposing buttocks as smooth and ample as peaches.

Ned cocked his head appreciatively before cracking Baines across the backside with his hand. The boy gasped in pain. Ned's hand tunnelled under Baines' belly and grasped the shaft of his cock, jerking it up and down with almost savage intensity.

Baines' breathing became a series of whimpered groans as Ned pumped at his cock. All the time he was biting and licking at Baines' ripe arse, his tongue exploring the dark, musty crack between the hairless cheeks.

He beat the boy again, leaving a bright red handprint on the exposed flesh. Baines cried out, half in pain, half in ecstasy.

Ned's hands flew to Baines' nipples and pulled cruelly at them. Already hard, they swelled further under Ned's fingertips.

He kissed the back of the boy's neck and ran his tongue the length of his spine. Then he sat back, enjoying the sight of the beautiful boy stretched out before him. His cock seethed with a life of its own, desperate for release.

He grasped Baines' wrists and, holding them firmly in one hand, plunged his cock into the boy's willing backside.

Baines almost shrieked but jammed his face into the pillow where his cries were stifled. He whimpered in delight as Ned thrust deeper and deeper into him.

Ned felt his hips ram aginst Baines' buttocks and he paused for a long, satisfying moment as he felt the great, burning weight of his cock completely encased by the young trooper's body.

Then, withdrawing slightly, he began to pump his hard cock in and out of Baines' soft flesh. Ned shivered with pleasure, moans of lust coming unbidden to his lips.

Baines thumped the pillows and gasped as Ned's body powered into his, feeling every stroke, every inch of his master's throbbing cock.

Ned pulled out of Baines' arse, making the boy cry out, then, grabbing the smooth globes of Baines' arse, rotated him round to face him. With a growl, he rammed his cock back into the boy.

Baines' pretty face was flushed, sweat dripping from his forehead His mouth hung dazedly open and he turned his gaze towards Ned, not knowing what he intended next.

Ned hooked the boy's legs over each of his shoulders so that Baines' feet banged against the thick muscles of his back then, forcing his mouth on to the boy's, thrust his cock still deeper inside the trooper.

Baines' hands fluttered around Ned's body and he squealed with pleasure. Ned kissed him furiously, biting and snapping at the boy's throat and nipples. Baines' thick hair lay plastered across his face, his head thrashing from side to side as Ned fucked him.

Ned felt his balls suddenly contract and a great scream of pleasure roared from him as he came, pumping Baines full of his hot, milky semen.

Baines pulled his master to him, grunting with pleasure, and rapidly rubbed his own cock against Ned's hard belly. He came on the instant, his jism squirting up to land like hot fat on the warm flesh of his lover.

Ned stayed inside the boy for a moment longer, enjoying the contractions of the boy's anus which played a sweet tune on his now-sensitive cock.

Then he withdrew, his breathing hoarse and shuddering. Baines lay with his eyes closed, a slack half-smile on his gorgeous face.

Ned sank back onto the pillows. Baines reached out a hand to caress Ned's face. Ned shifted his weight and pushed the boy roughly from the bed. He laughed callously, his body covered in ribbons of semen, his legs still in the sweaty stockings of battle which now hung loose around his shins.

Baines looked up from the floor, suddenly very vulnerable.

Ned smiled at him and tossed the parchment across the room. The boy picked it up.

'I'll give them my answer in the morning,' barked Ned. 'And to none but you, John Baines.'

The boy got up, smiling.

'And come early,' said Ned, turning over and pulling the blanket over him

The corridor leading to the King's chambers was long, cold and panelled in dark wood.

Lewis ran its length in his urgency to keep his appointment with His Majesty and almost collided with Edward Vane as the strange, white-faced Prosecutor emerged through the doorway.

'Mr St John,' sneered Vane. 'Are you late for something?'

Lewis pointed past Vane towards the door. 'His Majesty wishes to see me.'

Vane nodded. 'The King is giving us much of his attention today. I myself have just received sweeping new powers.'

'Oh yes?' said Lewis, anxious to get by.

Vane nodded. 'There are dangerous subversives out there. I must set out to track them down. Would you know anything about subversives, Mr St John?'

The Prosecutor laid his gloved hand against Lewis's cheek and stroked it.

Lewis jerked back, disgustedly.

Vane smiled. 'No, how could you?'

He looked Lewis up and down, apprising him lasciviously and then turned on his heel. Lewis frowned and tapped gently on the door.

The door was opened from within by a uniformed guard. Lewis hovered in the entrance and bowed low at the sight of the small monarch, who was busying himself with a sheaf of papers.

King Charles looked up. 'Ah, Mr St John. Please c . . . come inside.'

Lewis stepped inside, his heart racing. What was it to be? Some kind of honour, surely. But what had he done to deserve such reward? Merely kept His Majesty entertained these past few weeks. Perhaps the King recognised the importance of good morale and was about to reward Lewis for his sterling work in this field.

Wryly, Lewis thought that if His Majesty knew what a pleasure it had been, he would view Lewis's activities in a somewhat different light.

The King turned his huge, sad-spaniel eyes on Lewis then held out his hand for him to kiss.

'We thank you for your s . . . sterling work these past weeks, Mr St John. these have been dark times and we have often felt the wont of common pleasures. Your efforts in this f . . . field will not go unrewarded.'

Lewis smiled. 'I have done nothing but my duty, Your Majesty.'

Charles nodded. 'You know that we intend to ride for Chester?'

'Yes, Your Majesty.'

Charles nodded again and glanced down at his notes. 'We are given to understand that you have some military experience?'

Lewis felt a cold, clammy feeling wash over him. 'Your Majesty?'

'Before you entered the Governor's s . . . service you served as a soldier in S . . . Sweden and the Low Countries. Is it not s . . . so?' stammered the King.

Lewis sighed. He had hoped to have put his past behind him. To begin again in a role more suited to him than soldiering. But, he saw now, it was inevitable that the war would wrench him from his comfortable life sooner or later.

'Aye, Your Majesty,' he murmured.

King Charles flashed a rare smile. 'That is good. We are deficient in capable commanders.'

He rose to his feet, leaning on a long, black staff, its silver knob beneath his gloved hand. 'Mr St John, it is our wish that you ride with us for Chester, assuming, at once, the rank of captain.'

Lewis felt his guts churn. Almost without thinking he walked slowly forward and knelt at the King's feet.

'Your Majesty,' he said in a small, hollow voice. 'I don't know what to say.'

Eight

The autumn brought a flood of recruits to the King's cause as well as much needed money to pay his disgruntled army. Military success came too after Prince Rupert met a party of a thousand Parliamentary horse at Powick Bridge which he succeeded to scatter to the four winds. The Parliamentary commander, the Earl of Essex, determined that his men must never be so unprepared again and set about retraining his cavalry.

The victory was pleasing to Charles, who occupied Shrewsbury after Chester, yet still there had been no major clash between the opposing armies. This was soon to change . . .

A brisk October wind stirred the branches of the big, gnarled beech outside Humbleford's church. Its leaves, turned a glorious crimson, fluttered and fell to the graveyard path and caught in the long tresses of Cornelius Matthew's hair.

He pressed on towards the church, opened the heavy door and slipped inside, grateful to be away from the chilly outdoors.

The aisle was gloomy in the dusky light of the afternoon and something made Cornelius shiver as he made his way towards his room. There was something unpleasant in the air, some atmosphere of impending trouble which unsettled him.

He pulled his cloak closer over his trim body and entered his room, slamming the door behind him.

This place, too, seemed unusually dark and the cleric hurried to light a series of stubby candles in order to dispel the murk. Then he sat down on the edge of his bed and clasped his hands together in prayer.

Since Ned's departure, everything had changed. The war, which had seemed so unreal, so distant, only a few weeks before, now threatened to overwhelm them all.

Sir Harry rounded up all the remaining men of fighting age, including Miracle and the Melcombes' butler William, and pressed them into the service of Parliament. This left Cornelius practically alone save for the women and a gaggle of old men.

It meant, of course, that he was able to concentrate on his spiritual duties but Ned and Miracle's absence had left a huge vacuum in his life. He was also more than a little bitter that his dream of becoming Ned's master had been postponed, perhaps for ever. And, of course, he worried about his beloved's fate.

What if Ned were to die in battle? Or Miracle? What then?

Cornelius felt tears spring to his eyes and wiped them quickly away with the back of his hand. It wouldn't do to be so weak. they must all make the best of things and get through this terrible, dark time.

The wind outside beat against the windowpanes, making them rattle like extracted teeth in a jar. Cornelius looked up and shuddered again as he saw the candle flames sputter.

He got to his feet and poured himself a glass of wine. He was careless and the rich, red liquid splashed on to the pale wood of the window seat. Cornelius looked at it for a long time before becoming conscious of movement in the church next door.

Opening the door of his room a fraction, he peered out into the darkened interior of the church but could make out very little.

The rows of pews extended into the shadows and there were pools of meagre light thrown off by clusters of tall, thick candles.

Then Cornelius noticed something in the second row. It seemed to be a hunched figure, head bowed in prayer. He slipped out into the church, immediately conscious of the chill of the building.

Carefully, silently, he walked up to the dark figure and stood still. He could hear it murmuring a prayer and was just about to speak when the figure looked up and stared right at him.

139

Cornelius jumped. At first he didn't recognise the lovely, chiselled face but, as he grew accustomed to the dark, the cropped blond hair and narrow grey eyes became familiar.

'Christopher?' he said, amazed, staring at the boxer-soldier to whom he had made love some two months before.

Christopher nodded. 'Aye. It's me.'

He got to his feet and looked around fearfully. Then as if sure they were not seen, he kissed Cornelius gently on the cheek.

'I didn't expect to see you here,' continued Cornelius.

Christopher shrugged. 'I am to join Essex's men the day after tomorrow. We were training nearby. I thought I would come back to see you.'

'Me?'

'Aye. It is good to see a man of God before going into battle,' said Christopher pragmatically.

'Oh,' said Cornelius, a little disappointed.

'And besides,' whispered the soldier, clasping Cornelius' hand, 'I thought we could take leave of each other in a rather more . . . interesting way.'

It was Cornelius' turn to look about. At any moment the Reverend Peters might come in.

He looked back into Christopher's bright, humourous eyes, feeling his depressed mood lifting and a deep current of desire beginning to stir in his loins.

'Training, you say?' he asked. 'What news of Ned Melcombe?'

Christopher leaned over the pew and kissed Cornelius again, this time on the throat and chin. He spoke as he kissed, his handsome features glowing in the light of the candles.

'He's a captain,' said Christopher, 'and doing well. His men seem to . . . er . . . like him.'

He flashed Cornelius a knowing grin and the cleric felt a pang of jealousy stab at him. Brushing the emotion aside, he responded to Christopher's kisses with his own, setting his lips to the soldier's, his chin rasping over the bristly surface of Christopher's face.

'Captain Melcombe told me things,' said Christopher. 'Told me that you and he have a secret place.'

Cornelius knew that he should feel betrayed, that the temple was his and Ned's to enjoy together, but his heart leapt with excitement. He let his tongue move over Christopher's lips and murmured, 'What of it?'

Christopher's tongue connected with his and it was a while before he spoke, so much did he enjoy their passionate embrace.

'I should very much like to see it,' he said at last. 'It will give me sweet memories in the days ahead.'

The soldier reached out his hand as he had done on that far-off summer day and pressed the palm over Cornelius' crotch.

The cleric groaned and pushed his hips forward, pressing the stiff bar of his penis against the flat of Christopher's hand. He began to rub himself lasciviously, his balls contracting as lust overwhelmed him.

Christopher jammed his mouth over Cornelius' and they shared a hard, excited kiss, their breathing fast and staccato.

There came the noise of a latch being lifted and the unmistakeable shuffle of the Reverend Peters sounded through the church.

Cornelius pulled away from the soldier's kiss and leaned towards his ear.

'I shall meet you outside at ten o'clock tonight,' he hissed. 'You must not be seen.'

Christopher smiled, nodded and kissed him again before stealing away into the shadows.

The Reverend Peters appeared in the aisle and made his way painfully slowly towards Cornelius.

'Ah, hello, my boy. Did I hear you talking just now?'

Cornelius looked over the old man's shoulder and saw Christopher make his way silently out of the building.

'Talking?' he said at last. 'Oh no, just praying.'

He turned towards the altar and busied himself. The Reverend Peters mumbled something to himself and made his way into the vestry.

Neither saw the tall, powerfully built figure dressed all in black who moved out of the shadows and followed Christopher outside.

Sword clashed against sword. Two helmeted figures faced one another on the hillside. Their swords rang out again as they fought, armour glittering in the late afternoon light.

There was a breathy gasp of triumph and one of them forced the other to his knees, planted his boot squarely in the other's chest and kicked him down the hill. The soldier rolled and rolled, making the surrounding men laugh uproariously.

'Good! Excellent!' cried Sir Harry Melcombe. He clapped the victorious combatant on the shoulder then helped him to remove his helmet.

Ned Melcombe shook his long hair and grinned at his father. The fight had been a good one, requiring every ounce of skill he had learned in his two months' training. He was at last beginning to feel like a real soldier with the authority to order about far more experienced men.

He laid down his sword and Sir Harry, who looked pale and old beyond his years, ruffled his hair proudly.

'You're improving all the time, Ned. Tomorrow we'll join the Earl of Essex and then let's see what we can do about this troublesome monarch of ours, eh?'

Ned laughed and walked tiredly towards the cluster of out-houses and farm buildings which the Parliamentarians had seques-tered for their training camp.

There were three huge barns which had been converted into sleeping quarters for the troopers and two, smaller cottages for the officers.

As inexperienced as Ned knew himself to be, he was still glad not to have to share his quarters with two hundred snoring men. Instead, he had the room all to himself, the room where he had taken Trooper Baines up the arse and hoped to take many more. Memories of the boy's firmly muscled body sent little shivers of anticipation flickering up his spine.

Now though, he was pretty much exhausted. The afternoon's training had left him drained and he looked forward to a short nap before he dined.

Ned was about to step across the threshold of his cottage when none other than Baines appeared around the corner.

'Sir!' called the lad, excitedly.

Ned smiled slightly. 'Hello, John Baines. What can I do for you?'

Baines shifted a little uneasily. 'You asked me to do something for you, sir. Do you remember?'

'I have a lot to remember just now,' said Ned, a little testily.

Boldly, Baines laid a hand on Ned's arm. Ned scowled at him and Baines removed it as though he had touched fire.

'Forgive me, Captain,' said the lad. 'But you asked me to look out for any ... friends I might come across amongst the new recruits.'

Ned grew more cheerful at once. 'Ah yes. Yes, I remember. Well?'

Baines turned his big eyes on his captain and smiled shyly. 'I've taken the liberty, sir, of quartering them in the far barn.'

'All together?'

Baines nodded.

Ned restrained himself from laughing out loud. 'I always said you were forward, Baines. You'll go far.'

Baines gave a formal little bow and was about to move off when Ned stopped him. 'Nay, John,' he muttered huskily. 'Stay a little while.'

They walked on, the young soldier ahead of Ned. As Baines moved, Ned could see the outline of his buttocks beneath his britches.

Reaching out his hand, he squeezed Baines' arse and the lad cried out in delight, casting a cheeky glance over his shoulder.

They reached the barracks at last; a long, low, timbered building.

Ned knew that all the other occupants of the barn would be out on training manoeuvres. He, Baines and the new recruits would have the place to themselves. He looked around quickly to check they were unobserved, then kissed him full on the lips.

'Now,' he said. 'Go inside and line them up. I shall make a grand entrance.'

Baines opened the door and went inside.

Ned stood outside the closed door, his cock stiffening in anticipation. He could hear muffled voices and the sound of boots on bare floorboards. Finally, when all was quiet, he pushed open the door.

Baines was just inside the doorway as Ned entered the shadowy room. High windows spilled the last of the day's light on to the floor and a row of lamps illuminated the four newcomers.

Ned stood framed in the doorway, aware of the impact of his presence. To his surprise, however, one of the new recruits failed to stand stiffly to attention.

Peering through the gloom, Ned could just make out a suggestion of long, centre-parted hair and a pale, smooth forehead. He advanced into the barn and closed the big door behind him. This only served to darken the room further and it wasn't until he was quite close to the soldier that he recognised him.

'William!' he gasped with undisguised pleasure.

The Melcombes' servant said nothing, merely furnishing his former master with a small bow.

Ned grinned and began to strut up and down in front of them in traditional fashion.

'My father said he would be taking as many as possible into service but you ... How will the household manage without you?'

'My thoughts exactly, sir,' said William drily.

Ned glanced at the other three men. Two, though handsome enough, were unknown to him. The third, to Ned's delight, was Miracle Smith. Ned cast an appreciative eye over them all but his gaze soon returned to William.

'So, William. I find myself in command over you at long last.'

The former servant said nothing. Ned wondered yet again what could be going through the young man's mind. Could he really be so resistant to the pleasures of the flesh? It was time to find out.

'Bolt the door, Baines,' ordered Ned, shrugging off his coat.

Baines moved to the door and placed a heavy plank across it, barring entry.

Ned rolled up his sleeves and walked towards William.

'Stand over there, William,' he said quietly, pointing to the shadowed corner of the barn.

William obeyed without demur, keeping his face completely impassive.

Ned strolled towards the three new soldiers.

'I do not wish to know your names,' he barked. 'That is not why you are here.'

144

Miracle looked at him confusedly. Ned allowed him a little smile to show they were playing a game.

'Just let me say,' he continued, 'that if you please me then your life in this regiment can be made a good deal more comfortable. Is that not so, Baines?'

Young John Baines nodded vigorously.

Ned pointed a finger at the smallest soldier, a girlishly pretty boy with tousled blond hair. 'I request, therefore, that you, sir, take down your britches.'

The blond gulped nervously, his eyes flicking from side to side. Hands shaking, he unbuckled his belt and let his britches slide to his ankles, exposing bare, shapely legs.

'Well,' said Ned with mock-annoyance. 'Take them off.'

The soldier bent down and pulled off his trousers and shoes. His penis and balls were large and well-proportioned but were almost hidden by the tails of his shirt.

Ned moved to the next soldier, taller than the first; he was thick set and wild-looking with small, feral eyes. Ned simply nodded at him and the soldier dropped his britches without a word.

He had on stained and cheap stockings which fell down of their own accord. His legs, skinny but respectable, were covered in thick, dark hair. His cock, which was quite small, was almost buried in a dense mass of wiry black hair.

Ned raised an eyebrow appreciatively and turned finally to Miracle, whose chest was heaving nervously.

'Now you,' said Ned and the boy hastily struggled from his garments. Ned murmured appreciatively as he saw Miracle's athletic legs and thick, powerful cock. He looked down at the barn floor, blushing furiously.

Ned walked along the line of soldiers, brushing his fingers over their genitals with a delicate, teasing motion. Both the small blond and the dark, hairy soldier remained unaffected, their nerves preventing proper arousal. Unexpectedly, though, Miracle's big penis responded at once to Ned's touch. The boy closed his eyes and a little, gutteral groan escaped him.

Ned stopped and let his fingers close around the end of the

boy's cock. He squeezed at it till he felt it pulse and thicken beneath his touch, growing at once to an impressive length.

Smiling, Ned pulled back the boy's foreskin and gently tugged at his cock which rose vertically till it was almost flat against the boy's flat, hard young belly.

Ned rubbed his thumb over the lovely smooth head of Miracle's penis and then stepped back.

'Come,' he said gently. 'Strip me.'

Miracle swallowed, his breath quickening. He gave a self-conscious glance at his stiff cock and then followed Ned across the barn towards a pile of sacking which had been laid out on the floorboards.

Ned lay down on this improvised mattress and, much as he had with John Baines, allowed Miracle to take off his clothes.

He glanced over at Baines and saw that the lad was growing hard within his own britches.

'Baines,' he ordered, 'you come here and take off this man's clothes.'

Baines needed no encouragement. As Miracle pulled Ned's shirt over his head, so Baines knelt down and began to do the same to him. In seconds, the boy was naked, his swarthy torso and arms dappled with downy hair. His big, stiff cock was thrust over Ned's prone body.

Baines looked down at Ned who was now stripped to the waist.

'With your permission, sir?' he said.

Ned gave a little nod and Baines hurriedly pulled off his own clothes, revealing his own firm, lovely body. He had learned much from Ned in the past weeks and had grown considerably in daring.

As Miracle pulled off Ned's britches and rolled his stockings from his legs, Ned's own cock emerged, thick and strong, beating with its own tiny pulse.

Now there were three naked, erect men on the sacking mattress.

Ned pulled Baines and Miracle down to his level so that he had one on either side. Forcibly, he pressed their faces to each of his nipples and the two men began to suck greedily at them.

146

Ned sighed and jerked his head towards the other two strangers, who were looking down with lusty eyes.

'Now you two. Come here,' he ordered.

The small blond and his hairy comrade did as they were told, pulling off the remainder of their clothes and hurrying to Ned's side.

The dark one proved to be as hairy as his legs promised, his broad chest and thick arms covered in it like matting.

The blond immediately got to work on Ned's cock, taking it's head between his lips and gently sucking.

Ned stretched out, Baines and Miracle still attached to his nipples, and let the hairy soldier kiss him full on the lips.

He made a great, showy display of this, letting his tongue entwine with the lad's, his eyes flicking round to take in William's expression. As usual, the impassive youth showed nothing.

Ned pushed the soldier away. 'You will stay there, William. Stay there and watch just as you once watched me.'

Grabbing the soldier by the neck, he pushed him down onto his chest, indicating that he should take over Miracle's duties on his nipple. Then he pulled Miracle up to his mouth and kissed him violently. He probed with his tongue around the surface of the beautiful boy's lips then back inside his mouth, forcing down, down into his throat.

He pulled away suddenly, waved off Baines and the hairy soldier and shot a look of transported lustiness over at William.

'What say you, servant?' said Ned huskily, glancing down at the young lad still sucking his cock. 'Would you not like to join us?'

For answer, William shot him a look of such contempt that Ned actually felt himself turn cold. But he was not to be put off now. These men were his. His to control.

He turned back to Miracle with something like a snarl.

'On your knees,' he spat. 'On your knees before me.'

The boy obeyed, kneeling so that his hot prick stood straight up from his lap.

Ned moved so that he was sitting astride the soldier, then sat up on his haunches so that his own cock brushed at the dark man's mouth.

'I will take you in your mouth, my beauty. Just as I should have done back at the falls,' he chuckled, then glanced to his side. 'Baines, make free with that boy,' he said, indicating the blond. 'l wish to watch.'

Baines pulled the blond soldier into his arms and they rolled together into a position by Ned's side.

As they kissed, the skinny-legged, hairy soldier with the tousled hair was left sitting a little disconsolately, his penis drooping.

Ned laughed. 'My boy, don't let's have you wilting through lack of action.'

The boy looked up, his eyes bright with passion. 'What would you have me do, sir?' he said in a small, quiet voice.

'Why, use your imagination!' cried Ned, thrusting his big, veiny cock into Miracle's pert mouth.

He felt it slide inside the spit-moistened hole and the brief, stimulating scrape of Miracle's teeth on its sensitive head.

Then he seemed to have filled the mouth utterly, his cock forcing apart Miracle's jaws as he began to slowly pump in and out.

Unconsciously, Ned had closed his eyes. He let them flicker open now to see Baines and the young blond at work only a foot or so from him.

Baines was sitting on the soldier's lap with his back towards him, so that the cheeks of his arse were over the young man's tumescent cock. As Ned watched, Baines lowered himself on to it, gasping as he did so, his pretty face already flushed with arousal.

He placed the palms of his hands on the sacking and, with infinite slowness, began to raise and then lower himself on to the blond's penis.

Ned couldn't properly see the young soldier who had his cock rammed inside Baines but could hear his moans of pleasure.

Then the third soldier made his way towards them. Without a word, he positioned himself in front of Baines and laid down so that he could take Baines' cock in his mouth. He began to suck and gobble at Baines and the young trooper hissed in pleasure.

Seemingly aloof from it all, William stood with his arms folded, the last rays of the sun dappling his lovely face.

Ned stared at the three men before him and felt his own cock grow even stiffer inside Miracle's mouth. He sat up straighter on

148

his knees and grabbed the sides of the boy's face, pumping his cock remorselessly in and out.

Briefly, he thought of Cornelius and their Sunday ritual, just like this. He shook his head, his sweat-soaked hair sticking to his face, and looked again at the soldiers.

Baines had chosen them well. The blond's firm thighs and legs were visible beneath Baines' thrusting arse and the bobbing, shaggy head of the hairy young lad as he sucked at Baines' cock.

Ned was delighted to see that this soldier was even tugging at his own cock as he fellated Baines so that all three were rapidly pounding towards orgasm.

For himself, Ned was already feeling a delicious tingling creeping through every muscle. He stared down at Miracle, revelling in the boy's mute, wounded beauty. He was every bit as gorgeous as Ned had imagined, this plaything in whose mouth his big cock was lodged. He thrust ever deeper into the boy's willing throat.

He felt Miracle's tongue rasp over the smooth head of his cock then turned his head as he heard Baines crying out excitedly.

Baines was pumping himself up and down on the blond's cock with almost supernatural fury. His tongue hung slackly from the side of his mouth and his eyes were screwed up in concentration.

'Fuck me!' he gasped. 'Oh, fuck me!'

The blond soldier's hips were moving up and down in tandem with Baines' arse and the other's head. There was a chorus at gasping moans and the blond came inside Baines.

Baines, obviously feeling the man's hot seed shoot within him, came himself within seconds and Ned could see his semen shooting all over the hairy boy's mouth and face.

The latter then took his opportunity and kissed Baines full on the mouth. He jerked at his long, slender cock and then cried out as he came, his sperm spurting up onto the trooper's firmly muscled chest.

Aroused beyond endurance, Ned closed his eyes and fucked Miracle's mouth with increased passion.

He clamped his jaws together then opened them wide in a long, silent moan as a great, convulsive orgasm shuddered through him.

He tensed and felt his heart slamming in his ribs as his come jetted into the boy's mouth, seemingly for ever.

Finally he pulled out and collapsed in a sweating heap on the sacking floor. Eyes still closed he was hardly aware that Miracle was leaning over him, beating his own cock furiously.

Ned felt the boy's come slap onto his warm skin and smiled his lazy half-smile.

Opening his eyes, he found himself in the centre of a naked mass of bodies. Baines and the blond were locked in a passionate kiss. The dark, hairy soldier was lying on his back, his chest heaving exhaustedly. And Miracle was blinking in the gloom like a bewildered animal.

Vaguely, Ned was aware that William's face was inclined towards him. His voice, after such a long silence, sounded oddly authoritative.

'May I go now, sir?' he enquired innocently.

Ned felt his head sink to his chest. Shame overwhelmed him. What in God's name was he doing?

He nodded and William strode purposefully across the barn, lifted the bar from the door and slipped outside.

Ned looked about at the naked men he had been ordering about and heaved a huge sigh.

There was a trace of winter in the wind shrieking through the churchyard. Cornelius felt it as he hurried from the porch, wrapping his cloak tightly around his shivering body.

Beneath the material, he already felt strongly aroused as thoughts of his appointment with Christopher scurried through his mind.

It had been like this all through the tedious day in the church. Several times he had stopped in his work, a forbidden warmth spreading through his belly, a lusty smile creeping onto his face, his cock growing thick and hard within his britches.

Once, when the Reverend Peters had been standing with his back towards him, Cornelius had even let the head of his penis peek over the waistband of his britches and he had experienced a thrill of pleasure at this outrageous exposure. It made him want to laugh, to shout out, to throw off all his clothes and parade about the aisle of the church with his great, hot cock standing as stiff as the spire.

In fact, he had hastily tucked it away as the Reverend turned around and enquired after the hymns they were preparing for the following Sunday.

Now, as he made his way around the corner of the church, his whole body seemed to tingle from his cold-hardened nipples to the delicious lustiness building in his loins.

Christopher was standing next to his tethered horse, its breath streaming out like steam in the cold air.

Cornelius stole across the grass towards the soldier and Christopher swept him into his arms. They kissed passionately, faces almost swamped by the baggy cowl of the cleric's cloak. Then Christopher swung himself onto the horse and helped Cornelius up behind him.

With a short cry, Christopher dug his heels into the horse's flanks and they were away towards the Melcombe estate.

Soon, thought Cornelius, they would be inside the temple, playing the forbidden games that he and Ned had devised. Only this time, he, Cornelius, would be master and this lovely soldier his willing slave.

Cornelius snaked his arms around Christopher's waist and pulled himself closer. He kissed the soldier's neck and heard him groan gently in response. Within the folds of his cloak, his cock was straining for release.

Shuffling still closer in the saddle, Cornelius pushed his genitals against Christopher's back. He wanted to be inside him now, to plunge his stiff cock into the soldier's arse, to consume him utterly.

As the horse pounded across the fields, Cornelius was thrown up and down, only adding to his excitement. His cock rubbed against Christopher's back of its own accord.

Delving under Christopher's russet-coloured coat, the cleric let his hands trace the firm, defined outlines of the soldier's chest muscles then closed his fingers over them. He shut his eyes, letting the movement of the horse merge with the yawning desire he felt shuddering through him.

He pushed his hips forward, overwhelmed by the need to press his hard penis into the small of Christopher's back, to allow his foreskin to be pushed up and down by their movement on the saddle, to fondle the small, hard points of the soldier's nipples.

Christopher's head was oscillating from side to side as Cornelius covered his smooth neck in kisses. He groaned, as though ready to stop where they were and drag the cleric to the ground in a passionate embrace. He pushed himself back into Cornelius' arms and kicked again at the horse's flank.

'Soon,' murmured Cornelius. 'Soon.'

They raced on over the fields, bypassing the manor house, Cornelius whispering directions into Christopher's ear. Finally, they arrived at the temple, its entrance even more overgrown through months of disuse.

Christopher dismounted and Cornelius swung down behind him.

'This is it?' asked the soldier, peering into the gloom.

Cornelius nodded and, taking him by the hand, led him towards the temple steps. He opened the door with a large, black key and ushered Christopher inside.

The room was pitch black and it was some time before Cornelius managed to light sufficient candles to illuminate the place. He could see that Christopher was shivering and immediately set to work lighting the brazier which was all the heating they had.

The soldier looked about in undisguised wonder at the array of whips and manacles and the imposing table with its chains. He swallowed and exchanged glances with Cornelius. His grey eyes were bright with excited lust.

Within a few minutes, the coals in the brazier were glowing warmly and the room took on a pleasant orange hue. Cornelius rubbed dust from his hands and walked casually towards Christopher.

Setting his warm lips to the soldier's throat, he kissed him from jaw to collarbone till Christopher let out a low mumble of pleasure.

He let his hand stroke over Christopher's cropped hair, enjoying the bristly feel of its texture beneath his fingers. Then his hand travelled down the back of Christopher's neck and he pulled the young man towards him, kissing him fiercely. Tongue on tongue, they snapped at each other's mouths like animals with their blood up.

Cornelius dug his fingers into the soldier's scalp and, pulling back his head, rammed his hot tongue deep into his throat. His other hand was already pulling at the fastenings of Christopher's coat. He burrowed beneath the heavy material and on under the softer cloth of the soldier's shirt where his fingers again found Christopher's nipples and began to pinch at them.

Cornelius felt the soldier's breathing change to a regular, contented whispering. The cleric's mouth fastened on his chin and bit gently at the stubbled skin until Christopher groaned in delight.

Then, with sudden urgency, Cornelius pulled Christopher's coat from his body, wrenching it over his head and making short work of his shirt at the same time.

Stripped to the waist, the soldier stood blinking in the fiery light, vulnerable despite his strong, muscular build. He crossed his hands over his crotch, as though threatened, and did not smile as Cornelius looked at him, eyes blazing with lust and expectation.

'Tell me what to do,' said Christopher softly, compliantly. 'Tell me what you want and I will do it.'

Cornelius nodded, almost to himself, and crossed the room towards a huge brass-bound trunk. A suggestion of leather and metal glittered in the candlelight.

Cornelius came back carrying several items of bizarre-looking equipment. There was a small, black bag-like object which shimmered like silk in the light of the brazier and something very like a horse's bridle with a hard knot of leather on one of its thick straps.

Cornelius let them dangle from his outstretched hand and pointed towards the table.

'Get on there,' he ordered and Christopher meekly obeyed, clambering on to the table and lying flat on his belly on its cushioned surface. He stretched out his arms before him, as though guessing that Cornelius was about to chain him up and the cleric immediately did so, clamping manacles around his wrists so that he was securely fastened to the old table.

153

Christopher tried to crane his neck round so he could see what Cornelius was doing but it proved impossible.

In fact, the cleric was standing in silence, looking down at Christopher's broad, rippling back, enjoying the power he had over him.

He walked slowly, parallel to the table, his hand stroking over Christopher's britches and settling on the hard hemispheres of the soldier's buttocks. He rubbed at them for a moment and then slapped Christopher across the arse with cruel intensity.

The young man gasped, burying his face into the table's soft cushions.

Cornelius continued to stroke, his hand moving slowly, slowly up Christopher's spine, playing over the knots of muscle, the broad, flat expanses of his shoulder-blades and the downy nape of his neck.

Bending down, he kissed Christopher lightly on his hair, then pulled the soldier's head sharply up. In a moment, he had the bridle over the boy's head.

It was a contrivance of leather straps which covered the lower half of Christopher's face and buckled tightly around his head. The leather knot fitted neatly inside Christopher's mouth, almost filling it.

The soldier gagged momentarily and then nodded to show he was all right.

Cornelius moved down again, this time to slip the silk hood over Christopher's head. The cleric could see the strong outline of his jaw and cheekbones revealed beneath the tight fabric.

Manacled at the wrists, hooded and gagged, Christopher was finally ready for Cornelius' pleasure.

Taking a step back to drink in the details of the scene, Cornelius finally knew what Ned must feel like. Here was a beautiful youth, stripped to the waist and begging to be humiliated before surrendering his lovely, ripe arse to Cornelius' cock. He felt his own member swelling inside his clothes and advanced towards the table.

Taking the back of Christopher's britches in both hands he eased the garment down, exposing the orbs of the soldier's buttocks. There was a bright red weal across them left from the impact of his hand.

Cornelius smiled and spanked Christopher again, provoking a muffled cry from within his silk hood.

He eased the britches over Christopher's strong thighs and calves, pulling them over his shoes and finally flinging them into a corner.

The buckled shoes came off next, falling to the stone floor and revealing cloth-stockinged feet, dirty black shadow-footprints embossed on the soles.

Cornelius tucked his fingers under the tops of the stockings and teasingly rolled them off Christopher's legs, leaving him completely naked and bound on the table.

He glanced up. Now there was a clear, discernible hand-mark on Christopher's buttocks. Swinging himself up on to the table, he squatted at the soldier's side and, laying one hand on each of the boy's buttocks, gently parted them.

Cornelius was aware of his own prick, thrusting at the front of his britches, screaming for release and it was all he could do to prevent himself entering Christopher there and then. But he was determined to enjoy this as much as he could so, instead, he plunged his face into the cleft of the soldier's arse and began to lick urgently.

Within his hood, Christopher's moans became more audible as the cleric's tongue slivered over the sensitive tissue of his anus, probing inside, lapping over the mouth-like exterior, rolling over the peachy curves of his buttocks.

Cornelius plunged deep, his hair falling forwards over his face and brushing at Christopher's arse. He wanted to bury his face inside the soldier, to inhale his essence, to slip inside his soul. As he crouched, he could feel his cock jabbing into his own belly, hard and throbbing with need.

Finally, he lifted his face from Christopher's arse and slapped his hand repeatedly over the lad's buttocks. Every stroke brought a grunt of pained pleasure.

Cornelius slid over the table so that he was right by Christopher's manacled arm. He gazed at the youth's smooth, round biceps and began to lick at them, gradually moving down to his armpits.

Christopher struggled in his bonds, trying to pull away from a sensation he obviously found too much to bear. As his chest lifted from the table, Cornelius simply moved to his nipples, snapping and biting like a cornered beast.

The soldier cried out as best he could behind the leather gag and the silk hood. Cornelius moved up and kissed him on the eyes through the silk, the flat of his tongue leaving a wet trail over the boy's cheeks and jaw-line.

Cornelius swept back his hair with his hand and moved down the table so that he was kneeling at Christopher's feet.

'Now,' he said, a cruel smile playing over his lips. 'Now I shall take you up the arse.'

Christopher began to moan uncontrollably. Cornelius took out the little pot of honey from his coat and then threw the heavy garment into the corner where it landed on top of Christopher's abandoned clothes.

Now in shirtsleeves, the cleric began to daub the honey into the cleft of Christopher's arse, so that he was slick and ready for his cock.

When he was done he pulled off his own britches and began to smear the sweet liquid all over the strong, veiny length of his own ram-rod hard cock. The honey glistened over the smooth purple head and hairy shaft.

Then, placing both hands under Christopher's belly, he pulled the boy's arse into the air so that it was open and ready for him.

His hands lingered a while, feeling the hard ridges of the soldier's belly before moving to open wider the cheeks of his arse.

Then Cornelius reared up and thrust his cock straight inside.

Inside the hood, Christopher let out a great torrent of muffled oaths, all unheeded by Cornelius who was pressing himself deeper and deeper inside the soldier's hollow arse.

They began to move as one, locked tightly at cock and arse, rocking forwards and back as the cleric pounded himself into the soldier. He hooked his hands under Christopher's arms and back over his shoulders, giving him purchase as they made love.

Cornelius' hair was matted with sweat and he could feel its

saltiness stinging his eyes as he plunged his cock up inside Christopher's anus.

He groaned himself now, almost unconsciously, as he felt Christopher's buttocks pushing backwards into the hollow of his thighs.

Laying his head down on Christopher's back, he felt fused into this lovely youth, felt as though their spirits had merged, recombined into one engine of pleasure. At every thrust, his hard balls swung against the smooth flesh of Christopher's arse.

'Christ,' muttered Cornelius. 'Oh Christ, I want you, Christopher.'

The soldier muttered something from within the hood but Cornelius couldn't make it out.

He didn't much care. All he wanted was to fill this boy up, to feel his cock bursting inside the soldier's lovely, yielding arsehole.

His hands fell from Christopher's shoulders and he reached round to grab the boy's cock which was projecting, semi-erect, from his loins. Cornelius grasped it savagely and began to pump at its length in time to his own cock's thrustings within Christopher's arse.

There were more muffled cries, now settling into a steady rhythm as Cornelius fucked Christopher.

His hand around the rapidly swelling head of Christopher's cock, the cleric pounded at him, willing them to come together. The soldier's penis was stiff in seconds and Cornelius' shafting grew in intensity as he felt the boy harden in his hand.

His own cock thrust slickly in and out of the boy's arse, honey and sweat easing its passage.

Cornelius felt himself shaking, felt orgasm building like a damburst inside him. He hammered at Christopher's cock, urging him on and on as he felt his own climax thunder through his body.

'You're mine,' Cornelius gasped. 'Mine to own. Mine to enslave. Mine!'

A dazed drumming echoed through his mind and he gasped as he came, his semen gushing up into Christopher's arse. At once, perfectly, the soldier came too, and Cornelius felt his come splashing over his hand. He continued to stroke at the soldier's cock until Christopher's urgent moans told him he was sensitised beyond endurance.

Quickly, he scrambled up the table, took off the lad's manacles, then removed the hood and finally the gag.

Christopher's face was flushed and sweat-soaked but his eyes were like little fires of desire. He stared at Cornelius as though he'd seen a vision and then kissed him fervently, his warm lips tasting as sweet to Cornelius as the honey which had helped him fuck the boy.

They curled together into a tight ball, Cornelius enjoying the feel of the warm, naked boy in his arms.

A loud crash cut through the warm atmosphere of the room and both men sat up at once. Another crash sounded, coming from the other side of the door.

Cornelius pointed urgently at Christopher's clothes.

'Get dressed!' he hissed. 'We're discovered!'

He began to scramble back into his britches and Christopher threw on his coat but the pounding at the door continued, growing ever more rapid and soon the old wooden door was splintering.

Cornelius took a step back from the table just as the door gave way and fell apart. Five men tumbled inside, all dressed in rough approximation of Parliamentary garb. At their head, however, was a very tall, powerfully built man dressed from head to toe in black. His face was as pale as snow but eyes burned like black coals.

Despite his fear, Cornelius was able to register how extraordinarily handsome the stranger was but he felt compelled to cower in his presence.

The man swept around the room, his cloak stirring up little eddies of dust on the stone floor. He looked at the cabalistic symbols Ned had scrawled on the walls and shook his head. He then turned his piercing gaze on the half-dressed Cornelius and the still near-naked Christopher. His lip curled in contempt.

'What is this?' demanded Cornelius. 'How dare you –'

The stranger held up a black-gloved hand, silencing Cornelius. 'Dare, sir? *Dare?* I come in the name of all that's holy to lay charges of espionage against you, Mr Matthew. What I did not expect was to add to these charges of sodomy and witchcraft!'

Cornelius felt a wave of cold fear wash over him.

The man in black turned to his four colleagues. 'Get these . . . *creatures* out of my sight.'

Nine

————

On his way to church on 23 October 1642, the Earl of Essex received word that the King's army had occupied the brow of a ridge called Edgehill, only seven miles from his current position at Kineton. Soon, both fourteen-thousand-strong armies faced each other . . .

Lewis St John cleared his throat and cast a worried glance at the ranks of soldiers surrounding him. Under the bleak, white autumn sky, the King's men presented a colourful, if shambolic sight. Some wore green coats, others red or russet. Many officers, in their own clothes, seemed absurdly overdressed for battle.

Settling, himself, for a sober grey coat and britches, Lewis sighed and pondered his fate. Finally, honour had come to him but at what cost? It would be precious use to him if he ended up face down in the mud of this miserable field. No, there had to be more to ambition than this.

A double line of pikemen shifted uneasily, their attention fixed on the Parliamentary army across the way. Their weapons glinted dully, clattering together as the men nervously shifted their weight.

Lewis turned in his saddle as he heard nearby voices raised in anger.

Two men on horseback were arguing so fiercely that it seemed they might strike each other. One was a stern-looking man with a

160

pasty, grey face whom Lewis knew to be the Earl of Lindsay, the other, Lewis realised with a sharp intake of breath, was the King's nephew, Prince Rupert.

This was the first time he had set eyes on the famously dashing young man and was delighted to find that the rumours about his personal beauty were well-founded.

Rupert, a man of extraordinary military skill and ambition, was known to be arrogant beyond belief, alienating many whose advice would have been valuable to him. But looking at him now, Lewis thought there was nothing such a youth might not achieve.

His face, slender and pointed with an attractive dimple in the chin, was as smooth and pale as fine china. He seemed to have the same, huge, brown eyes of his uncle but with more fire and less melancholy. His hair and brows were glossy and black and his dark red lips turned permanently upwards in an amused, rather condescending smile.

Dressed in fine, sky-blue silk from head to toe, he carried a small white poodle on his lap which never stirred despite the vehemence of his arguing.

'I will not countenance it!' cried the Earl of Lindsay, his grey features colouring with rage.

'There's little to argue about,' shouted Rupert, tossing back his head. 'I take my orders from none but His Majesty.'

Lindsay shook his gloved fist in the Prince's face. 'We shall see,' he barked. 'How am I expected to fight when I do not control my own cavalry?'

The Prince shrugged and stroked his poodle as if he hadn't a care in the world. He glanced around at the assembled troops and suddenly caught Lewis's eye

They made contact in that brief moment and Lewis felt his throat go dry as the Prince stared at him. His regal features remained unmoved until he allowed Lewis a tiny, knowing smile. Then he turned back to Lindsay with another shrug.

'Take it up with the King, my lord. I have a battle to win.'

With that, he turned his horse and headed off up the hill.

Lewis felt suddenly excited by the prospect of the battle, the colours and smells already impinging on his senses. He straightened in his saddle, copying Prince Rupert's swagger and placed one hand on his hip.

The Earl of Lindsay spotted him and beckoned him over. Lewis jabbed his heels into his horse's flanks and moved across the field.

'Look after things here a while, Captain St John I must speak with the King.'

Lewis nodded, a smile creeping to his lips and a thread of adrenalin coursing through his veins. Being a cavalry officer was a fine thing if one could acquit oneself with some style and avoid being killed.

He began to think again of Prince Rupert, imagined running his fingers through his glossy black hair, watching those heavy, sensuous eyelids close as they kissed.

His clothes felt suddenly, pleasantly constrictive, as though every part of him, from nipples to cock, were suddenly sensitised. He placed a gloved hand on his chest and brushed over his coat, feeling the warmth of his flesh beneath.

It would be a wonderful thing to win this fight then retire in triumph to the Prince's tent and allow His Highness to strip him. Then to feel those soft, full lips wrapped around his cock.

There was a loud explosion some way off and Lewis was startled from his reverie. His horse whinnied and stumbled. He reined it in and glanced quickly to his right where a plume of smoke was rising. The enemy had fired their first canon.

The Earl of Lindsay emerged from the King's tent, his face grave. He stalked to his horse and rode away. Immediately afterward, the King and Prince Rupert emerged, the former dressed in a splendid black velvet coat lined with ermine.

He stood still and rose to his not very imposing full height. 'The foe is in sight,' he announced in a high, clear voice. 'The best encouragement I can give you is this. C . . . come life or death, your King will bear you company, and ever keep this field, this place, and this day's service in grateful r . . . remembrance.'

There was a loud cheer from the assembled ranks and the King mounted his horse ready to inspect his troops. Rupert rode alongside him and once again exchanged a glance with Lewis as he passed.

Lewis felt himself blush and hurriedly looked away. He had to concentrate on the task in hand. The main priority was to win and to survive. Anything which might come later was merely a bonus.

The King gave the order for the first cannon to fire and the weapon spat out in fury towards the Parliamentary lines. As Lewis watched Rupert's retreating back he crossed himself and looked up at the bleary, cloud-thick sky.

'O Lord,' he said solemnly. 'You know how busy I must be this day. If forget you, do not you forget me.'

There was a huge, screeching roar and the enemy cannon began its reply in earnest.

The walls of Cornelius' prison were thick and black with age. A constant stream of brackish water seeped through the stonework and puddled on the wet floor.

Sighing wretchedly, Cornelius sat with his knees tucked up under his chin, his wrists and ankles manacled. He had sat like that for a whole day, without once setting eyes on another human being. What on earth could they have in store for him?

A key grated in the door and it swung open. Weak daylight fell into the room, silhouetting a tall, powerful figure.

Cornelius felt his throat go dry and peered into the gloom. The figure remained where it was, hand on the door, then moved inside, slamming the door behind it. Still Cornelius could make out nothing of its features. Only when it spoke, in a voice as dark as the dungeon, did Cornelius recognise the stranger as the man who had so rudely disturbed his and Christopher's pleasure.

'Good afternoon,' said the newcomer, striding towards Cornelius. 'And how does the day find you?'

There was not a speck of colour on him, from his black tunic and cloak to his boots. Even his handsome face was chalkily white as though drained of anything approaching humanity.

He had a high, smooth forehead and raven-black hair which hung to his shoulders. His brows were like two question marks arching over his pitiless eyes and a long, straight nose. His mouth, thin and livid red like a wound, was contorted into a sneer.

'I am Edward Vane. You do not know me, priest,' he said in a quiet, dangerous voice. 'But I know you.'

'How can you know me?' countered Cornelius.

Vane laid a long, thin finger along the line of his own jaw as though pondering. 'I have been tracking your movements these several months. I know you to be a spy –'

'That's a lie!' cried Cornelius.

'Silence!' hissed his tormentor.

He swept further into the room and glared down at the cleric.

Cornelius looked up into the burning black of his eyes. He could see a tiny pulse beating in the stranger's muscular throat.

'Do not forget that you are my prisoner, priest, and that I bear the authority of the King.'

Vane leaned towards Cornelius so that his face was inches from the cleric's. Cornelius could smell the strong, masculine odour of his body. There was a gentle fluttering in his belly and he sank back against the wall, oddly aroused.

'I knew you to be a spy,' continued Vane, 'but now I must add to this charges of sorcery and . . . unnatural practices.'

Cornelius felt a cold sweat break out on his forehead. 'What do you propose?' he said in a small voice.

'Propose?' thundered Vane. 'Why, to hang you! What else?'

Cornelius felt his heart hammer in his chest.

Vane's face came closer still until it was right by Cornelius' ear. 'What else?' he repeated, his hot breath whispering over Cornelius' skin.

Cornelius felt himself tingle with an irrational excitement. His penis begin to grow hot and thick in his britches.

It was a little after one that afternoon when King Charles himself lit the fuse which began his army's response. For a smoky hour or so the rival cannon spat destruction at one another until Lewis heard Prince Rupert sound his trumpet and lead his cavalry in a charge against Parliament's left wing.

The enemy scattered, terrified, but Lewis was dismayed to see that the Prince failed to follow up his assault and watched as the cavalry chased the Roundhead soldiers across the fields to Kineton.

Shaking his head at this folly, Lewis rallied his own men and, with a short blast on his trumpet, led his thundering horse into battle.

All was noise and confusion. Lewis cried out as a musket ball whistled past his ear, then reared his horse into the air and slashed with his sword to virtually decapitate his would-be assassin.

Through the smoke and the blur of colour, he could see the enemy's pikes glinting in the sunlight. His horse ploughed on through the mud, Lewis lashing out with his sword at every Roundhead trooper he could spot.

He caught a glimpse of the Earl of Lindsay whom, he had discovered, had resigned his commission after his shameful treatment at the hands of Prince Rupert. The older man was off his horse now, fighting hand to hand and Lewis lost him in the baying mob as he lunged to attack once more.

A young Roundhead of no more than sixteen years threw himself bodily at Lewis's horse. He was such a pretty thing that Lewis hesitated a fraction before cleaving half of his face off. The boy crashed to the ground, blood pouring from his wound and Lewis's horse stamped over him.

He whirled round in his saddle. The disappearance of the Prince's cavalry together with those assigned to a man named Wilmot had left the King's infantry dangerously exposed.

Lewis blasted on his trumpet again in an effort to rally his men but the sound was lost in the cacophony of battle.

He stood up straight in the saddle and then ducked as another musket ball seared the air just by his ear. Sweeping back his blond hair, he urged his horse forward once more.

In spite of the mortal danger in which he found himself, in spite of the terrible scenes enacted before him, Lewis realised that he hadn't felt so alive in years. Adrenalin coursed through his body and he grinned as he thrust out his sword again and again. His body felt as though it were on fire and he bellowed a curse on the King's enemies as he thundered into the Roundhead ranks.

There was a deep, formless lustiness building in his bones. He banged repeatedly up and down against the hard leather of the saddle, his buttocks aching, as he drove his mount forward. His cock swung loosely in his britches and then began to grow firmer and longer.

Lewis was aware of all this but so lost in the heat of the battle that he almost took his arousal for granted. As he swung his sword down repeatedly, chopping the enemy into gory chunks, he whooped with excited, feverish delight.

Before him he saw a Parliamentarian horse, felled by a cannon ball, it's rider sprawled under it and trapped beneath it's mangled hind legs. The rider was unconscious, his pale face splashed with blood, his long, dark hair matted with mud and sweat.

Lewis raised his sword to pierce the young man's throat. Then he stopped as though time had stood still. He looked again at the rider and felt a strange, cold sensation creep over him as though icy fingers had wrapped themselves around his heart. The trapped soldier below him was Ned Melcombe.

'I am no spy,' cried Cornelius hoarsely. 'And no witch. Such talk is lunatic.'

Edward Vane pushed his face even closer to Cornelius, his eyes glittering like jet. 'But you cannot deny the third charge, can you?' he growled. 'I caught you and that boy ... enjoying one another. Is that not so?'

Cornelius hung his head. There was no denying it, of course. Vane had caught him and Christopher in the most obvious of positions.

Vane pulled away and turned his back on the cleric. 'But do not despair, Mr Matthew. You were a man of God, were you not? There is such a thing as forgiveness.'

Cornelius looked up.

Vane glanced over his shoulder and smiled cruelly. 'At a price.'

Cornelius felt his heart beat faster still. He seemed to sense that Vane had something in mind a little out of the common. He knew that he should be afraid, that he should be thinking of some way to get out of this fearful mess. Yet all he could think about was the powerful, darkly handsome man standing before him and the insistent hardness of his own cock.

'I can only pledge my loyalty to my God,' he stated boldly. 'What else?'

Vane opened his cloak and pulled out a large cloth bag. He tossed it to the floor and there was a metallic clatter on the stone floor.

'What's this?' asked Cornelius.

'Evidence,' said Vane. He bent down and tipped up the bag. An assortment of items from the temple fell to the floor, among them the leather gag, the silk hood and several flails.

At the sight of them, Cornelius felt his prick grow hard as wood and he shot a quick glance at Vane.

'What would you have me do?'

Vane shook his head. 'You will do nothing, my boy. Nothing except obey me.'

He picked up the bridle and then grabbed Cornelius' long, copper-coloured hair. Wrenching back the cleric's head, he fitted the leather and metal object over his face.

Cornelius gagged as he felt the fat leather knot which was inset in the gag fill his mouth. He swallowed and managed to get his teeth around it just as Vane tightened the buckle behind his head.

He swallowed again, feeling his mouth filling with saliva. It was like having a hard leather cock rammed into his mouth. His breathing began to quicken.

He looked up at Vane who was towering over him. The Prosecutor threw off his cloak, revealing a firm, broad torso encased in a black shirt. His nipples, erect like bullets, were discernible through the cloth. His hand flew to his britches and he pulled out his cock in one swift movement.

Cornelius gasped. Vane's penis was huge, like a piece of smooth, carved oak, it's engorged purple head wide and flat, its shaft ribboned with projecting veins.

The sight of the great organ made his jaw open and he tried to speak but the leather strap across his face prevented it. He could feel his jaw beginning to ache at the presence of the fat leather knot inside his mouth.

He mumbled incoherently as Vane moved forward and pushed the end of his cock against the soft skin of Cornelius' face.

The cleric closed his eyes, inhaling the gorgeous, musky smell of Vane's massive cock. He longed to take it into his mouth, to curl his tongue around its length, but the tight gag prevented it.

Vane took hold of the shaft of his cock and guided it so it slid over Cornelius' face from forehead to nose, leaving a sticky trail of pre-come.

Cornelius opened his eyes.

'Oh, you are a lovely one, aren't you?' hissed Vane. 'I've seen many a witch in my travels but you are a rare thing indeed. I shall enjoy you.'

Cornelius swallowed. Spit ran from his mouth as he bit into the leather knot which filled it. He felt desire wash over him like a warm tide. He wanted this cruel man to take him, to abuse him utterly.

Vane pulled back, his great cock bobbing in Cornelius' face, and picked up the silk hood from the dungeon floor.

Cornelius made a small cry as Vane slipped the hood over the cleric's head, then all was darkness.

His breathing rate increased at once and he could hear his own swallowing as he champed excitedly at the leather gag. The hood completely covered his face, tight over his eyes and ears, gently squashing his nose.

Manacled at hand and foot, he sank down to the floor and waited.

There were muted sounds all around him which he took to be Vane's footsteps on the stone-flagged floor. He turned his hooded head towards the sounds but could see nothing at all through the silk.

Lifting his hands, he heard the gentle chink of the manacles and then gasped as he felt Vane's weight suddenly press down on him. He sank onto his back and let his head come carefully to rest on the floor.

The Prosecutor was all over him, pulling at his shirt and britches, his hands kneading and squeezing Cornelius' flesh. The cleric felt a warm nuzzling at his ears and shuddered in response.

Vane was kissing his hooded face, his tongue and lips tracing the outline of Cornelius' jaw and cheekbones. He could feel the sexy bristliness of Vane's chin scratching at his own.

Moaning, Cornelius relaxed further, enjoying the tremendous heaviness of the dark-robed man on his chest. He felt a sudden cold on his chest and realised, dimly, that his shirt had been torn open. His nipples felt raw and exposed until Vane's mouth closed over them, fiercely chewing and sending bolts of electric desire shooting through Cornelius' body.

He felt his back arch spontaneously and spread his hands wide and flat over the dungeon floor.

There was an insistent prodding in his belly which he took to be Vane's huge, stabbing penis as the Prosecutor bore down upon him.

Cornelius tried to open his mouth but still the tight gag prevented him. He so wanted to see Vane on top of him, yet found the hood's dark, forbidden pleasures excitable beyond words.

What would it be like to be chained up like this, naked and hooded and be serviced from behind by all manner of men? And never knowing or caring who they were? Simply to feel their beautiful, stiff cocks sliding up inside him, pleasuring him to extremes. These mystery lovers would have no idea of his identity, either. All they would see would be his slender, manacled body, oily with sweat, his head masked in black.

Cornelius felt his own cock rise under the weight of Vane's body and there was a muffled grunt of pleasure from the Prosecutor.

There was a savage tugging at his waist and Cornelius knew his britches had been ripped off as efficiently as his shirt. Now he lay naked on the dirty floor, chained at hand and foot and completely at the mercy of this great, dark man.

For a long moment, Cornelius lay like that, his chest heaving up and down with excitement. He tried again to speak but felt his tongue pressed down by the strong leather gag. He wanted to shout out to Vane, to beg him to worship his body, to plunge his cock deep, deep inside his welcoming arse.

Then, suddenly, his legs were pushed upwards and he felt Vane nestle within his thighs. The huge penis hovered over his groin, Vane's bollocks, heavy and hairy as exotic fruit, flopping on to the cleric's thigh.

Cornelius groaned with awakened desire and spread his legs wide so that Vane could enter him. His arse felt as open and moist as if it were intended for Vane's cock. Lifting his hooded head, Cornelius let out a slow murmur of appeal.

He gasped as the massive, stiff prick finally entered him, and there was a marvellous sensation of tight fulfilment. Beneath his closed eyelids he seemed to see red sunbursts as Edward Vane thrust his cock deep into his arse.

Thoughts and images scurried through his mind like racing demons. For so long now he had desired to master over Ned, to invert the roles they had played for so long. Denied this, he had taken Christopher the soldier, mastered him, possessed him. Yet now he wanted nothing so much as to be utterly debased by this cruel, dangerous stranger. To bend his will to Edward Vane's. To worship his cock and his body. How could two such conflicting passions exist within him?

He pushed his hips forward now to impale himself further on the Prosecutor's gargantuan organ which felt like it must split him open.

Tugging at the chains which bound him, he tried to smile beneath his gag. The restriction excited him, he knew, just as Ned's tying him to the temple table had excited him but this was something new. He felt like this should never end, that he should remain in Vane's service for ever, always at his beck and call. Ready to service him whenever he chose.

Cornelius groaned again, his teeth champing into the gag as Vane drove steadily into him, slipping his hands under the cleric's buttocks and lifting him up.

Waves of ecstasy powered over him and he grunted repeatedly as Vane's cock slammed into his arse, slapping his back against the hard stone of the floor. He felt his own cock standing proud.

Cornelius felt a delicious longing to wrap his long legs around Vane's waist, to pull him forward so that the Prosecutor's great penis tunnelled to the limits of his arsehole. But the heavy chains around his ankles held his legs down and he lay spread-eagled as Vane fucked him mercilessly.

The cleric began to pant like a fevered beast, his chest heaving up and down under Vane's body, till his ribs felt bruised and crushed. Vane pulled back and then thrust in again with a savage intensity as though Cornelius were merely a vessel for his lust.

Through the hood, Cornelius could hear Vane's hoarse panting as he approached his climax, but the combination of sensory deprivation from the hood and the pleasure burning within his own body made him hardly aware of it.

Rocking his hips on the cold floor, he felt the great, wide head of Vane's cock sliding within him till his anus tingled with pleasure.

His head was pounding as desire flooded through him like an unstoppable force. He wanted to rip away the gag and scream as Vane filled him but instead he held tightly to his chains and thrust himself down onto Vane's immense prick.

With a throaty roar, Vane pumped his hot seed into Cornelius' arse, driving deep into him as orgasm lashed at his senses.

He stayed like that, his cock still hard as stone, as Cornelius writhed around him, desperate for release. Then Vane withdrew, leaving a hollowness in Cornelius which he could scarcely bear.

Whimpering beneath the mask, Cornelius expected his own cock to be grasped now in Vane's big, masculine hands or even to be sucked between those cruel lips. But no release came.

Instead he felt the silk mask pulled from his face and Vane's quick fingers unbuckling the gag.

For a moment, he was confused. The darkness of the room and Vane's body over him combined to bemuse his senses. His cock was still stiff and upright against his belly.

He turned appealing eyes to Vane but the Prosecutor ignored him and unfastened the bridle from Cornelius' head.

Despite his lust, Cornelius was grateful for the release. He worked his aching jaw up and down and looked up again at Vane in silent appeal.

The Prosecutor slipped his softening cock back inside his britches and pulled on his cloak. He smiled slightly, then, out of nowhere, cracked Cornelius across the face with the back of his hand.

Shocked and stunned, Cornelius fell back against the walls, still naked and still chained at wrists and ankles.

With that, Vane swept from the room, locking the heavy door behind him.

Cornelius felt his face burn from Vane's blow. He lifted his hand to his cheek and his chain tinkled on the floor. He felt frightened and bemused yet still his burning desire for Edward Vane surged through him.

He brought his hands together as if in prayer and found that he was able to grasp the shaft of his beating cock. He could stand the suspense no longer. If Vane would not satisfy him then he must satisfy himself.

Wrapping his fingers around the head of his penis he began to swiftly pull his foreskin back. He spat on his fingers and rubbed excitedly at the membrane beneath the head, feeling satisfaction gush through his taut muscles.

Pushing back against the wall, he formed a fist with his hand and began to pump furiously at his cock, grunting rhythmically as he did so.

He closed his eyes and remembered once more the sensation of being hooded and gagged. The sense of helplessness had been wonderful but the presence of Vane's great hot dick inside him had been even better.

Air hissed between his clenched teeth as he felt his climax rapidly approach. He was far too aroused to play this long. He needed to come, to watch his semen jet onto the cold, wet slabs of stone.

He pushed back further till his naked arse, still burning from Vane's cock, slapped against the wall. Then he felt himself dropping into blissful darkness. His body convulsed and his movements became jerky as he came. Eyes still closed, he felt rather than saw his come streak from his cock, then murmured as the hot liquid pooled over his fist.

The battle had descended into something approaching savagery. The King's standard was captured by the Parliamentarians, its bearer, Sir Edmund Verney, killed with his severed hand still grasping its bloody shaft. The Earl of Lindsay fought bravely at the head of his own regiment, swearing that he would never fight under such undisciplined youths as Prince Rupert again. He was never to have the chance, dying of his wounds late in the day.

As night fell, Ned Melcombe found himself under a blanket inside a large, dark tent. He was trembling and staring ahead as though deep in shock, his lovely face blanched white except for the spattering of someone else's blood which covered his cheeks.

He had seen much that day which would have driven any rational man insane. Such slaughter . . . He could hardly comprehend it. He had thought himself prepared for the realities of war, thought himself a proper soldier now, fearless, undaunted. But when he saw a Royalist sword take away the life of Trooper Baines he had felt as though the blade had cut through his own guts.

Baines had fallen in silence to the wet ground, his pretty face disappearing into mud to be trampled on by the approaching enemy.

Watching from his horse, Ned had suddenly seen the boy as he had known him, so vibrant and full of life, his hard, warm body under Ned's, his ripe arse open for Ned to take with his cock. Now all that, and all that sweet boy's promise, were gone, to turn to dust on the field of Edgehill.

Enraged, Ned had redoubled his efforts, slashing away with his sword from his mount, taking down as many of the King's men as he could.

Then a musket had reported and his horse fell under him, twisting and trapping him. He had struggled to get out from under the beast but found he could not.

Desperate and terrified, he had looked about wildly, knowing that, through the smoke and confusion he would soon be spotted by the enemy and cut down.

Head bleeding, he looked over the battlefield, through the piles of corpses and clouds of smoke. Around him, the battle went on. Dimly, he heard the clash of pikes and the roar of charging troopers. But he seemed detached from it all, like a ghost trapped at the scene of its own death. Finally, the scene had spun around him and he sank into darkness.

The tent in which he awoke was oddly still and silent, its dark brown walls fluttering fitfully in the evening wind. The structure was large, with room for several to walk upright in, but Ned, lying on his improvised bed, was the only occupant.

He turned his head to look around and swore as pain scythed through his forehead. He raised a hand to the wound and found that it had been carefully dressed.

Looking down, he realised to his surprise that he was naked beneath the blankets. He sat up, his chest muscles bunching, and, this time, carefully inclined his head to take in the details of the tented room. He could see a glow beyond the walls which he took to be a brazier. Its warmth spread into the tent and he felt none of the chill of the evening. There was a small table by the bed-side on which a basin full of water stood. Several blood-stained towels and the muddied remnants of Ned's clothes and his bloodied sword were piled neatly nearby.

Speculations raced through his mind. Where had he been taken? And by whom? Could someone have come for him? Miracle Smith? Yes, surely it was the strong, beautiful farmboy who had scooped him up from the battlefield and brought him here. Or perhaps he had been captured and was now behind enemy lines.

Ned's ears pricked up as he heard someone approaching. With sudden decision, he pulled the blankets back over him and pretended to be asleep.

The tent flap was pushed aside and someone entered, their tread light but assured.

Ned kept his eyes closed and listened as the newcomer walked close to his bed. Then he leapt out from under the blankets, grabbed his sword and grabbed the stranger from behind.

Despite Ned's arm around his neck, the man struggled to speak. 'You ... really ... are the most ungrateful of masters ...' he spluttered.

Ned swung him round in shock. 'William!'

His former servant coughed and rubbed at his throat. He was dressed in a long white nightshirt that made his tanned, beautiful face and long chestnut hair seem all the more vivid. He looked at Ned, standing naked with his sword drawn and cocked an eyebrow.

'I should put some clothes on, sir. You'll catch your death.' He reached under the table and produced another white gown which he tossed to Ned.

Ned laid down his sword and struggled into the garment. It was thin and translucent and his hard, firm body was visible through it.

'You saved me?' he asked. William nodded, pouring a goblet of wine for Ned which was rapidly guzzled down.

'Where are we, then?' said Ned, sweeping his arm around to indicate the tent.

'Far from the field,' murmured William. 'This is a place I know. A monastery. I knew it as a boy. We'll be safe here.'

Ned reached for his coat and britches. 'Safe? Safe, William? We have to get back.'

William touched him lightly on the arm and Ned felt a little thrill of pleasure race through him.

'No, my lord,' said William. 'Stay awhile.'

Ned let the clothes fall to the floor. He watched as William poured himself a goblet of wine which he drank swiftly, his lips stained red.

'Was the day ours?' queried Ned.

William shrugged. 'It's hard to say. There was much devastation. On both sides. Let things settle a little. We shall return tomorrow at first light.'

Ned sat down on the edge of the bed. 'Why have you brought me here, William?'

The servant sighed. 'I think you deserve some time alone.'

'Alone?'

William smiled slightly. 'I can keep you company if you wish.'

Despite his confusion, despite the shock of the dreadful day and of John Baines cut down, Ned found William's words electrifying. Within his nightshirt, his cock began to stiffen and rise.

Immediately, Ned folded his hands over his erection and cleared his throat.

William walked towards him and sat down right by Ned. He ran his hand through Ned's hair and set his lips lightly to Ned's.

A tingle of pleasure ran up Ned's spine.

'What . . . what is all this about, William? Why now?'

William looked down. His own body was visible through the thin muslin of the nightshirt and Ned could see how wiry and well-defined it was.

'You want me, don't you?' said William.

Ned nodded dumbly.

'And I, you,' murmured William, placing his warm hand on Ned's thigh. 'Since that first day when I came to Humbleford.'

Ned smiled excitedly. 'But you were always so cold. So . . . arrogant.'

William gave a rueful smile. 'That, if I may say, is the pot calling the kettle black.'

Ned laughed. It was true, he knew. He thought again of William's look of scorn inside the barn with the soldiers. In his effort to be in control of his destiny and of those he liked to dominate sexually he had turned himself into something of a monster.

'I knew,' continued William, 'that I could never let you be master of me. That I must have you as an equal.'

Ned frowned. 'I always said you were an uncommon servant.'

'Uncommon I am,' said William, straightening his shoulders. 'Until today I was the eldest son of the Earl of Lindsay.'

Ned's Jaw dropped open. 'What?'

William shrugged. 'It's true. We quarrelled some years ago and he cut me off without a penny. The fact that I support Parliament and he the King meant that our differences were never likely to be reconciled.'

Ned was finding all this difficult to take in. His penis, untroubled by britches or underwear, rose and thickened steadily under his nightshirt. He wanted William so much, the feeling physically hurt him.

'What do you mean, until *today* you were Lindsay's eldest son?'

William looked into the middle distance. 'My father died today on the field of Edgehill.'

Ned opened his mouth to sympathise but William held up his hand.

'No, don't worry. I hated him. It is no loss. It is gain. I am now the Earl of Lindsay and able to see you, dear Ned, as my equal.'

He pulled himself into Ned's arms and they kissed. Ned felt his heart race and a surge of lust and fulfilment rose from his loins and up through his body till he felt he would sing out.

Ned opened his mouth wide and let William's tongue roll around inside. He tasted so good, so sweet; as sweet as the wine they had both quaffed.

Tracing the outline of William's jaw with his hand, Ned pulled him round and they fell backwards onto the bed. William's gentleness was blissful. All kinds of new sensations flooded through Ned. He wanted his servant so much, felt rough desire pound at his senses and stiff cock, yet the simplicity of William's delicate kisses brought forth unexpected emotion in him.

Quite suddenly and uncontrollably, he began to cry.

William pulled his lips away from Ned's and frowned. 'What is it?'

Ned shook his head. 'I don't know. I . . .'

He trailed off, feeling hot, salty tears roll down his face.

Images flooded his mind. He saw Thomas, he saw young John Baines, he saw all the dead of the battlefield. Then he saw Cornelius, his lovely face smiling up at him, trusting, honest, loving.

Cornelius' image cleared to reveal William, sitting before him in his muslin shirt, so vulnerable and beautiful.

Ned shook his head and kissed William lightly on his rose-bud lips. 'I was just thinking,' he said at last. 'I . . . I feel as though I have wasted half my life in idle folly. That I have been half a man. And have treated many with such contempt . . .'

William placed a finger on Ned's lips and shushed him. 'We all play games,' he said. 'Hide and seek. Games of bluff. Sometimes we find that we have been playing the bluff on ourselves.'

He kissed Ned again and Ned felt desire surge through his every muscle.

Sighing, Ned entwined his tongue around William's and caressed his long, dark hair. Then his hands swept underneath William's shirt and fluttered over his smooth skin, stroking at his breast, at his thighs and around to clasp his firm, rounded buttocks.

William pulled himself deep into Ned's arms and they kissed again. Ned felt like he was melting, that all his worries and anxieties were being soothed away by William's caresses.

Gently pushing back William's head, Ned began to lick and kiss at his neck, his tongue leaving a glistening trail in its wake.

Then he felt William's hands move under his nightshirt and clutch at his warm, hard torso. With gentle movements, William rubbed the soft mounds of his nipples until Ned groaned in pleasure.

Suddenly, he felt the shirt being lifted over his head and he was naked once more, his big, stiff cock standing proud. William lowered his head to Ned's nipples and began to suckle them.

Ned whimpered as his nipples began to grow more swollen and sensitive. William's lips toyed with the darkening mounds, pulling them up from the warm flesh of his chest.

Then William moved straight down and took Ned's cock deep into his mouth.

Ned sighed in ecstasy as he felt the youth's lips close around the broad, hot shaft. William's head bobbed up and down rapidly as he sucked, his tongue flickering over the solid, delicate skin of Ned's cock.

Bolts of desire cracked like whiplashes through Ned's body. He lay back further still and groaned as William sucked his pulsing, shuddering cock.

For a brief moment, William withdrew his lips, but only to pull his own nightshirt over his head. Then he returned to his action on Ned's penis, biting, sucking, licking.

Ned's eyes fluttered as he drank in the details of William's body, the body he had so long yearned to see. The boy was as tanned as his face and hands promised; a rich, honey colour which contrasted with the milky smoothness of Ned's own flesh. He seemed completely hairless save for a dark nest of pubic hair and a comically small spread across the firm, flat pads of his pectorals. His cock, slender and hard as iron, nestled gently against Ned's leg.

William lay on top of Ned now and Ned was surprised to find he didn't resist. Normally, he would have had to have been master of the situation, have turned William over and rammed his cock straight into the boy's willing arse. But now he wanted William to soothe his pain, to make him forget.

He gasped suddenly as he felt William slip a finger into the tight entrance of his anus. The walls of his arse closed around the warm digit and he felt a low rumble of pleasure building at the base of his spine.

No one had been there since Lewis St John. Not even like this. But he wanted it now. Wanted William's gentle finger to slide in and out of him, to push him over the edge into orgasm.

William pulled away again to kiss the hard lines of Ned's belly and the soft, concave shapes of his thighs. Then he pulled himself up the bed so that they were eye to eye. He kissed Ned deeply and Ned could taste the saltiness of his own cock on William's lips.

Ned felt himself swooning with joy and lust. He wriggled a little so that William's finger moved within his arse.

They lay there, kissing, locked together and William moved to lie on top of him. Slowly, he began to rock back and forth, his cock pressed against Ned's.

Ned sighed and moaned, his head rolling from side to side as he felt the delicious pressure of William's body on his. He thought of young Trooper Baines and melancholy suddenly overwhelmed him. He closed his arms around William's body and held him tight and close.

William moved over him like a ghost on water, his prick stimulated by the movement just as was Ned's.

Ned's hand moved down the smooth hollow of William's spine and came to rest on his taut buttocks. He grabbed both in his hands and pushed at William, helping him to rock up and down, up and down, over his body.

'I want you so much,' sighed Ned. 'I need you so much tonight.'

William nodded and smiled but his face was set into a frown of concentration. He began to grunt rhythmically.

Ned closed his eyes and concentrated on the lovely warmth of the boy on top of him and the feelings of pure desire he was experiencing.

There was a gorgeous rapture building within him and he pushed his hips upwards, wanting to bang himself against William's hard body.

The boy began to gasp and suddenly sat back on his haunches, grabbing the shafts of his own cock and Ned's and rubbing them both with his fisted hand.

Ned's head jerked from the pillow and his jaw dropped open as eddies of pleasure rippled through him. He felt as though he would burst, that he was a sun-hot vessel of desire, waiting to explode. He tensed, feeling his back arch and his feet curl, then shouted out as a huge, deep, blissful orgasm thundered through him.

His come shot up his body, splashing on his chest and on

William who continued to pump at Ned's cock in tandem with his own.

Ned gasped at the intensity of the feeling. He raised his hands in helpless appeal. He could stand no more.

But then William screwed his eyes tight shut and moaned through gritted teeth as he too came, his sperm thudding into Ned's face and trickling down the contours of his cheeks.

At once, William clambered off Ned and came to rest by his side. They embraced and kissed deeply, then Ned buried himself in the boy's arms. Tears came again, but they were tears of relief and pleasure and satisfaction.

Ten

———

Cornelius woke shivering. He had pulled back on the meagre garments he'd been wearing but Vane's assault had left them ragged. He had slept fitfully but was unsure now whether even it was day or night.

He pulled his shirt tightly around him and wrapped his arms about himself.

His wrists and ankles were sore from the constant chafing of the manacles and his arse still smarted from the presence of Vane's massive cock inside it. It was not an altogether unpleasant sensation, Cornelius had to admit, but he knew that Vane meant him no good and that the sooner he found a way out of this wretched place, the better.

The feelings he had experienced alarmed him. He knew he should be repulsed by Vane, knew he should fear him, yet his deepest desire was to abase himself before the dangerous Prosecutor, to be his slave just as he was slave to Ned Melcombe.

The thought of Ned made Cornelius shiver. His brow furrowed and he sighed, remembering the beautiful man to whom he was devoted. Yet, was Ned so different to Vane? Had he ever treated Cornelius with anything but contempt and indifference?

Cornelius was beginning to realise now that he wanted much more out of life than to be someone else's plaything. He enjoyed, needed even, to be used and humiliated by his lovers but there were times when he had to be in control too. It had to be a partnership of equals.

His mind began to drift back to that golden afternoon by Greenacre Falls. Could anything be more different to his current situation? Then he had finally got Ned on equal terms. Who knows, if the war had not interrupted, they might have built something real and lasting by now. He remembered Ned's face when he had lost the wager over the wrestling bout. There had been a wild, almost savage intensity about it. Then Cornelius had felt confident enough to take the bonny Christopher up the arse, to make the lad his, to lick and chew at his downy flesh . . .

But it was useless to think like that. He had to find a way out of this prison and probably flee the country. Certainly Vane would have made it impossible ever for him to return to Humbleford. He had no idea where he was being kept. There had been a long journey in a closed and shuttered coach after his arrest but as to his final destination, nothing was clear.

A key turned in the lock and the door was thrown open. Two burly men, whom Cornelius recognised from Vane's raid on the temple, bustled inside and quickly and efficiently removed his manacles. He was tempted to make a run for it there and then but one of the men twisted his arm behind his back and threw a small sack over his head. Within seconds another pair of manacles, this time terminating in a ball and chain, had been clamped around his wrists.

Cornelius felt a painful push in the small of his back and moved across the room, dragging the ball and chain behind him. The guards laughed at the sight of him and Cornelius reflected ruefully on how recently he had been wearing a hood quite unlike this one.

He made painfully slow progress along a stone-flagged corridor, constantly pushed and chivvied by the guards until they arrived at another chamber. Cornelius was dragged through the entrance and was immediately aware that the room was very, very hot.

He stood stock still, his breath rasping beneath the sack and let his manacled hands drop down in front of him.

There was a familiar crackling, popping sound close by which

Cornelius took to be a fire. He made no movement until the sack was pulled from his head and he was left blinking into the gloom.

He was inside another prison cell but this one was much longer and wider, its walls black but dry due to the oppressive heat.

To Cornelius' horror, the place seemed to be dotted with instruments of torture. Although he couldn't put a name to any of them, nor divine their function, the collection of winches, blades and chains did not bode well. He felt his stomach begin to churn.

In the centre of the room, sitting on a large throne-like chair, was Edward Vane, his proud, cruel features dappled with the orange glow of the fire which roared in a huge hearth at the top of the room.

'Welcome,' murmured Vane, his voice as smooth as silk.

Cornelius said nothing but fear and a terrible excitement were already coursing through him. He held his hands close to his crotch lest his already growing erection should betray him.

'Yesterday,' said Vane evenly, 'you died.'

His words made Cornelius go cold all over. 'What do you mean?'

Vane cocked his head to one side and laid a gloved finger on his cheek. 'I mean that Cornelius Matthew, cleric of the parish of Humbleford, who had been arrested on suspicion of sorcery, was killed whist attempting to escape.'

Cornelius shrugged. 'No doubt you'll let me know what you are talking about in the fullness of time.'

Vane got to his feet and strode across the room. He took Cornelius' face in his hand and smiled evilly.

'No, sweet,' he hissed. 'I shall tell you now. You are officially dead. Nobody knows where you are. And, therefore, you are mine. For ever.'

Cornelius pulled his face free and glared at Vane. 'There has been no trial. Where is your evidence? You cannot do this.'

Vane laughed harshly. 'It's done. I have so many powers these days that I sometimes frighten myself. And no one is going to miss a treacherous sodomite like you, are they?'

Cornelius suddenly felt very small and vulnerable. He let his head sink to his breast. 'You mean to keep me here? As your slave?'

Vane nodded gleefully, his face splitting into a horrible grin. 'But don't worry, Cornelius. It won't be so bad. There'll be compensations.'

He walked towards a long table which was covered in a large, dirty tarpaulin. 'Food, wine . . . company.'

Vane pulled the tarpaulin from the table and Cornelius gasped at what was revealed.

Spread-eagled on his belly on top of the table like a mounted starfish was the figure of a man. He was clothed from head to toe in shiny black leather. It covered his feet and muscular legs, his chest, arms and hands. A tight leather mask completed the effect and he was chained at wrists and ankles just as Cornelius had been.

Looking more closely, Cornelius could see that the leather costume wasn't quite complete. There was a large hole in between the man's buttocks, exposing a sliver of white skin.

The figure began to moan miserably as soon as he was revealed.

Vane grabbed hold of Cornelius' hands and tried to pull him forward. The cleric resisted and Vane pulled again, his hand brushing over the front of Cornelius' ragged britches.

As he felt the big, stiff erection, Vane let out one of his short, barking laughs. 'Dear me, we are eager, aren't we?'

He pulled Cornelius forward until he was standing at the top of the table. Now he could see that the leather mask had two eye-holes and another opening for the mouth. Two blue eyes stared up at Cornelius in desperate appeal.

Despite himself, the image excited Cornelius and he felt his swollen cock grow larger still inside his britches.

Vane undid a catch at the back of the mask and whipped it off. 'As I said,' he muttered. 'Company.'

The flushed, sweating face of Christopher was revealed. There was an ugly bruise across his forehead and his lovely lips were dark with dried blood.

Cornelius stared down at the soldier, wanting to apologise and free him and fuck him all in one crazed thought.

Vane walked around the table and cracked Christopher across the backside. His hand sounded like a pistol-shot on the taut leather covering the boy's buttocks. Christopher groaned and then gasped sharply as Vane prodded his finger deep into the soldier's arse.

'This one has already proved very versatile,' hissed Vane. 'It's good to know that we have not been recruiting virgins into our armies.'

He pulled out his finger and laid his head on Christopher's arse. Then, with a savagery that made Cornelius catch his breath, he bit into the soldier's buttock.

Christopher howled in pain yet Cornelius could see that he was also enjoying it.

Vane looked up, his lips glistening with saliva, and grinned. 'I can see it in your eyes, Master Matthew. You want to escape. You want to resume your place in the parish and yet you want to stay. There is something inside you – and in this one – that makes you want to obey me.'

Cornelius could not deny the evidence of his own hard prick. He raised his hands, forgetting for a moment that he was manacled. 'Are you seeking my consent, Vane?' he said.

'Hardly,' spat the Prosecutor. 'I only want you to know that I can see right through you. You can protest all you wish but you are mine.'

Vane walked to the door and rapped on it twice. It opened and the two burly guards came in. One was carrying something which glistened in the firelight, the other began to remove Cornelius' shackles.

For an instant, he stood free and thought wildly of making a break for it. But how could he escape these men?

The other guard approached him now and Cornelius saw that he carried a leather costume just like the one which encased Christopher.

Cornelius backed away but the guard grabbed and began to rip off the cleric's clothes. He stood there naked, his hot cock hard and sticking up against his belly.

The guard began to unfold the leather costume.

As he looked at the weird garment, Cornelius felt a thrill of forbidden excitement run through him. He put on a show of protest as the guards forced him into the thing but was secretly excited.

They pulled it over his feet and he wriggled his toes, enjoying the sense of enclosure. As it slid over his calves and thighs, his cock throbbed with anticipation.

The thing laced up the front and it was as tight over his muscular chest as everywhere else. He slipped his arms into it and pulled the gloved ends onto his hands.

A guard prepared to put the mask over him but Vane held up his hand. 'Not yet,' he whispered.

He walked over to Cornelius and stroked his leather-clad thigh. There was a thick, diagonal shape in the crotch of the garment where Cornelius' stiff cock lay.

Vane made a low, approving grumble deep in his throat and hissed through his teeth. 'Mine.'

Cornelius' head was spinning. He had to escape and soon. Vane was clearly insane and could have something unimaginably horrible planned for both him and Christopher. Yet his heart and his cock were pounding with forbidden desire. He loved the feel of the exotic costume he was wearing and loved to see Christopher lying there on the table, chained and abased. And he wanted the handsome, cruel Vane to take him there and then.

Vane pointed a bony digit at Christopher's recumbent form. 'Release him,' he spat.

The guards unlocked Christopher's manacles and he sat up, breathing hard, sweat glistening on his forehead. He looked at Cornelius and a silent understanding passed between them. His penis was obviously stiff within the tight restriction of the leather costume as was Cornelius'. Whatever the risks, whatever the dangers, he wanted to be a part of Vane's perverse game too.

Vane grabbed Christopher by the arm and slung him across the room where he came to rest by the roaring fire. So tight was his costume that he looked as though he had been dipped in tar, muscles, nipples and stiff cock all clearly defined. He shot a defiant look at Vane who chose to ignore it.

The Prosecutor turned to Cornelius and pointed to the floor. 'You too. Kneel before me.'

Cornelius turned away and Vane slapped him across the face. Cornelius' flesh stung like fire but a contradictory lust leapt through his veins.

'*Kneel!*' ordered Vane, pushing Cornelius to the floor at Christopher's side.

The two men knelt before Vane, resplendent in their glistening leather costumes, their faces slick with sweat.

Vane strutted up and down before them, removing his shirt to reveal a massive, hairy chest and arms like coiled rope. 'Now,' he mused, kicking off his boots and unfastening his britches. 'Which is it to be?'

His trousers flopped to the floor and he pulled them over his feet.

Cornelius felt his breathing quicken. Vane's legs were as thick as tree trunks and covered with dark hair. His massive cock was standing up at right angles to the big, heavy sack of his balls, themselves surrounded by a virtual forest of hair.

Vane moved closer to his two slaves and let the wide, purple head of his penis brush over their lips.

Its touch made Cornelius shiver with pleasure. He wanted so much to take it into his mouth but he could not afford to appear so willing. If Vane were to keep him alive then he would have to remain a challenge.

Christopher had no such qualms. No doubt aroused beyond reason by Vane's attentions, he flicked out his tongue as Vane's cock brushed by him and licked at it.

At once, Vane moved his penis back towards Christopher and thrust it into the boy's mouth.

He grunted in pleasure as Christopher began to suck at him then snapped his fingers for the guards.

They seemed to know what to do and dragged Cornelius to his feet, clamping the manacles back around his wrists and standing him by Vane's side.

Vane pulled the cleric close to him and cracked his hand across his leather-covered arse. Then he let his hand creep into the slit between Cornelius' buttocks and pulled him closer still. With his other hand he unlaced a portion of Cornelius' costume so that his cock projected from it.

'You too,' he hissed, pointing at Christopher.

Cornelius frowned, confusedly. Vane pushed him in the small

of the back so that Cornelius' cock prodded into Christopher's cheek.

Then the cleric nodded and allowed Vane to guide his big, hard cock into Christopher's mouth.

Now the soldier had two ram-rod hard penises crammed into his mouth and he sucked at them both as though his life depended on it, which, for all he knew, it very probably did.

Cornelius felt his balls pulse inside his leather costume. They had not been released when Vane opened the front of the garment and he felt their presence keenly. They felt ready to burst, so full of seed did they seem.

He watched the shaft of his cock disappear then reappear from the warm, red hole of Christopher's mouth. It felt so good to be inside him, to have that gorgeous, wet warmth surrounding his flesh and to feel his cock rubbing against Vane's massive erection which threatened to overwhelm Christopher on its own.

As they both fucked the soldier's mouth, Vane continued to paw at Cornelius' body, his hands stroking the leather-encased outline of his arse and thighs.

His face was set into a cruel mask as though he derived no pleasure from this ritual but simply had to undergo it.

For his part, Cornelius could not disguise the delicious sense of power which the performance gave him. He closed his eyes and thrust his hips forward, pushing his cock deep, deep into Christopher's mouth.

Vane began to grunt spasmodically and his impassive face at last showed signs of some emotion. He seemed about to come when he grabbed Christopher's face and suddenly pulled both his and Cornelius' cock out from the boy's mouth.

With a strange, wild cry he kicked at Christopher so that he fell forward onto his face, then grabbed Cornelius and, turning him round, thrust his huge cock straight up and into the cleric's yielding arse.

Cornelius cried out but Vane reached round and pulled back his long, coppery hair. With his free hand he pointed down at Christopher.

'Now, fuck him!' he ordered, thrusting his cock into Cornelius with frightening urgency.

Christopher was on his knees and thrust his backside into the air so that Cornelius could slide into him.

Soon, all three were arranged on top of each other and Cornelius couldn't help but remember the similar coupling he had enjoyed with Simeon and Solomon what seemed like a life-time ago.

Cornelius powered into Christopher's arse and he felt pleasure beating at his senses. Already sensitised by the attentions of the soldier's mouth he felt as though he could come almost immediately but he held back. He wanted to enjoy the sensation and he stared down at Christopher's glistening, leather-covered arse thrusting up and down with his cock inside it. Then he pushed back and felt himself deliciously impaled by Vane's enormous, thick member.

Cornelius bit his lip as he felt an unstoppable orgasm rise like a curtain of fire through him. He opened his eyes again and saw the real fire before him. It seemed as though he were twisting in its flames, pleasure and pain merging within him.

His heavy balls throbbed inside their leather prison and he gave three or four quick short thrusts into Christopher's arse as he came, sending his semen shooting up into the soldier's sweaty arse.

From behind, Vane grabbed him and he felt a big, warm hand close over his face. He cried out as Vane's hand closed over his mouth, sweat dripping down his face.

His cock slipped from Christopher's arse and the soldier rolled over onto his back where he managed to work his own cock free from its leather encasement and beat quickly and urgently at its slender length.

Cornelius moaned in delight as Vane's cock moved rapidly within him. Then the Prosecutor's movements became jerky and savage. He seemed to draw arousal from the sight of the leather-clad Christopher frantically pumping at his own cock. As the soldier came, crying out as gobs of hot seed splashed over his black costume, Vane shot his load into Cornelius' arse, forcing the cleric down to his knees as he withdrew.

Vane staggered backwards then waved quickly for the guards to attend to Christopher and Cornelius.

Within seconds, both had been masked and Cornelius found

himself looking out through the small eye-holes of the strange leather object. They were both chained to the wall and Vane rapidly dressed again, as though anxious to re-assert normality.

The guards brought food and drink for the slaves and Vane again swept from the room without a word.

Their chests heaving with exertion, Cornelius and Christopher sank back against the wall and looked at one another.

Eleven

Lewis St John unbuttoned his coat and sank down onto a plump, well-cushioned chair. He was weary to his very bones and closed his eyes, letting the hazy May sunshine that spilled through the window illuminate his pale features.

In the months following Edgehill, the King's attempts to take London had been repulsed and he had finally set up his headquarters here in Oxford.

For Lewis, this meant some relief from the constant round of skirmishes and minor battles which his life now seemed to comprise. In addition, his promotion to colonel had meant more responsibility though he had ended up with far more splendid quarters than his captaincy would have allowed.

He pulled off his boots and settled back into the chair.

The window was open and the scents of early spring were wafting into the large, pleasant room. Slowly, his mind began to drift.

He saw himself back on the field of Edgehill, amidst the smoke and clamour. He was threading his way through the corpses that littered the ground, looking around as though in search of something.

There was a horse lying nearby but the rider Lewis expected to see trapped beneath its legs was missing. Turning, he suddenly saw the boy, Ned, wasn't it? Yes, Ned. The son of that old fool he and his family had visited years back. The boy had changed, certainly, but Lewis remembered him well enough to recognise the thin, adolescent face and frame within the man. And he was nostalgic, or foolish enough, to let the boy go and not consign him to the death he and his Roundhead friends deserved.

But there was more to it than that and Lewis knew it. He thought of Alexander, the gorgeous actor he had slept with in Nottingham and that strange look he'd worn the morning Lewis received his commission from the King. What was it? Reproach? Disgust? Or was there something else? A strange sense that he could see where Lewis was heading and did not have the heart to tell him, like a seer bearing bad news.

Lewis murmured in his sleep and drifted. He saw again the bright, hot summer he had spent with Ned Melcombe, remembered holding him down as his cock thrust deep into his young arse.

A confused, sad look crept over Lewis's dozing face yet the warmth of his penis in his loins soon sprang into urgent, solid life.

He stirred, inclining his face towards the sunshine, and murmured as he felt a gentle lustiness tingle through him.

Yes, he had enjoyed Ned. Of course, the boy had simply been one of many but that summer held special association for him. It had been when he'd crystallised his philosophy of life. That to achieve power over other men was what made him tick. That their humiliation and ultimate enslavement to him were fundamental to his sexual desires.

The figure of Ned in his dream shifted from boy to man, like a sputtering candle-flame but led the way off the field of battle towards what appeared to be a huge barn.

They drifted inside, Lewis aware of his big, burning erection as the spectral figure of Ned took his hand and led him inside.

The barn was cool away from the summer heat and Lewis felt a sheen of sweat develop on his skin as the change in temperature affected him.

In the dream, he seemed to be stripped to the waist and wearing only a pair of leather britches, his prick pressing against the waistband.

Ned lay down on a bed of hay and rolled onto his belly, pulling his linen britches down and exposing his firm, ripe young arse.

Lewis's hand dropped to his crotch and he unlaced himself, allowing his cock to flop out. In seconds it was rising to its full, impressive length, throbbing and pulsing.

But then there seemed to be someone standing before him and Lewis could no longer see Ned. He moved his head but found the newcomer blocking his path.

Lewis's eyes snapped open and for a moment he didn't know where he was. But, though the warm sunlight of his room brought him rushing back to reality, he found that someone was indeed standing over him.

He pulled back his head and a dark, beautiful face swam into focus before him.

'You will think me very forward, I'm sure,' drawled Prince Rupert, 'but I take it you don't object?'

Lewis scrambled to his feet. 'Your Highness,' he sputtered.

Rupert waved away the formalities. 'No, no. Let's have none of that. We're men of the world, Colonel St John. We have both seen something of life, have we not?'

Lewis felt his head spin. This was so unexpected. He had only seen the Prince a few times since the battle of Edgehill. They had exchanged smiles and furtive glances but no more. Now the King's favoured nephew was in his apartments.

Rupert threw himself down into a seat and sighed. 'God, I find this war wearisome. Sometimes I think I shall take me back to the Continent and away from you English altogether.'

Lewis still stood before the Prince, his heart thumping. 'That would be a great loss to us all, Your Highness.'

'Well,' smiled Rupert, his swarthy face lighting up. 'That's very kind of you to say. Of course, this wet little country does have its compensations.'

He stared deep into Lewis's eyes and did not look away.

Lewis felt his face flush and broke the contact. Rupert let out a short laugh.

'I did not take you for a shy one, Colonel,' he said quietly.

Lewis could think of no reply. Instead, he moved towards a big, wooden dresser which was pushed against the panelled wall.

'A drink, sir?' he enquired. Rupert nodded.

The Prince was dressed sumptuously in red velvet decorated with gold brocade. His long, rich hair spilled to his shoulders and hung over his large, devastating brown eyes. He took a goblet from Lewis's outstretched hand, drank its contents in one go and held out the goblet again.

'More,' he said.

Lewis poured more dark, red wine into the goblet. Then the Prince patted his knee. 'Join me.'

Lewis looked about, not quite sure what to do. Surely the Prince did not mean for him to sit on his knee?

As if in answer, Rupert opened his legs wide and patted them again. 'Come,' he ordered, drinking more of the wine.

Lewis needed no further invitation. He crossed the room and straddled the Prince's legs, his cock growing thick and hard within his britches.

He was facing Rupert and the Prince grabbed him roughly by the shirt and pulled him forwards into an embrace. The feel of his soft, soft lips sent Lewis into raptures. Their tongues entwined and Lewis closed his arms around the lovely young man, feeling like a schoolboy enjoying his first, illicit kiss.

Rupert pulled away and drank more of the wine, then set his lips back onto Lewis's, allowing the rich liquid to pass between them. It spilled from their mouths and dribbled down both their chins and onto Lewis's creamy smooth neck.

He groaned in delight as he felt Rupert's tongue slip under his lips, exploring every contour of his mouth. The warmth in his loins was like a furnace now and he had to shift his buttocks on Rupert's legs as his erection grew ever more stiff.

Suddenly, Rupert opened his legs and allowed Lewis to slide through to the floor. He smiled callously and then his handsome features became more stern.

'Colonel St John,' he whispered. 'I want you to take out my cock and suck it. Do you hear me?'

Lewis nodded and reached up to undo the fastenings of the Prince's britches. His hands shook slightly as he unhooked the elaborate pins. A boiling lust washed over him. He so wanted to taste Rupert, to suck at his cock, to feel his royal seed sliding down his throat.

He pulled down the Prince's britches and stockings and laid his lips to the inside of Rupert's thigh. The soft, white flesh was firm and muscular and the Prince let out a little moan of pleasure as Lewis's mouth kissed him there.

Looking up, Lewis could see the impressive sacs of Rupert's hairy balls and the long, slender rod of his penis which was standing up and leaving a little stain of pre-come on his scarlet coat.

Lewis trailed his tongue up Rupert's thigh and on to his warm balls which shivered and contracted at his touch. Then he made his way up the length of the Prince's cock, his saliva wetting its hard shaft until he reached the engorged purple head.

He let his tongue tickle at the glans and Rupert gasped in delight, his hands grasping Lewis's hair and tugging harshly at it.

Lewis's hands fell to the Prince's warm thighs and squeezed at them just as Rupert pulled at Lewis's hair.

Then he opened his mouth wide and took the full shaft of Rupert's cock into him.

The Prince took in a sharp breath and Lewis let his tongue play over the stiff shaft, servicing him with practised skill.

And yet Lewis suddenly found himself feeling oddly unmoved. He knew he should be euphoric and thrilled. This was an extraordinary, unexpected event. That he should be here, taking the lovely, legendary Prince into his mouth, pleasuring him, teasing him to his climax. It was scarcely believable.

Lewis, though, found himself thinking crazy, irrational thoughts. Was this all he had come to? A royal plaything? A pretty but foolish cock-sucker for this arrogant Prince?

Rupert thrust his hips forwards and gripped the padded arms of the chair until his knuckles whitened. Lewis frowned and tried to concentrate on Rupert's cock. He relaxed the muscles of his throat so that the Prince could penetrate him still further. He could feel his own cock straining for release and wanted to undo his own britches, allowing his erect organ to protrude into the air. But he could not.

As he sucked at Prince Rupert, he felt his own erection begin to diminish.

Rupert's hands were clawing into his scalp now, the Prince throwing back his head and exposing his fine, slender throat. Again, he pushed himself forwards to fuck Lewis's mouth as though he were taking a woman.

His guttural cries should have excited Lewis, should have made him beat desperately at his own cock, but he let his penis shrink within his trousers, not caring a whit for it.

The Prince went suddenly stiff and cried out as he came, his cock pushing to the very limits at Lewis's throat and pumping, pumping a river of hot seed into him.

Lewis sat there like a zombie until Rupert gradually withdrew from his mouth and collapsed backwards into the chair, his chest heaving with the exertion.

Lewis himself fell back, swallowing the Prince's semen, his face a mask of confusion.

Rupert closed his eyes and let out a long peal of delighted laughter. 'Well, well, Colonel St Johns –' he began.

'Please. Lewis, sir.'

The Prince shrugged. 'Very well. *Lewis*. I congratulate you. That was one of the best I have ever received. From a boy.'

He got rapidly to his feet and tucked his penis back into his britches. Then, bending down, he kissed Lewis lightly on the lips. 'Come to my apartments tonight, Lewis. There may be sport for you.'

So saying, he swept from the room in a blaze of scarlet.

Dazed, Lewis got up and then sat down in the chair Rupert had just vacated. It still smelled of his exotic, foreign perfume. Lewis closed his eyes. This was all wrong, all wrong. Why did he suddenly hate himself for what he'd become?

He closed his eyes but found sleep impossible. He stayed awake long into the night, his weary eyes burning.

Humbleford had changed. Ned could see that the moment he and William reached the brow of the hill which overlooked the quiet Oxfordshire valley.

Ned shifted in his saddle and gazed down at the little village. It was unnaturally quiet and the upturned hayricks and broken cart-wheels which littered the approach spoke of some disturbance.

William's horse snorted loudly, breaking Ned's reverie. He looked round and exchanged glances with his former servant whose pretty face was fixed into a grave frown.

'What do you think?' asked William.

Ned shrugged. 'We had best be careful. There are Cavalier scouts all around. Humbleford might be theirs for all we know.'

'Then perhaps we had better not go down.'

'We came back for a purpose, William. It's high time I faced up to my responsibilities.'

William nodded and smiled. 'Of course.'

Ned clicked his tongue and his horse moved forward down the slope of the hill.

His mind was full of confusion. In the last few months, he had served Parliament well but found his appetite for conflict waning daily. He longed for the peace and security of his old home but this seemed permanently out of reach until, at last, his regiment came near to Humbleford again and he had been granted leave to put some of his affairs in order.

Ned fingered the black sash of mourning which he wore around his waist. His father, who had never really got over the death of his beloved Thomas, had succumbed to a brain-fever earlier that month. Now Ned really was Squire of Humbleford. But what would remain of the pretty village once they reached it?

He had found great solace in William's company but knew that their time together was drawing to a natural end. As Earl of Lindsay, William had achieved quick promotion and his undoubted military skills were in demand by Colonel Cromwell himself. Soon he would leave Ned's side and, before he did, young Melcombe wanted the boy to be near him during this hour of need.

'Where will he be?' asked William as they rode towards the village. 'Still at the church?'

Ned shrugged. 'It's a good place to start.'

They had come, not only to visit the manor and check the status of Ned's inheritance, but to see Cornelius Matthew.

'I have done many a grave disservice in my time,' Ned had said to William, 'but none so much as to that poor, gentle boy. I must make amends. He has loved me through it all.'

And there was worse to come. The beautiful Miracle Smith had lost his life in the service of Parliament, felled by a musket ball to the heart.

Sometimes Ned felt like an old man steeped in blood. All he ever seemed to know was carnage and destruction. Only William's soothing arms kept him from losing control.

They made their way into Humbleford, the May sunshine peeking through a cloud-scudded, china-blue sky.

The clusters of cottages showed signs of attack with loose bricks littering the ground. The hayricks they had spotted from the brow of the hill had been set alight and there were dead animals quietly putrefying in the shadows.

The church seemed relatively undamaged, though its clock-face had been shattered by cannon-fire.

Ned and William dismounted quietly and made their way towards the porch. The door was barred by a plank which looked as though it had been ripped from a pew. Ned made short work of it and they stepped through into the cool, dank interior of the church.

It was wrecked. From the altar to the windows, stretched a debris field of broken pews and shattered glass.

Their boots crunching on the floor, Ned and William walked slowly up the aisle.

'Ned?' William said. 'Look at this.'

Ned walked to William's side and bent down to examine an ominous dark stain on the floor. It was blood.

Ned and William looked at each other and William put a comforting hand on Ned's shoulder.

They both turned sharply at a noise from the area of the knave.

'Who's there?' called Ned.

There was a shuffling sound, as though a particularly large rat was moving through the darkness. Ned sprinted down the aisle and dragged a small, frightened figure into the light. His shock of white hair was mussed up and his wrinkled face contorted with fear.

'Peters!' cried Ned. 'It's the Reverend Peters.'

The old priest peered myopically at Ned and smiled. 'Is that —? No, it couldn't . . . is it? Young Melcombe? Is it you, Ned?'

Ned nodded his head vigorously. 'Aye. It's me. What happened here?'

'The King's men?' put in William.

Peters nodded. 'Aye, they came. But they were not the worst. It was the witchfinder, Vane. They have wrought destruction that the Cavaliers would blanch at, they —'

Ned took the old man by the arm. 'Gently, my friend. Tell me, where is Cornelius?'

The Reverend Peters looked down at the glass-strewn floor. 'Ah, poor boy, poor boy.'

Ned felt a wave of fear prickle over his skin. 'What is it?'

Peters fixed him with a steady gaze. 'It was terrible. There was talk of him consorting with the Devil. Of espionage and dealings with young men. Such arrant nonsense.'

Ned looked at William. Not all of it was nonsense, he thought to himself.

'What did they do?'

'Arrested him,' continued Peters. 'Then, when he tried to escape their wickedness, they . . . they killed him.'

Ned felt suddenly dizzy as if the whole, black, black experience were about to overwhelm him. He righted an upturned pew and sank onto it, putting his head into his hands.

William touched him gently on the cheek and then turned to the old man. 'This . . . witchfinder . . .?'

'Edward Vane,' murmured the Reverend Peters.

'This Vane, then. Where is he now?'

Peters looked up and the light from the church windows leant his crumpled features a spiritual glow. 'I hear he is at Oxford with the King.'

They reached the manor house as dusk was falling. It had sustained great damage but whether this was due to the Cavaliers' action or madness of Edward Vane's men was difficult to gauge.

The Reverend Peters, who seemed to be virtually the only soul left in Humbleford, fed them as best he could before retiring to his ruined vestry.

199

Now Ned and William found themselves in the parlour they had so often shared. The room where Sir Harry had told Ned that he must be acting Squire, then that he must take his brother's place. The room where William had watched as Ned played with his own cock and pleasured himself with the wooden phallus.

Both men looked around, overwhelmed by memories.

'I've checked the upstairs rooms,' said William at last. 'There's little left except the mattresses.'

Ned nodded. 'Well. We must have sleep, regardless. Let's fetch one down.'

They hefted a mattress from Ned's destroyed bedroom down into the parlour and drew the ragged curtains.

Ned sank down onto the mattress and sighed. William sat by him and held him tightly in his arms.

'You mean to go to Oxford, don't you?' said William.

Ned nodded. 'I must. For his sake.'

William caressed Ned's soft cheek. 'Then I will come with you.'

'No, no. I cannot allow you.'

'Why not? We've come this far together.'

Ned smiled and kissed William softly on the lips. 'I know. But this is something I must do for Cornelius. I must get revenge on this man, Vane. And I'll stand a far better chance alone. Besides . . .' He let his hand run through William's hair. 'Besides, Cromwell needs you.'

William smiled. 'You will always be very special to me, Ned. You know that?'

Ned nodded. 'Of course. And you to me. But our destinies do not lie together.'

William smiled. 'No. I believe your heart was always with another.'

Ned let his head rest on William's lap and felt tears spring to his eyes. He knew it now, of course, he knew it though it was too late. It was Cornelius, lovely, loyal, patient Cornelius whom he had always loved. But he had been too blind, too arrogant ever to see it. Now it was too late and the gentle cleric was dead at the hands of Edward Vane.

William stroked his hair as the tears poured. After a while, Ned lifted his head, his eyes puffed and red and kissed William, tasting the salt of his own tears as they streamed down his face.

William embraced him and they kissed again. This time, their tongues found their way into each other's mouths and Ned allowed William to push him back gently onto the mattress.

When William pulled away and began to nibble at Ned's neck, Ned sighed deeply, feeling the pleasure soothe his hurt.

'Will you hold me?' he murmured. 'Hold me through the night. Love me?'

William smiled. 'My dear Ned,' he whispered and set his lips to the muscular skin of Ned's throat. He tickled and stroked the soft flesh, the hot point of his tongue jabbing at the soft underside of Ned's jaw and Adam's apple.

Ned groaned and relaxed backwards on the soft mattress. He wriggled out of his shirt, exposing the hard lines of his battle-weary body.

William wrapped his arms around him and held him in a tight embrace, his lips pushed hard against Ned's mouth. Then William took off his own shirt and pressed his warm, honey-coloured body onto Ned.

They lay there, breast to breast, wrapped in a gorgeous embrace, William rocking gently backwards and forwards over Ned's body. His prick felt hot and hard against Ned's belly.

Ned wanted to be naked and began to struggle out of his britches. William helped him and pulled off his own in one or two quick movements. They wore no stockings as the ride to Humbleford had been hot and sweaty and so now lay naked on top of each other.

Ned grasped William's pert buttocks in both hands and rocked him up and down. What he wouldn't give to have Cornelius back. To allow the cleric to be master of him like this. He had once sworn that no one save Lewis St John would ever take him up the arse again but now he wanted Cornelius to be here to do just that.

With a pang of sadness, he realised that was impossible. But, at least, here was the lovely William. So strong and alive.

'Now, Ned,' said William quietly. 'Now you must take as you always wanted to.'

He kissed his former master full on the lips and then turned over onto his belly.

'No,' said Ned, turning him back. 'Let me see you, William. I want to see you as I enter you.'

William smiled and sank back. He opened his legs wide and Ned sank down on top of him, his great, hard prick insinuating itself into the cleft of his arse.

Breathing regularly but with a quiver of excitement, William raised his buttocks slightly so that Ned could enter him.

Ned groaned with delight. How long had he wanted this? To take the insolent boy up the arse, to feel the perfect, pert globes of his buttocks speared by his tumescent cock.

Now it was happening at last and Ned let his breath stream hotly through his clenched teeth as he pumped his penis deep into William's body.

Once Ned was inside him, William wrapped his legs around Ned's body and used his strong thighs to push his lover into him.

Ned growled with pleasure and pressed his lips to William's firm nipples, running his tongue over their delicate surfaces, nipping and biting like a man possessed.

He felt that he wanted to pierce William's very soul with his burning prick, to tear him apart as he thrust and thrust again.

William's head thrashed from side to side on the mattress and then he looked up, fixing Ned with a kind of awed wonder on his face.

'I'm inside you,' mumbled Ned. 'I'm inside you with my cock.'

William nodded, clamping his eyes shut in ecstasy as Ned powered into his arse.

'Inside me,' he murmured. 'Oh, Ned. Fuck me, Ned. Fuck me.'

Ned snarled with renewed energy, letting his lithe body stretch out over William. His big, solid penis slid gracefully in and out of William's arse, pushing him to the point of orgasm and rubbing simultaneously over William's own cock which was jammed like a warm fleshy pole against the hard plane of Ned's belly.

Ned shivered with pleasure as desire boiled in his loins. He moved faster and faster inside William, his cock flying in and out of the boy's anus but never quite leaving it.

William's legs gripped tightly around him, urging him on and on and then the boy's arms were around him, pushing Ned's face down to his breast so that he might suckle his nipples.

'Oh, Ned,' cried William, his face flushing red. 'Ned.'

Ned's brow furrowed with effort. He felt like a man lost in fever as his muscles spasmed and a gorgeous, blissful orgasm flooded his senses.

He felt his come shoot up inside William and arched his back over the boy, his head hanging down, dripping with sweat.

Still William gripped him. 'No, don't stop. Don't stop.'

Ned pulled his penis out of the boy's arse but allowed himself to be gripped by William's arms and legs and rocked over the boy's firm body, the ridges of his abdominal muscles rubbing at the swollen cock beneath.

William opened his mouth wide in a silent scream as he came, his jism exploding under the firm lines of Ned's belly.

Doused in come, they fell back together onto the mattress and held each other close.

Ned could think of only one thing to say for the months of support and love and pleasure William had given him.

He nestled his head on the boy's sweat-slicked chest and breathed, 'Thank you.'

Oxford seemed to Ned more like a garrison than a city. As he approached, on foot but leading his horse by its bridle, he craned his neck to look beyond the fortifications of the city walls.

He approached a huge, portcullised archway which was guarded by no less than four of the King's soldiers and came slowly to a halt.

About a dozen people were milling about him, most of them merchants of one kind or another. There was an old man with a huge basket of wine bottles on his back who was deep in conversation with one of the guards. A woman and a clutch of dirty children were clamouring to be let in.

Ned was dressed in an inconspicuous and filthy brown coat, which was of a similar hue to his britches and stained stockings. By contrast, his boots were well-heeled and tough as he expected to be doing a good deal of leg-work that day.

He had plastered mud into his long hair and across his face and carried a quantity of silver plate on the back of the horse which he had recovered from a secret hiding place within the manor house.

Approaching the portcullis, one of the guards held up a hand to stop him.

'Hold, there,' said the guard, smiling. 'And what are you? Pilgrim, merchant or thief?'

The guard laughed, exposing broken black teeth.

Ned indicated the basket of silver plate with a mud-dirtied hand. 'I've brought plate for His Majesty's coffers,' he said. 'I'll give anything for the King, honest I will. Just let me inside. Them Roundheads are everywhere. An honest man isn't safe outside these walls.'

The guard cast a wary eye over Ned's cargo and seemed to consider his words. Certainly the King was strapped for funds. He had ordered the melting down of Oxford University's finest plate in order to help pay his mutinous soldiers.

He nodded and laughed good-humouredly. 'Very well then. In you go. But remember who let you in if you come into any more of this stuff.'

Ned thanked him and led his horse through the gateway and into the city proper.

Oxford was teeming with life. Despite the war, ladies and gentlemen of high rank continued to parade around in sumptuous fashions, their opulence contrasting with the squalid low-lifes selling their wares all about.

And everywhere there were soldiers, brawling, drinking, laughing. Ned hadn't seen so many enemy troops outside of a battlefield. He kept his head bowed and led his horse up the cobbled street away from the entranceway.

He was already missing William's comforting presence but his fear was overlain by his thirst for revenge on the man who had taken away his precious Cornelius.

There was a small, rather lop-sided tavern at the junction of two streets up ahead. Ned tied up his horse outside and, taking down the basket containing the silver plate, struggled inside.

A low, evil-smelling room met his gaze and he staggered

towards the nearest empty table, the basket in his hands. Several pairs of very interested eyes lit up at the shining silverware which crashed to the table.

Ned caught the eye of a serving girl and ordered a pint of ale. He sat down, looking about into the dark corners. When the drink came, so did a small, weasel-faced man with a permanent, crooked smile plastered on his face.

'You're new, friend,' he said. 'May I offer you a drink?'

Ned said nothing, merely indicating his ale.

'Well,' said the newcomer. 'Perhaps another after that.'

'Perhaps,' said Ned.

The man sat down without invitation and nodded towards the basket of plate. 'You should be careful with that, friend,' he warned. 'There are some very dishonest folk in Oxford since the war began.'

'You don't say,' said Ned with a smile.

He sat back in his chair and wiped beer froth from his lips.

'You may be able to help me,' he said, fixing the weaselly man with an appealing look.

The stranger spread his hands as though to show he had nothing to hide. 'Honoured to be of service.'

Ned downed more ale. 'I seek Edward Vane,' he said in a low whisper.

The weasel-faced man went very pale. 'The Witchfinder?' he hissed, aghast.

'The Prosecutor, aye,' replied Ned.

The man began to get to his feet. 'I can't help you.'

Ned restrained him gently and nodded towards the basket of silver. 'It's all yours. If you help me.'

The man sat down and looked from Ned to the basket and back again. He licked his lips and frowned.

'Here,' said Ned, catching the serving girl's eye again. 'Let me get *you* a drink.'

There were six of them now, arranged in a chained row against the wall. All wore the same, tight-fitting leather costumes and masks and all, without exception, were sunk into abject despair.

Cornelius could scarcely remember a time when he had not been enslaved to the evil Edward Vane.

Every day it was the same. He would spend the night in a comfortable cell, with access to books, good food and washing facilities. Then, as dawn broke, he would be forced into the weird leather suit and taken to the fiery room where he and Christopher and the four others who had joined them in captivity were restrained all day long. Sometimes Vane appeared and used one or all of them for his sport. Other times he did not appear at all and they lingered in an agony of suspense.

Whatever excitement he might once have derived from this abasement had all but evaporated. Cornelius wanted only to escape. His one hope was that the war would go Parliament's way and he would be released.

Cornelius raised his arms and his chains clanked. He moved closer to Christopher and looked deep into his icy grey eyes which could just be made out through the holes in his mask.

It seemed hard to imagine now that they had once enjoyed each other so freely, that Cornelius had felt Christopher's taut, defined muscles beneath his belly as he slid his cock into the soldier's arse.

'Do you think he will come today?' he whispered.

Christopher shrugged, his voice muffled by the leather mask. 'Hard to say. There was nothing yesterday. But he seems busier these days. I wonder whether that's good news or bad.'

Cornelius could only agree. If Vane tired of them or they became a dangerous liability, he could have them put to death and no one would be any the wiser.

They had some information on their side, however. Over the months they had gleaned that they were in Oxford and that the King had established himself there. In addition, the war was said to be going against the King.

Vane was sometimes absent for a week or more, during which they led something approaching a normal life. One such period had recently ended, and when Vane returned he seemed less swaggering and slightly frightened, perhaps recognising that a man such as he would receive short shrift from a triumphant Parliament.

The door was flung open and Vane strode into the chamber,

his jet-black cloak streaming behind him. Without a word, he sat down in his opulent chair and stared at the six men he had enslaved. None of them, Cornelius included, dared look at him. To do so brought punishment of an unpleasant kind.

Vane clicked his fingers and one of his guards walked over to his chair. Vane whispered in his ear and the guard came over towards the captives. He walked along the leather-clad line and paused before Cornelius who felt himself grow cold all over.

The guard unshackled his manacles and then left Cornelius kneeling on the stone floor, feeling oddly exposed. His fellow captives looked at him anxiously.

Vane spoke at last. 'Look at me,' he bellowed across the room.

Cornelius looked up and Vane pierced him with his night-black eyes.

'I do not know which of my pets you are,' said Vane. 'It really doesn't matter. But you will come towards me now.'

Cornelius began to get to his feet, his leather costume creaking.

'No!' barked Vane. 'On your knees.'

Cornelius sank back to the floor and then began to move slowly across the flagstones towards Vane's chair.

With every movement he felt his hatred of Vane grow more intense. He wanted to jump up and run at him, tear at his face, make him suffer. But he knew the guards were armed and that his situation was hopeless. Perhaps, one day, there would be a chance.

With agonising slowness, Cornelius crept towards Vane's chair. When he reached it, the Prosecutor put out his foot and kicked Cornelius backwards, laughing cruelly. Then he extended both legs so that his feet rested by Cornelius' masked head.

'Now,' he ordered. 'Lick my boots.'

Cornelius was determined to feel nothing. Not even a little thrill of pleasure at Vane's words. He would resist it. He would.

He knew now that his desires were nothing without love. He could still find a monster like Vane attractive but refused to grow hard within his leather costume.

Inwardly proud of himself, Cornelius raised himself up on his knees and began to lick at the soft, black leather of Vane's boots. His tongue lapped over the surface, leaving a wide trail of spittle and the taste was harsh and salty, as though Vane had been walking through wet grass.

He licked all over the surface, and then began to run his tongue up Vane's leather-encased calves. Vane suddenly reached out and, pulling Cornelius up by the head, pressed his masked head into his lap.

Cornelius could feel the stiff rod of Vane's cock lying in his lap under the protection of his black britches. What would happen if he fastened his teeth around it and simply didn't let go? What would Vane do then?

Thoughts of revenge filled his head but Vane's crotch was warm and sensuous, doubly so with Cornelius' face hidden beneath the leather mask and, despite himself, Cornelius began to get aroused.

Vane lifted up his legs and wrapped them around Cornelius' trunk, pulling him down onto him with the strong muscles of his thighs.

His face was fixed into a kind of manic snarl as he clicked his fingers again and his guards assumed positions around the room.

Cornelius was unable to see but heard various items being removed from their housings. Vane's legs dropped and he found himself being pulled round so that his back, and his exposed arse, were towards the Prosecutor.

Now he saw what the guards had done. There were five of them lined up behind the other slaves and each carried a whip. The slaves were on all fours with their penises exposed through the lacings of their leather costumes. Each was nearly or completely erect, as obviously incapable of resisting their dark instincts as was Cornelius.

Vane took out his own cock and began to play it over the leather-clad cheeks of Cornelius' arse. He produced a whip himself and cracked it in the hot air.

'This will be our last game, my sweets. Enjoy it while you may.' He cackled insanely.

Cornelius felt his stomach flip over. It was as they'd suspected. Events had made the city too hot to hold Vane. He was about to quit the place and dispose of any unpleasantries, including them.

Pushing Cornelius forward, Vane cracked the whip across the cleric's buttocks.

Cornelius caught his breath as the blow stung his leather-covered flesh. The whip cracked again and the same, searing pain assaulted his senses. Yet his cock grew stiff as the pain ebbed away and he found himself longing for its feel against his arse again.

As though Vane's action had been a cue, the guards began to flog the other five slaves, the whips smacking off their arses with a sound like musket fire. And each one took hold of his cock and began to beat at it.

Vane looked on, a triumphant leer on his handsome face. He whipped Cornelius again, this time with such force that the cleric fell to his knees.

As though inspired, Vane threw down the whip and advanced towards Cornelius, his enormous penis standing out straight in front of him like a sword of flesh.

He grabbed Cornelius by the shoulders and then thrust his cock into the slash in the leather which covered the cleric's backside.

Cornelius grunted in a mixture of pain and pleasure as he felt the great weapon impale him. His own cock insinuated itself through the lacing of his costume and, almost unconsciously, he began to fondle at its head.

Filled to the hilt by Vane's massive cock, he gave in to the strange experience. It might well be his last.

Ned moved through the darkened streets with practised stealth. Divested of his silver plate and with his horse securely stabled he felt able to move freely about the city. Apart from one or two groups of rowdy men and the ever-present soldiers it was reasonably quiet.

He was following a route given to him by the weasel-faced man in the tavern who, after several jugs of ale and a hefty amount of silver plate had gone off to establish the whereabouts at Edward Vane.

Returning after an hour or so, the man whispered a series of instructions to Ned on the strict understanding that they were not to be enacted until after dark.

Ned had then found himself somewhere to sleep and quartered the horse before sitting by the river to await nightfall.

He had plenty of time to think through his situation. After the war, in the event of victory, his property would be returned to him and there would be compensation for the damage done by the Cavaliers. But what of the damage done to his life? He had been jolted out of his complacency by the horrors of the conflict and realised, too late, that the one who truly loved him was lost to him for ever.

Despite his grief, the thought of Cornelius made him feel a deep, pleasurable lust. He remembered again their times in the temple, even the brief time when the cleric had come to the manor. If only he had got past his own arrogance and not used Cornelius merely as a plaything. What he would give now to share a big, soft bed with the cleric, to fall into its crisp, white, downy embrace and tell Cornelius that he loved him, then to kiss him, to entwine their tongues together, to take Cornelius' cock in his mouth and up his arse.

But that was beyond all reason. All he could do was make amends a little by taking the evil life of the man who had killed Cornelius.

Ned crept past a row of thatched cottages towards a large, square, stone building which he took to be the Prosecutor's headquarters. The weasel-faced man had promised that he would be met there and taken inside. The rest was up to him.

The night was turning chilly and Ned pulled his scruffy coat tight around him.

There was a low hooting sound from close by which sounded so artificial that it could only be some kind of signal. Ned looked around to locate it and then did his best to imitate the sound.

At once, a nondescript man dressed in ragged clothes appeared from around the side of the cottages and beckoned to Ned.

Ned followed and the man led the way towards the sturdy-looking stone structure. There was a big, brass-embossed door inset in the wall which the stranger opened with a particularly heavy-looking key. Than he and Ned slipped inside into complete darkness.

By instinct rather than vision, Ned followed the little man down some kind of corridor until they emerged into a better lit, airy chamber with four torches fixed to each corner.

Ned stood there, waiting for the man to speak.

'Where now?' he hissed.

As soon as he saw the look in the man's eyes he knew something was wrong. The little fellow scurried away as footsteps rang out through the room.

Ned let out a heavy sigh as the weasel-faced man appeared from the corridor, flanked by two heavily armoured soldiers.

Without a word, one of them marched up to Ned and cracked him across the head with the hilt of his sword. The room span and all went black . . .

Cornelius felt as if he were about to explode. Edward Vane's cock was pumping in and out of his arse at the same time as he was furiously rubbing at his own genitals.

He could feel the hot tip of Vane's massive penis within him, moving about, arousing the sensitive flesh of his anus.

Vane had hold of his hips and was pulling Cornelius back and forth on his cock, eliciting little gasps of pure pleasure from the cleric.

'Christ,' murmured Vane as he pumped in and out of Cornelius' tender arse, his hips slamming against the leather-covered globes of the cleric's buttocks.

. Around them, the five other slaves continued to be flogged by the guards. And, as they were flogged, they violently masturbated, their livid, swollen cocks jutting out defiantly from the soft black leather which covered the rest of their bodies.

One of them, furthest from where Vane was fucking Cornelius, suddenly cried out and came, his jism shooting to the floor and puddling around the cracked flagstones. As he sank down, exhausted, the guard behind him redoubled his efforts, cracking the whip over the slave's buttocks.

Cornelius watched as another came and then another but still the guards whipped them.

He knew his own climax to be near and wondered what fate lay in store for him. But all he could think about now was the immensity of the cock plunging into him and his own penis, so hard and hot in his leather-covered hands, pumping towards orgasm.

Christopher, his body sagging, came next, his semen landing on the slave next to him who came himself on the spot. Now the guards moved as one unit, rhythmically flogging the five slaves.

Cornelius suddenly stiffened, feeling his muscles popping with effort and was then overwhelmed by a tide of pleasure. He felt his seed race up the length of his cock and then came all over his hands, his semen spilling down his leather-encased legs.

Vane shouted something incoherently and plunged his cock even deeper into Cornelius' arse. With his hands on the cleric's hips, he banged back and forth, his cruel mouth set into a thin line of concentration.

Then he let out a weird, banshee-like wail as he came and Cornelius felt the Prosecutor's sperm shoot up into his arse like a river of lava.

Dripping with sweat, Vane sank his head to his chest but kept tight hold of Cornelius.

The cleric stayed absolutely still lest any movement incur Vane's dangerous wrath. But, finally, the evil captor pulled his cock from out of Cornelius' arse and fell back into his chair.

As one, the guards ceased flogging the slaves and stood back against the wall.

There was none of Vane's usual haste to rearrange himself. He sat there, his eyes glazed, with his massive, fat cock hanging outside his britches, dribbling with come.

'As I said,' he whispered hoarsely, 'that was our final game. I must leave here. And I cannot take you with me. Though it grieves me to say so.'

He flashed a demented smile and looked around the room at the exhausted, leather-clad slaves.

'So,' he continued, standing and running his hand over Cornelius' back. 'You must all die.'

Ned woke in altogether different circumstances. He was in a sumptuously decorated room. Rich velvet drapes covered the tall windows. There was a big, four-poster bed hung with damask silk and a cheery fire glowing in the corner. Were it not for the fact that he was bound and gagged, Ned would have thought himself to be dreaming.

He looked slowly about at the orange-hued room, looking for

some clue as to his whereabouts. There was none forthcoming though something about the sheer luxury of the place raised dark suspicions in Ned's mind.

The door opened and Ned started. A young man swayed slowly towards him, his face in shadow. He looked down but Ned could still not distinguish his features. Then the newcomer sat down in a chair in the shadowed corner.

'My men say you came looking for Edward Vane. Is that right?'

The voice was slurred, obviously drunk.

Ned didn't react. Instead he looked steadily ahead.

The newcomer tried again. 'You look and stink like a peasant but I don't think you are one. You're far too pretty for that.'

Overwhelmed by curiosity, Ned peered into the darkness. At last, the young man got up and walked unsteadily into the light. He was very attractive with dark, almost saturnine features and large, spaniel eyes. Ned had seen him once before, on the field of Edgehill but never thought to meet him in person and certainly not in such circumstances.

Prince Rupert put his hand on his hip and, with the other, stroked the poodle Ned now saw revealed in the crook of his elbow.

'You know who I am?' said the Prince, stifling a burp.

Ned nodded slowly.

'Hmmm,' muttered Rupert. 'But I don't know you. What are you doing here, I wonder. Are you on a mission to kill me? Or to kill the King perhaps?'

It didn't seem as though he expected Ned to answer and he made no move to release Ned's gag.

Rupert put the poodle on the floor and it scurried away. Then he walked up to Ned and Ned leaned backwards, overwhelmed by Rupert's presence. 'I have a new friend,' he said, running his hand through Ned's muddied hair. 'I wonder if he can suggest what to do with you.'

The Prince bent down and licked Ned from his chin to his forehead.

Ned could smell the wine on the Prince's breath but felt his cock stiffen at the handsome man's touch. He looked up into Rupert's eyes and tried to speak. Perhaps the Prince was a reasonable man. Perhaps he would listen and understand his story about Vane and Cornelius. Ned cared nothing for his own life now, but if he could only explain, only get some measure of revenge.

Rupert straightened up and walked out of the room, closing the door behind him with a soft click.

As soon as the Prince was gone, Ned began to look around for some means of escape. He couldn't rely on Rupert's whim. There had to be a reliable exit in case he had to leave in something of a hurry.

His legs weren't bound and he struggled to his feet. He managed to make it as far as the window before he heard footsteps approaching and raced back to his position on the floor.

The door opened and Rupert entered with someone else. Whoever they were remained in the shadows.

'What do you think?' said Rupert casually. 'He's a bonny one, isn't he?'

The newcomer mumbled something and Rupert frowned.

'Don't be such a faint-heart. Go and look. He won't bite.' The Prince turned to Ned and smiled. 'You won't bite, will you my lovely?'

Still the newcomer stayed where he was until Rupert took his arm and practically dragged him across the carpet towards Ned.

Ned looked up into a face he had never thought to see again. The blond hair and dark brows were unmistakable, as were the razor-sharp cheekbones and glittering blue eyes. He was older, of course, but not too dissimilar from the man who had haunted Ned's dreams for ten years.

Ned tried to speak, tried to say Lewis St John's name but a tiny movement of Lewis's eyes silenced him.

'Aye, he's a rare one, Your Highness,' said Lewis, turning back towards the Prince.

Ned's head was reeling. In the midst of all this to find Lewis again. It was beyond words. He struggled to keep still in his kneeling position on the carpet.

Rupert continued, 'My spies say he was trying to find the Prosecutor.'

'Vane?' said Lewis. 'Why?'

Rupert shrugged. 'For whatever reason, he bribed my man with a great deal of silver.'

Lewis looked over at Ned, his face impassive. 'What are you going to do with him, sir?'

'Hmm? Oh, I don't know. That's why I asked you over here. I thought we could have some . . . sport.'

So saying, Rupert staggered drunkenly across the room and removed Ned's gag. Ned spat out a ball of fluff and then grunted as the Prince kissed him full on the lips. Then, removing Ned's bonds he spoke again.

'What's your name?'

Ned shot a glance over at Lewis. Should he use an alias or be honest? But Lewis's expression revealed nothing.

'Ned, sir,' he murmured at last.

The Prince inclined his head. 'Ned. Hmm.' He shrugged. 'Now then, Ned. Something about your demeanour tells me you are not a fervent supporter of His Majesty King Charles so I suppose I should have you killed on the spot.'

Ned tensed but Rupert wasn't finished. 'However, something about your reaction to my kisses also tells me you might just give my friend and I some amusement. Then, afterwards, we can discuss why you came here and all sorts of dull things like that.'

Ned let out a sigh of relief. He looked again at Lewis but he had moved back into the shadows.

Rupert extended his hand and Ned took it, rising to his feet.

The Prince smiled and led Ned towards the capacious four-poster bed then spoke over his shoulder to Lewis. 'Come along, Lewis. We don't have all night.'

Lewis hung back a moment more and then strode across the room.

Rupert was already on the bed and removing his clothes. Ned sat by him, looking and feeling awkward until the Prince pulled him down onto the mattress and planted a fervent kiss on his full lips.

Ned felt his cock stiffen on the instant and sank back into Rupert's embrace. Yet, despite the Prince's beauty, all his thoughts were turned towards Lewis, the lover whom he had once thought so precious.

Lewis was undressing slowly with his back towards them and Rupert looked up testily. 'You're not a nun, Lewis. Come here!'

He reached out for Lewis and, in doing so, overbalanced and toppled out of the bed. He hit the floor with a dull thud.

Ned was momentarily panicked until he realised that the Prince was simply dead drunk and sound asleep. He curled into a foetal ball and began to snore gently.

The situation in which Ned now found himself was so bizarre that he almost laughed.

He sank back on the divan and watched as Lewis approached him. He was still fully dressed, save for his boots.

Lewis slid into bed beside Ned and for a long moment they simply stared into each other's eyes.

'What . . . what are you doing here?' said Lewis at last.

Ned sighed, feeling completely overwhelmed. 'It's too long a story. I . . . never thought I'd see you again, Lewis. I can't believe this is real.'

Lewis shook his head. 'It isn't. It can't be. We're set on different paths.'

Ned thought of the similar words he'd used with William. 'All these years I've thought of you as my ideal,' he whispered. 'And I would never open myself to anyone.'

'Is that why you're here?' asked Lewis gently.

Ned nodded slowly. 'In a sense. I did someone very precious to me a great wrong. I've come to seek vengeance on his behalf.'

Lewis sank back onto the pillows and Ned rested his head on his old lover's firm chest. Lewis sighed. 'It's Vane you want?'

'Yes.' Ned felt his words vibrate on Lewis's chest.

Lewis sat up and pulled Ned to him. They kissed for what seemed like an eternity, tongues curling together until finally Lewis pulled away.

'I've seen you since,' he confessed.

Ned frowned, puzzled. 'Where?'

'At Edgehill, would you believe.'

'Edgehill!'

Lewis nodded. 'Aye. I found you under that horse of yours. I recognised you at once and I knew I should have let you die. But

I couldn't. I remembered that summer we spent together. I remembered what you had meant to me.'

He looked deep into Ned's dark eyes and Ned felt his heart melt at the intensity of that look.

'All my life I've sought advancement. Walked over everyone who's ever cared for me. I seem to remember telling you that was the only way to get on.'

Ned nodded. He could hear Lewis's heart beating in his chest.

Lewis sighed again. 'Then, when I saw you, it was like someone had thrown cold water into my face. I remembered your sweetness and your simple love and I wondered how I could have come so far from that bliss.'

He kissed Ned again but this time it was a chaste kiss, as though they were old, close friends. Ned pulled him closer and they embraced again.

Ned looked at Lewis and smiled. 'It's strange,' he said. 'Perhaps you won't believe me but . . . I know just what you mean. I've dreamt of this moment for ten years. But now I need your help to avenge the one I really love.'

Lewis nodded slowly, smiled and kissed Ned once more on his full, red lips. Then he clambered from the bed, stepping over Rupert's recumbent form and moved towards the door.

'This way,' he whispered. 'I know where Vane hides. And I have one or two scores to settle with him myself.'

Ned followed him and, together, the former lovers crept from the room.

Cornelius was back in line with his fellow slaves, all cowering against the wall, shackled at wrists and ankles. His arse was glowing from the presence of Vane's massive cock but now he was in real fear of his life.

Vane had pulled on his cloak and was standing before the great fireplace, rolling his head around as though possessed. His guards stood loyally by, swords at their waists.

'I shall have to find others, you see,' Vane muttered to himself. 'And it's so difficult. So difficult to find the ones who can endure the pain and enjoy it at the same time. It's taken me months to find you, my pets.'

He swept the room with his coal-black gaze, looking for the last time at his leather-covered slaves.

'I could be fair, I suppose. Turn you loose.'

There was a gentle clanking of chains as the slaves sat up. Vane smiled sourly. 'But that wouldn't be right. After all, you are all agents of the Devil and I have a reputation to preserve.'

Cornelius sank to his knees, convinced now that they were all doomed. As Vane droned on, he thought of how different his life might have been. If he and Miracle Smith had somehow made a life together. If things had ever worked out between he and Ned Melcombe. But that would never have been possible. Ned had always been too much in love with himself to care for anyone else.

Vane had not yet finished. 'I could be merciful and let you all die quickly. But that wouldn't quite fit the rules of our games, would it? We can't turn soft after all we've shared together, can we?'

He turned to his guards. 'Where are the priest and the soldier?'

The guards came up behind Cornelius and Christopher and dragged them to their feet. They were pushed towards Vane, movements hampered by the chains around their ankles.

Cornelius felt his heart slamming in his ribs. This was it. He was being led to his death. He wished now that he had made a break for it or had clawed out Vane's eyes when he had the chance. But there had been enough regrets. Better to just get on with it.

He stopped in front of Vane, feeling the heat from the fire even through the leather costume.

Vane produced a large, vicious-looking dagger from his belt and held it aloft so that the blade flashed in the firelight.

He looked at Cornelius and Christopher and smiled evilly. 'You two were my first here in Oxford. Therefore, you shall die first.'

He stretched out his hand and let the point of the dagger pierce the soft leather covering Cornelius' belly.

Suddenly, the door was flung open and revealing, to Cornelius' astonishment, Ned and a tall, beautiful blond man he did not know.

Cornelius spun round and gasped as he saw Ned. It seemed

218

impossible that he could be here. But Ned could hardly be expected to recognise Cornelius in his leather mask. Instead he fixed his eyes on Vane.

'Edward Vane!' he bellowed.

Vane looked round, shocked and alarmed. His guards moved forward but Ned's blond companion roared at them to get back.

'I am Colonel Lewis St John! Stand back! Stand back, I say!'

He stormed into the middle of the room and took in the scene of depravity with an anguished frown. 'What in God's name is going on here?'

He fixed his gaze on one of the guards and pointed at the slaves 'You! Release them! Release them all!'

Terrified, the guard did as he was bidden, unshackling the four slaves who remained chained to the wall.

Ned walked up to Vane and pointed to Cornelius and Christopher. 'These too.' He gently pushed them away so he could confront Vane.

Cornelius wanted to cry out, to tell Ned that he was alive but he was too overwhelmed to speak. Instead, he watched as Ned marched towards Vane, his lip curling in detestation.

'You killed him, you bastard. You killed Cornelius Matthew. Well, now it's your turn to die.'

He raised his sword and Vane lashed out with his dagger. Lewis moved forward to help but, before they knew what was happening, the four released slaves rushed forwards with a deafening cry of triumph. They ripped their leather hoods from their faces and ran at full pelt towards Vane.

Ned rolled out of the way as the four powered into Vane. The evil Prosecutor tried to fight back, tried to stab at them with his dagger but they overwhelmed him and, with a great roar, thrust him backwards into the fireplace.

At once, Vane's cloak caught light. He cried out but his screams were silenced as flames engulfed him, blackening his skin and consuming him completely. He fell backwards into the fire, a rolling ball of flame, letting out a terrible, dying scream which echoed through the chamber.

Ned fell backwards and the brave Colonel St John caught him. The four slaves sank to their knees, sobbing with relief.

Christopher removed his hood and Ned's expression betrayed his surprise. Smiling, Christopher pointed to the only leather-clad figure still masked. Ned walked forward and gently removed it, revealing the flushed, beaten but still lovely face of Cornelius Matthew.

Cornelius smiled and fell into Ned's welcoming arms.

The morning light was like pure gold, falling in hazy shafts through the window of the manor's parlour and onto Cornelius' sleeping form.

Ned lay with his head propped on his hand, gazing down at the beautiful boy he had so abused and whom he had never expected to see again.

Gently, he stroked Cornelius' lovely hair and laid his lips on the smooth, milky flesh of his neck. He wanted to kiss him for ever, to apologise for all the years of hurt. A burning love overwhelmed him and he scooped up Cornelius in his arms, holding him as tight as if his life depended on it.

Cornelius' eyes blinked open and he looked up into Ned's face. For an instant he seemed troubled but then his face cleared. He kissed Ned on the lips and let his tongue worm its way inside Ned's mouth, exploring the moist, sensuous warmth.

As he sank back onto the pillow he let a sigh of pure contentment slip from his lips. 'For a moment I thought myself back there,' he said with a shudder.

'No,' said Ned. 'Nevermore. It's over.'

He pulled Cornelius to him and squeezed him till his heart filled with joy. 'I thought I'd lost you, my love. Can you ever forgive me?'

Cornelius smiled. 'Forgive you, Ned?'

Ned nodded gravely. 'Aye. Because I never saw how much you meant to me. Never knew how much you cared for me.'

Cornelius cocked his head. 'We were playing a game,' he said quietly.

'Aye,' said Ned. 'But all the rules were biased in my favour. It'll never be like that again, I promise.'

He kissed Cornelius with a passion which surged through his every bone. His heart lifted as though it were about to fly from his body and he pressed his chest against his lover's in a tight embrace.

They were both naked beneath the clean sheets and Ned felt Cornelius' penis stiffen against his belly. He laughed delightedly and curled up alongside his lover, his own cock hardening as it lay alongside Cornelius'.

Then Cornelius rose up and positioned himself on top of Ned, his cock pressing down against the hard, flat plane of Ned's belly. Once, Ned reflected, this would have been unthinkable. Now he welcomed it as he had never welcomed anything before.

He closed his eyes as Cornelius sank down onto him. The pressure of the cleric's wonderful cock was simply beautiful. Desire and lust and love battled for supremacy within Ned's mind as he kissed Cornelius again, moaning gently as his tongue traced the outline of the cleric's jaw.

Cornelius moved down and took each of Ned's nipples in turn into his mouth. He sucked at them, pulling them up between his teeth, nipped and nibbled at their sensitive flesh until Ned thought he would go mad with desire.

He wanted to kiss Cornelius again but the cleric wouldn't let him. Instead, he trailed his tongue the length of Ned's body, taking each of his heavy balls into his mouth.

They were both panting with urgency now, a need to have each other after so long apart and after years spent in a half-love.

Cornelius clamped his mouth on the great, throbbing rod of Ned's cock and began to suck at him like a loosed demon.

Ned's head thrashed from side to side. It was perfect, just perfect. He had had so many men in his time but there was nothing to compare to the feelings of pure love he felt for Cornelius. The emotion only amplified his desire and, as Cornelius kissed and licked at his cock, he sat up and breathed into the cleric's ear, 'My love. Make love to me.'

Cornelius left Ned's penis for a moment and kissed him again, his tongue joining with Ned's in a dance of hot desire.

Then he lifted up Ned's legs, exposing the tight, hairy hole of his arse.

'Lick me,' begged Ned. 'Lick me there.'

221

Cornelius held on to Ned's knees and laid his head down so that his tongue could move slickly in and out of Ned's anus.

Ned gasped at the new sensation, wriggling around so that Cornelius' tongue pierced him. He locked his hands around Cornelius' head and moaned as the cleric's tongue played a sweet tune inside him.

As he licked, Cornelius' hands moved up Ned's broad, taut chest and began to play with his erect nipples. Ned found this triple attack on his senses pushing him into sheer bliss and cried out Cornelius' name over and over.

He looked down, feeling the young man's hair brushing against his balls.

Cornelius looked up and smiled. 'What is it?'

'I want you inside me,' said Ned gently.

Cornelius' brows shot up. He was genuinely astonished. 'Are you sure?'

Ned nodded. 'I've never been more sure. Take me there, please, Cornelius.'

Cornelius seemed to consider a moment then moved up to kiss Ned long and full on the lips.

He slid from Ned's chest and lay down, then encouraged Ned to move on top of him. His cock stood up straight and hard and proud. 'Ride me,' he said.

Ned felt his throat go dry and a little shudder of excitement pass through him. He swung himself onto Cornelius' body and rested his buttocks a moment on the firm plane of his lover's stomach. Cornelius opened his legs wide and took hold of his thick cock. Then, as Ned moved backwards, he manoeuvred the glistening purple head into the mouth of Ned's anus.

He placed his other hand on Ned's muscular forearm and pushed him gently down.

Ned cried out. It was like being stabbed with a blade of fire. His jaw fell open as he sank down onto the shaft of Cornelius' cock and he held his hands out in front of him, opening and closing his fists.

'No . . . no,' he gasped, his face contorting.

'It's all right. Shhh,' soothed Cornelius and, indeed, after a few moments, Ned felt himself relax and the rest of Cornelius' cock slid smoothly into his arse.

His hands dropped down to his own stiff penis and he held himself for a long time, luxuriating in the feel of Cornelius' cock within him. He felt full and alive and wonderful.

He reached back and found one of Cornelius' knees which he used to lever himself back up the shaft of his cock and down again. It felt incredible to be shafted again.

With his other hand he slowly masturbated himself, drawing his foreskin back in measured beats. The dark, forbidden thrill pulsing through him made him giddy with pleasure.

The soft walls of his anus distended as Cornelius pushed his proud organ deep into Ned's body. Then Cornelius took hold of Ned's cock and began to pump at it himself, allowing Ned to concentrate on the column of hot pleasure inside him.

He felt his head buzzing with unfamiliar sensations. This was what it had been like with Lewis St John but what was he now but a memory, a false idol that Ned had set up to hide behind. He was nothing. Nothing compared to his dear Cornelius.

As he pushed himself up and down on Cornelius' rigid cock, he remembered his times spent in the temple with the priest. The thought of Cornelius chained and naked aroused him. He saw again the coppery hair matted with sweat, the taut globes of his buttocks red from the lashings he'd received.

He felt his cock grow stiffer yet between Cornelius' fingers as he was drawn ever closer to orgasm. A ragged, intense pleasure was coursing through him as he felt the twin sensations of his own cock and of Cornelius' thrusting up inside him.

Sinking down once more onto the shaft, he spread his hands over the mattress and grasped at the surface. A cascade of desire seemed to flow over him, like the water at the Greenacre Fall that faraway day.

Cornelius was moving faster and faster inside him now, his big, solid penis gripped by the walls of Ned's anus. Ned could feel his seed threatening to blast from his cock at any moment and prayed that Cornelius was about to come too. Surely he couldn't stand such pleasure much longer.

He looked down into Cornelius' face and saw that his eyes were screwed tightly shut.

'Oh, my sweet,' gasped Ned. 'Take me. Come inside me. Now. Now.'

Cornelius opened his dazzling eyes and smiled, his breath hissing between his teeth. Then his face contorted into a mask of ecstasy and he howled Ned's name as he jetted his semen deep into Ned's arse.

Sweat coursing down his flushed face, Ned gasped as he felt Cornelius' warm come inside him. He shifted all his attention to his own cock and threw back his head as Cornelius' hands jerked at his organ, rubbing over the sensitive head, pushing him closer and closer and closer.

Cornelius' cock was still stiff within him and he rode it with his buttocks, hearing his flesh slap on Cornelius' firm thighs. Then the room span about him and he opened his mouth in a silent scream as he came, his sperm streaming over Cornelius' body and slapping into his lovely face.

Cornelius let it trickle down into his mouth and lapped greedily at it. Ned watched his sperm form a jagged white line on Cornelius' lips and then smiled at his lover.

Carefully, he raised himself and Cornelius' softening cock slid from him.

At last, Ned looked over at his lover and smiled. 'You know I must return to my regiment?'

Cornelius nodded. 'Of course. But you will come back. We can't have gone through so much only to lose you in battle.'

Ned grinned. 'If you have faith, my love. Then I have faith.'

'Meantime,' said Cornelius, 'I must help to get the village and the church back in order.'

'It won't be easy,' said Ned.

'Of course not,' said Cornelius, smiling. 'Don't you know there's a war on?'

Twelve

Prince Rupert turned towards the window and looked out over the streets of Oxford, tutting angrily.

'There's much you can do,' he said. 'His Majesty has been most impressed by your service.'

Lewis nodded, a gentle breeze fluttering through his shining blond hair. 'I know that, sir. But I feel my talents would be better suited elsewhere.'

Rupert turned to him, scowling. '*Where?*'

Lewis shrugged. 'That's for me to discover, sir.'

Rupert looked him up and down, his eyes lingering on Lewis's dark brows and smooth, beautiful face.

Lewis could see that he still aroused the Prince and that Rupert was loathe to let such a bonny pet go.

'This doesn't have anything to do with . . . what passed between us?' asked Rupert warily.

Lewis shook his head. 'It was a pleasure, sir. But I think we should look upon the Vane episode as our last *collaboration*.'

Lewis had told a very convincing story. The Prosecutor, Edward Vane, had been killed by a lone assassin who had smuggled himself into the citadel. Both he and Prince Rupert had seen the man but he had confounded them and escaped to kill Vane. Lewis tactfully left out the part about Prince Rupert attempting to seduce the assassin and then falling asleep, dead drunk. It wouldn't do to have confidence in the King's security undermined.

For himself, Lewis had resigned his commission and decided to move abroad. He saw no future for himself in England.

Rupert looked at him again and an expression of great sadness seemed to cloud his face.

'You don't think we're going to win, do you, Lewis?'

Lewis smiled, kissed the Prince's hand and went out, leaving Oxford for ever.

He sailed to France on the very day that the King's men were soundly defeated at the battle of Marston Moor.

In his new life, he kept his ear to the ground and heard of the King's execution and the establishment of an English Republic under Oliver Cromwell. He thought often of the lesson he and Ned Melcombe had unexpectedly learned and resolved to be a better, more humble man.

He turned his face from England towards the Continent and other adventures . . .

IDOL NEW BOOKS

Also published this month:

THE VELVET WEB
Christopher Summerisle

The year is 1889. Daniel McGaw arrives at Calverdale, a centre of academic excellence buried deep in the English countryside. But this is like no other college. As Daniel explores he discovers secret passages in the grounds and forbidden texts in the library. The young male students, isolated from the outside world, share a darkly bizarre brotherhood based on the most extreme forms of erotic expression. It isn't long before Daniel is initiated into the rites that bind together the youths of Calverdale in a web of desire.

ISBN 0 352 33208 5

CHAINS OF DECEIT
Paul C. Alexander

Journalist Nathan Dexter's life is turned around when he meets a young student called Scott – someone who offers him the relationship for which he's been searching. Then Nathan's best friend goes missing, and Nathan uncovers evidence that he has become the victim of a slavery ring which is rumoured to be operating out of London's leather scene. To rescue their friend and expose the perverted slave trade, Nathan and Scott must go undercover, risking detection and betrayal at every turn.

ISBN 0 352 33206 9

WE NEED YOUR HELP . . .

to plan the future of Idol books –

Yours are the only opinions that matter. Idol is a new and exciting venture: the first British series of books devoted to homoerotic fiction for men.

We're going to do our best to provide the sexiest, best-written books you can buy. And we'd like you to help in these early stages. Tell us what you want to read. There's a freepost address for your filled-in questionnaires, so you won't even need to buy a stamp.

THE IDOL QUESTIONNAIRE

SECTION ONE: ABOUT YOU

1.1 Sex (we presume you are male, but just in case)
Are you?
Male ☐
Female ☐

1.2 Age
under 21 ☐   21–30 ☐
31–40 ☐   41–50 ☐
51–60 ☐   over 60 ☐

1.3 At what age did you leave full-time education?
still in education ☐   16 or younger ☐
17–19 ☐   20 or older ☐

1.4 Occupation _____

1.5 Annual household income (if you don't mind telling us)
under £10,000 ☐   £10–£20,000 ☐
£20–£30,000 ☐   £30–£40,000 ☐
over £40,000 ☐

1.6 We are perfectly happy for you to remain anonymous; but if you would like us to send you a free booklist of Idol books, please insert your name and address

_____

_____

_____

_____

SECTION TWO: ABOUT BUYING IDOL BOOKS

2.1 How did you acquire this copy of *The King's Men*?

I bought it myself (from a bookshop) ☐	My partner bought it (from a bookshop) ☐
I borrowed/found it ☐	It was bought through mail order ☐

2.2 How did you find out about Idol books?

I saw them in a shop ☐

I saw them advertised in a magazine ☐

I read about them in _____

Other _____

2.3 Please tick the following statements you agree with:

I would be less embarrassed about buying Idol books if the cover pictures were less explicit ☐

I think that in general the pictures on Idol books are about right ☐

I think Idol cover pictures should be as explicit as possible ☐

2.4 Would you read an Idol book in a public place – on a train for instance?

Yes ☐   No ☐

SECTION THREE: ABOUT THIS IDOL BOOK

3.1 Do you think the sex content in this book is:

Too much ☐   About right ☐

Not enough ☐

3.2 Do you think the writing style in this book is:

Too unreal/escapist ☐   About right ☐

Too down to earth ☐

3.3 Do you think the story in this book is:

       Too complicated   ☐   About right   ☐

       Too boring/simple   ☐

3.4 Do you think the cover of this book is:

       Too explicit   ☐   About right   ☐

       Not explicit enough   ☐

Here's a space for any other comments:

SECTION FOUR: ABOUT OTHER IDOL BOOKS

4.1 How many Idol books have you read?

4.2 If more than one, which one did you prefer?

4.3 Why?

SECTION FIVE: ABOUT YOUR IDEAL EROTIC NOVEL

We want to publish the books you want to read – so this is your chance to tell us exactly what your ideal erotic novel would be like.

5.1 Using a scale of 1 to 5 (1 = no interest at all, 5 = your ideal), please rate the following possible settings for an erotic novel:

       Roman / Ancient World   ☐

       Medieval / barbarian / sword 'n' sorcery   ☐

       Renaissance / Elizabethan / Restoration   ☐

       Victorian / Edwardian   ☐

       1920s & 1930s   ☐

       Present day   ☐

       Future / Science Fiction   ☐

5.2 Using the same scale of 1 to 5, please rate the following themes you may find in an erotic novel:

Bondage / fetishism ☐
Romantic love ☐
SM / corporal punishment ☐
Bisexuality ☐
Group sex ☐
Watersports ☐
Rent / sex for money ☐

5.3 Using the same scale of 1 to 5, please rate the following styles in which an erotic novel could be written:

Gritty realism, down to earth ☐
Set in real life but ignoring its less pleasant aspects ☐
Escapist fantasy, but just about believable ☐
Complete escapism, totally unrealistic ☐

5.4 In a book that features power differentials or sexual initiation, would you prefer the writing to be from the viewpoint of the dominant / experienced or submissive / inexperienced characters:

Dominant / Experienced ☐
Submissive / Inexperienced ☐
Both ☐

5.5 We'd like to include characters close to your ideal lover. What characteristics would your ideal lover have? Tick as many as you want:

Dominant	☐	Caring	☐
Slim	☐	Rugged	☐
Extroverted	☐	Romantic	☐
Bisexual	☐	Old	☐
Working Class	☐	Intellectual	☐
Introverted	☐	Professional	☐
Submissive	☐	Pervy	☐
Cruel	☐	Ordinary	☐
Young	☐	Muscular	☐
Naïve	☐		

Anything else? _____

5.6 Is there one particular setting or subject matter that your ideal erotic novel would contain:

_____

5.7 As you'll have seen, we include safe-sex guidelines in every book. However, while our policy is always to show safe-sex in stories with contemporary settings, we don't insist on safe-sex practices in stories with historical settings because it would be anachronistic. What, if anything, would you change about this policy?

_____

_____

SECTION SIX: LAST WORDS

6.1 What do you like best about Idol books?

_____

6.2 What do you most dislike about Idol books?

_____

6.3 In what way, if any, would you like to change Idol covers?

_____

6.4 Here's a space for any other comments:

_____

_____

_____

_____

Thanks for completing this questionnaire. Now either tear it out, or photocopy it, then put it in an envelope and send it to:

Idol
FREEPOST
London
W10 5BR

You don't need a stamp if you're in the UK, but you'll need one if you're posting from overseas.